NOT SINCE JAY ANSON'S OWN BEST SELLER, **THE AMITYVILLE HORROR,** HAS THERE BEEN A TERROR-SHOCKER LIKE THIS!

And then, as David watched, the house began coming apart . . . One long plank became the side of a guillotine. Another beam was the upright of a cross on which a man was being nailed, upside down. David saw people being beheaded, impaled and burned alive. Every stick of wood in that blue house was figuring in the torture or execution of a human being. . . .

David tried to run, but his feet would not move. Coming straight at him was a shiny brass chandelier, like the one he had in the living room of his apartment. From it dangled a piece of white cloth shaped into a crude hangman's noose. The noose lifted gracefully in midair and settled around his neck. He felt the fabric closing around his throat. He tried to scream, but the noose was too tight. He could make no sound at all!

666

JAY ANSON

PUBLISHED BY POCKET BOOKS NEW YORK

With acknowledgment and thanks to Tam Mossman for his editorial contribution to this work.

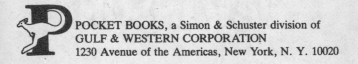

POCKET BOOKS, a Simon & Schuster division of
GULF & WESTERN CORPORATION
1230 Avenue of the Americas, New York, N. Y. 10020

FOR LESIA

Again there was a day when the sons of God came to present themselves before the Lord, and Satan came also among them to present himself before the Lord.

And the Lord said unto Satan, From whence cometh thou? And Satan answered the Lord, and said, From going to and fro in the earth, and from walking up and down in it.

—Job, 2:1–2

David had to get a grip on himself. He couldn't let

Prologue

SEATTLE (September 10, 1978)—A yellow-and-white frame house, site of a brutal double killing five years ago, was placed on a low-bed trailer yesterday and trucked to Puget Sound.

Early this morning, waterfront residents watched as the two-story house was winched aboard a barge and towed out to sea. The house's actual move was made shortly after midnight, when roads along its route could be closed to traffic.

The Victorian-style home at 666 Bremerton Road had remained empty since 1973, when James Beaufort committed a double murder inside. The brutality of the killings shocked this quiet residential section of the city. Beaufort's attorney denied that his client was physically strong enough to have committed the slayings. But in a surprise development at his trial, Beaufort confessed to both murders in open court.

The former city councilman testified that he had

1

rented the dwelling for Patricia Swenson, a secretary in his office. Beaufort had asked his wife for a divorce so that he could marry Miss Swenson, but she refused. Shortly thereafter, Beaufort caught his brother-in-law, Edgar Sutton, alone with Miss Swenson. In a jealous rage, he slaughtered them both.

"I thought he had talked her into leaving me," Beaufort testified. Since 1974, he has been serving a 20-years-to-life sentence at McNeil Island Federal Penitentiary.

"The house was a wonderful example of mid-19th-century architecture," said a spokesman for Spatz Realty, who had leased the house to Beaufort originally. "But those killings made the place impossible to rent. Prospective clients felt the place was 'spooky.'"

"Also, there was a problem with curiosity seekers. People would just drive up in front of the house and stare, or get out and take photographs. Tenants thinking of renting worried that they'd have no privacy."

According to Spatz Realty, several offers to buy the home had been received over the past several years. But they were all refused by the owner, who is listed on the tax rolls as a Mr. Coste.

The owner's address is given as in care of Spatz Realty. But no one at the real estate office recalls meeting him in person. They claim he transacted all his business by mail and by telephone, and added that the lot at 666 Bremerton Road is now for sale.

Since the killings, police stated, the house had suffered minor vandalism. A stained-glass entryway and ornate bay windows had been boarded up, to prevent damage. Several times, neighbors spotted a flickering red light inside and called the fire department. But there was never any evidence of smoke or fire damage.

Mr. Coste did not inform Spatz Realty where the house's new site will be. The company hired to move the structure could not be reached for comment.

1

Tuesday, April 10, 1979

TEN DAYS IN THE CARIBBEAN were just what Keith Olson needed. He had spent most of the winter renovating an old farmhouse over in Dobbs Ferry, and he really wanted a breather before his next job. So he and his wife, Jennifer, had flown down for some sun and deep-sea fishing on Grand Bahama Island.

Keith was looking forward to getting back to work, however. Spring was always a busy time for Olson Custom Carpentry. The cold Hudson Valley winters left plenty of roofs and downspouts in need of repair. And with real estate prices spiraling so high these days, more people were fixing up the houses they already owned—adding a room, or finishing off the attic or basement. In May and June, Keith usually had more work than he could handle. Now, if only his wife could get her own career going again.

Two years before, Jennifer had been working as an interior decorator in Manhattan. But when she married Keith, she had closed up her office and moved out of the city. Now she and Keith lived in the Town of New Castle, just above Ossining. But Jennifer had found she wasn't happy unless she was planning some room in her mind, leafing through wallpaper samples and swatches of fabric.

Having nothing to do all day left her depressed and irritable. So since Christmas of 1978, she had been looking for interior-decorating assignments. She had even placed an ad in the local paper, but no one had called in reply. Here in upper Westchester, jobs simply weren't that easy to come by. And as the winter wore on, Jennifer had been growing increasingly discouraged. But Keith noticed that the warm tropical sunshine had helped cheer her up.

Their BWIA flight landed at Kennedy International Airport shortly after 4 P.M. Keith didn't bother looking for a skycap to carry their three suitcases out of the baggage-claim area. He had played football in college, and now, at thirty-three, he was still built like a fullback, with strong, broad shoulders and a barrel chest. He carried their luggage to the pickup area, then walked to the long-term parking lot where he and Jennifer had left her blue Datsun. Then he loaded up the car back at the terminal and took the Whitestone Bridge north to the Saw Mill River Parkway.

They were almost home when Jennifer turned to him. "Do you mind if we have David up for dinner tomorrow night?"

"So soon?" Keith asked. "It seems like we're feeding David M. Carmichael almost every two weeks." Down in the Bahamas, he and Jennifer had both been too sunburned to make love; and of course they had dined out every night. Now Keith had been looking forward

4

to a few evenings alone with her at home, with no waiters, no fuss . . .

"But we haven't seen David since March," Jennifer reminded him.

"Yeah," Keith laughed, "March thirty-first! But sure, go ahead and invite him. I don't mind." But back when he had first married Jennifer, Keith had felt very uncomfortable about his wife's warm friendship with the Manhattan antiques dealer.

At six feet, David Carmichael stood two inches taller than Keith. And David's rugged extraordinary good looks had made Keith feel competitive and ill at ease. David was forty-two—nine years older than Keith, twelve years older than Jennifer. But the extra years had only made him better-looking. His full head of hair had turned a distinguished gray, and he kept himself trim and athletic by spending at least an hour at the indoor racquet club every afternoon. An elegant man, he always wore hand-tailored blazers, silk ties and expensive shoes. And as a dealer in eighteenth-century antiques, he was perfectly at home in the rich, sophisticated world that Jennifer used to inhabit.

The first time Keith had met David was when Jennifer had dragged him down to New York for an auction at Sotheby Parke Bernet. In the exhibition rooms, the three of them had seen a lampshade of green stained glass. It reminded Keith of the lamps that used to hang in a German ice cream parlor over in Ossining; and Jennifer really seemed to like it. He told her that if she wanted the lamp for their wedding anniversary on May 7, he'd bid as high as four hundred dollars.

David and Jennifer gave each other a strange look, but neither one said anything. Later, Keith checked the sale catalog. That nice green lampshade was a signed piece by Louis Comfort Tiffany—estimated to sell at between fifteen and eighteen thousand dollars! So for

Keith, the world of art and antiques was a glittering maze that David and his wife knew all about, but where Keith himself couldn't follow.

A little before six o'clock, Keith pulled into their driveway at 712 Sunset Brook Lane. Jennifer headed straight into the kitchen to defrost a couple of shell steaks for dinner. Keith hefted the suitcases again—one under his left arm, one in each hand—and staggered up the stairs and into the bedroom.

It was good to be home, he thought. He and Jennifer had bought this old red-brick house two Aprils ago, just before they got married. Then Jennifer sold her co-op apartment on the East Side and moved most of her furniture up here to New Castle. Their furnishings made a funny mixture—Jennifer's Mission Oak and modern designer furniture beside Keith's plain old tables and chairs. But her skill with colors and fabrics made it all work—without making the house so feminine and luxurious that Keith felt uncomfortable.

Suddenly he heard Jennifer's voice from downstairs in the kitchen. "Keith!" she called. "Come down here!" She sounded worried.

"Coming!" he shouted back. He bolted out of the bedroom and ran down the stairs, two at a time. But when he entered the kitchen, there didn't seem to be anything wrong.

"Hey!" he panted. "What's the matter?"

"Look." Jennifer pointed to the window over the sink.

He and Jennifer owned just over an acre of land. But their house seemed even more private, because Sunset Brook Lane was almost completely wooded. Behind their house was a deep gully sloping down to a little brook where ferns and wildflowers grew every summer. And their kitchen had a great view of the western horizon. Keith and Jennifer often liked to eat dinner at the kitchen table so they could watch the sunset.

But now when he glanced out the window, he couldn't believe his eyes. Directly across the gully, where Sunset Brook Lane doubled back on itself, stood a two-story house. It hadn't been there when he and Jennifer had left on vacation.

"There goes the view," Jennifer said sadly.

But Keith was amazed. "That's impossible!" he exclaimed. "There's no way you can put up a house that fast. The land wasn't even cleared ten days ago!"

"Are you sure?" Jennifer asked. She and Keith didn't usually use the western spur of Sunset Brook Lane, unless they were headed for the Taconic Parkway.

"I'm positive!" Keith insisted. "I drove over that way just two weeks ago on my way to Dobbs Ferry. There weren't any foundation markers laid out, no bulldozers. Besides, that's Clyde Ramsey's land. He'd never want to build there."

He squinted against the late-afternoon glare. The oaks and maples weren't in leaf yet, and the setting sun was just slipping down behind the front porch of the new house. It seemed to be barely a hundred yards away, right on the edge of the gully. And from its silhouette, he could tell it had a mansard roof, and a large porch, complete with pillars, to the left. He couldn't see any shades or blinds—evidently the new tenants hadn't moved in yet.

Keith glanced over at the clock above the stove. It was six ten. The sun would be setting in about fifteen minutes. "Jennifer, you mind if I walk over and take a look at that new place? I just can't imagine how it's possible to build a house so quickly."

"As long as you unpack first," she said. "Your sports jackets are going to grow mold if you don't."

Keith nodded and climbed back upstairs. The night before, a series of tropical thundershowers had swept Grand Bahama Island. Now, when he unlocked his suitcase, he felt the humidity trapped inside. His sports coats were crushed and wrinkled, but if they had to go to the cleaner's, Keith wasn't going to miss them. He wasn't much of a jacket-and-tie man.

Placing his empty suitcase at the back of his closet, he quickly changed into blue jeans and work shoes. April weather was still nippy up here in New Castle, so he reached for the heavy quilted jacket he wore when he and Jennifer went skiing in Vermont. No point risking a cold with his busy season coming up.

When he came back downstairs, Jennifer was by the sink, placing the frozen steaks on a rack for broiling. She had tanned beautifully, and the bright sun had filled her chestnut hair with highlights that were the color of honey. The sun had already vanished behind the new house, but the light from the western sky shone through her hair and turned it to a soft and lovely gold. She wasn't the most beautiful woman he had ever seen, but she was certainly one of the finalists.

Was that why he was so jealous of her? he wondered. It bothered him a bit that Jennifer had been married once before, when she was twenty-five. Her divorce had been final a full five years ago. But even so, Keith didn't like being compared with somebody he had never met. And it didn't help things that one of Jennifer's closest friends was David Carmichael—a handsome, polished, unattached man who made one hell of a lot more money than Keith did.

He kissed his wife and looked at her face for a moment. Her eyes had little rings of yellow around the pupils, like two little solar eclipses. He didn't have to worry about Jennifer, he told himself. She and David

8

were just old business associates, who'd known each other for years. . . .

"I won't be long," he told her. "I just want to have a look at that house before it gets dark."

Jennifer smiled back at him. "Try to find out who owns it. Maybe they'd like to let me decorate the place once it's all fixed up."

Keith unlocked the kitchen door and stepped outside. Jennifer waited until he was a good distance along the path that led across the gully. Then she lifted the telephone on the kitchen wall and dialed Manhattan. But there was no answer. Could David be working late at the gallery on East Fifty-seventh Street? She hung up and dialed again.

Jennifer recognized the crisp English accent of Miss Rosewood, David's secretary. "David M. Carmichael; good afternoon."

"Hi, this is Jennifer Olson. Is David still there, please?"

"One moment, Mrs. Olson. Let me see if he's available." And then there was a dead silence—Miss Rosewood had placed her on hold.

Jennifer waited. It was always mildly annoying to be treated like a stranger by a woman who had known her for years. But the English-born Miss Rosewood was very proper and guarded her employer with ruthless loyalty—especially now that David was single again.

"Jennifer!" It was David's voice. "How are you?"

"Wonderful, David, and you? Why are you working so late? Am I calling at a bad time?"

"On the contrary," David laughed. Then he lowered his voice. "I have a Beverly Hills producer here who wants to buy his wife a tenth-anniversary present. She prefers a pair of armchairs at sixty-five thousand dollars. But he's leaning toward a Louis Sixteenth writing table at eighty-five thousand. Says it's more practical!"

9

"For your sake, let's hope he convinces her," Jennifer said. "But say, Keith and I just got back from Grand Bahama. I want you to see us before my tan starts to peel. Are you free for dinner tomorrow?"

David glanced at his desk calendar. Wednesday evening he was supposed to have dinner with a senior curator from the Metropolitan Museum. But he could always cancel. He would much rather see Jennifer—and Keith too, of course.

"Sounds good," David said. "What time do you want me?"

"Oh . . ." Jennifer paused. "Around six thirty is okay."

"Six thirty it is," David said. That meant he'd have to leave the gallery about four, take a cab home, shower and shave. . . .

From the Olsons' house at 712, Sunset Brook Lane ran north, then curved sharply south again to form an inverted U. If Keith had wanted to get to the new house by walking along the road, it would have meant crossing the short concrete bridge at the top of the Lane—a walk of nearly half a mile. It was much faster to hike straight across the gully separating the new house from his own kitchen door.

A light breeze was blowing. The skin on Keith's face—sunburned only the week before—felt dry and stiff. Down at the bottom of the gully, where the ferns grew in summer, the brook was low and not making much noise. Apparently it hadn't rained since that incredible downpour they'd had the night before they flew out of Kennedy.

Crossing the stones that protruded above the water's surface, Keith paused. Here on the other side of the stream, the air seemed darker. It had that slightly evil greenish tinge Keith had often seen right before a thunderstorm.

Keith glanced up. The house loomed above him, blocking the sun. Keith shrugged and started climbing the steep bank. He soon reached the other side of the ravine. Directly in front of him loomed the wood-frame house, on a narrow expanse of bare soil that had been bulldozed flat. It was painted yellow, with white trim, and the slopes of the mansard roof were finished in slate. There couldn't be much of an attic, Keith thought, just a shallow crawl space that could attract squirrels and mice.

The house had been set at right angles to Sunset Brook Lane, so that its front door faced due south. Keith stared in amazement at the ornate Queen Anne-style wooden trim under the porch roof. You didn't see gingerbread like that on houses anymore.

There wasn't any garage, but right in front of the front porch, a wide strip of soil leading to the road had been covered with bluestone gravel. That, Keith supposed, was where the owner would have to park his car. But there was no automobile there now. Nor were there shades or curtains on any of the windows. The scalloped clapboards were carefully shaped in imitation of semicircular shingles, but they definitely needed a fresh coat of paint. Keith could see dents, scratches and chips everywhere—even twenty feet up on the side of the building.

Then Keith noticed the enormous tire tracks. Some heavy vehicle had left smears of clayish soil out into Sunset Brook Lane. Now he understood. This house hadn't been built—it had been *moved* to its present site!

He walked closer and peered at the lowest row of clapboards, just above the freshly poured concrete

11

foundation. Yes, there were the scars of the jacks that had lifted the house off its original underpinnings. Whoever had handled the work had certainly known what he was doing. Keith almost regretted having been away on vacation. He would have loved to be here to watch this two-story structure get eased onto its new foundation.

But why had it been moved *here*, of all places? There was practically no backyard to speak of. And just beside the front porch, the land sloped steeply down to the brook at the bottom of the gully. After going to all that trouble, why had the owner picked such a narrow, awkward plot of ground?

Keith walked around the porch so that he could view the house from the road. A massive bay window jutted out from the wall fronting on Sunset Brook Lane. Roofed in slate, the bay contained three separate panels of glass. Each was about three feet wide and nearly six feet tall. Apparently the house had been angled so that this window would catch the afternoon light. Maybe whoever owned this place liked to watch sunsets too?

Climbing up onto the front porch, Keith saw the entryway panels on either side of the front door. Each was composed of little six-sided panes of glass, held together with strips of lead. The six-sided panes were perfectly clear. But the top and bottom of each panel bore a strip of bright red stained glass.

Over the door was a semicircular fan window, also composed of leaded glass. In the middle of the fan was a large disk of blood-red glass. From it, strips of leading radiated out like sunbeams. It looked just like the setting sun, about to drop beneath the horizon. And right in the middle of the red circle, in big black numerals, was the house number—666.

Keith and Jennifer lived at 712. A house on this side

of Sunset Brook Lane could take any number down to 640—that was the number of Mrs. Woodfield's place, about a quarter-mile down the road. Looking more carefully, Keith saw that the numerals were strips of lead enclosing the disk of red glass. Was that why this house had been moved to this precise location—so that the house number wouldn't have to be changed?

Then he heard a soft click. Right in front of him, the front door swung inward, ever so slightly. That's odd, Keith thought. He hadn't felt any breeze. But if the door was unlocked, there had to be someone inside after all. Keith would have to meet their new neighbor sooner or later; and now was as good a time as any.

He pressed the doorbell, but there was no sound from within. Apparently the electricity hadn't been hooked up yet. He pushed the door with his hand, and it swung inward, noiselessly, on its hinges.

Directly to his left, a steep staircase with an old-fashioned banister led up to the second floor. Straight ahead, a narrow hallway ran directly to the back of the house.

"Hello!" Keith called out. But there was no answer.

He stepped into what must have been the living room. But the ground floor was absolutely bare, without a stick of furniture. Also, there were no light bulbs. Some thrifty soul had removed the ceiling fixtures in the hall and living room, so that the only light in the place was coming through the windows from the outside.

At the back of the living room was a small alcove, with a fireplace in one wall and a door in the wall adjoining. Keith pushed at the door, and saw that it led to the kitchen at the back of the house. In there were a modern-looking refrigerator and a stainless steel sink.

He retraced his steps. The living-room floor was of

oak and looked positively ancient. But the walls—which Keith had hoped would have some attractive wood paneling—were of the cheapest possible wallboard. Keith shook his head. Didn't the owner give a damn about the interior? If he wanted to go the prefab route, he could have at least used decent Sheetrock.

One part of the ground floor did have paneling, though—the staircase. At first, Keith assumed that the two sliding doors under the stairs led to a coat closet. But in place of knobs, the doors had huge iron rings, all pitted and worn. Keith took hold of them and pulled, and the doors slid sideways into the paneling. Behind them was a strange little six-sided room.

Keith stepped in. Right ahead of him were the three panels of the bay window he'd seen from outside. But whoever had designed this room must have had hexagons on the brain! The floor, perhaps twelve feet across, was of white and cream-colored marble, inlaid in a series of interlocking hexagons. The same pattern was repeated on the paneling on either side of the sliding doors, and underneath the leaded windows. And then there were the windows themselves.

Each section of the bay window was made up of six-sided panes of clear glass, about seven inches across, joined by strips of lead. Most of the panes had little scratches that seemed to form some kind of overall pattern, but it was too faint for Keith to make out. Those little scratches were almost as transparent as the glass itself. And the sun was almost on the horizon now, shining right through the bay window and creating too much of a dazzle.

Keith climbed upstairs. The banister was of fine old mahogany, but the stairs were nothing special—just old, stained boards with a splinter here and there. At the head of the stairs was the bathroom, and to the right, a sizable dressing room or small bedroom. Farther to the right—back toward the front porch—was the master bedroom. One wall of it was finished in the same wood paneling that formed the side of the staircase downstairs. The other three walls, though, were finished in that same crummy wallboard.

Glancing out the bedroom windows, Keith got a good view of his own house, barely a hundred yards away. This new house stood on slightly higher ground, and so it was easy to see right into his and Jennifer's own second-floor bedroom. Too bad; they'd have to remember to lower the venetian blinds at night.

He was about to walk back downstairs again when he heard a sharp *clang!* behind him. It sounded like metal hitting metal, as if someone had dropped a bolt into a galvanized bucket. Keith turned around. Right behind him was the bathroom. Inside was an old-fashioned bathtub of cast iron, standing on its four clawed feet.

He walked over to the bathtub's high, rounded rim and looked inside. Lying on the rust-stained enamel at the bottom of the tub was a dark brown coin about the size of a fifty-cent piece. It had been just a bit too large to roll down the drain. Keith leaned over and picked it up. To his surprise, it was almost hot to the touch, as if it had been resting next to a light bulb. But there weren't any bulbs in the house—in fact, the electricity hadn't been hooked up yet.

Where had the coin fallen from? Keith looked up at the ceiling over the tub, but the plaster was completely intact. Had the coin been balanced on the tub's rim, and been jarred loose by Keith's footsteps?

He carried the coin over to the bathroom window to look at it in the light of the setting sun. As he held it, the heat seemed to retreat within it. Now Keith wasn't really positive whether it had been warm at all. On one side was *S C,* in big capital letters and between them, a shape that looked vaguely like an umbrella stand. Keith wondered what the *S C* stood for. South Carolina?

It had to be a foreign coin, he thought. On the other side was the worn profile of a man with a long, thick neck. Around the profile was a circle of letters, but they were so worn that Keith couldn't make them out. In fact, the coin wasn't in very good shape. It had that green and bumpy look old bronze gets after being buried in the earth; and the edge was badly dented in several places.

But even so, there was no point in leaving it in the bathtub. Keith slipped the coin into the pocket of his quilted jacket.

At the head of the stairs, he glanced out the window. The sun was right on the horizon now. It would be getting dark any minute—time to get back home before Jennifer started worrying about him.

Keith descended the stairs and stopped in his tracks. He had left the front door wide open when he walked in here. Now it was closed again. And just then, he heard a low noise—a hiss, maybe a sigh?—from the hall behind him.

Turning around, he saw a wide ruby-red shaft of light fanning out from between the sliding doors. Curious, Keith walked back down the hall and peered into the six-sided room.

Outside the bay window, the deep red sun was right on the horizon. Only a few minutes before, the clear glass panes of the bay window had been completely transparent. Now they were glowing red, stained the same color as the dying sun.

He stepped into the room and gasped in astonishment. Somehow, the glass seemed to be collecting the sun's rays and amplifying them. The floor, the paneling—in fact, the entire room—was bathed in the crimson glow. Keith looked down at his hands, now blood-red. His quilted jacket, blue in ordinary daylight, glowed a deep purple.

Then he noticed the nearly life-sized human figures in each of the three windows. Those weren't scratches, but minute lines carefully etched into the glass. And now that the panes were glowing red, the pattern superimposed on them was clearly visible.

The figure in the left-hand window wore a long-sleeved tunic, leggings and a strange kind of half-shoe, half-sock. He looked a bit like one of those brass rubbings that Jennifer had brought back from a trip to England. Graceful and handsome, he was facing right and smiling broadly, extending his left hand toward the woman depicted in the middle window.

Like the Grinning Man, she seemed to be dressed in a costume out of the Middle Ages. Lifting the hem of her skirt, she was stepping—or maybe dancing— toward the Grinning Man. He was beckoning her to come with him, and she—with a coy smile on her face—was accepting his invitation.

Now Keith understood the reason for all those separate panes in each window. If a single sheet of etched glass, nearly six feet by three, got broken, then some artist would have to etch an entire panel to replace it. But small panes were much easier to replace. Now if some kid threw a rock at the window, the owner would need to commission only two or three six-sided panes at the most. Clever! And that etching was really masterly, he thought. Too bad you couldn't appreciate it except at certain times of the day, like this. . . .

And then his eyes fell on the third, right-hand window.

Both the Grinning Man and Willing Maiden were etched in profile. This other man was depicted full-face.

His mouth was contorted in grief, and big stylized tears ran from his eyes. Obviously this guy wasn't too lucky in love—the Grinning Man was stealing his woman away from him. But rather than doing anything to stop her, he was just standing there, crying over the situation. Damned fool!

But there was something oddly familiar about the face. Keith stepped closer. This man's face was contained within a single pane of glass, as if a six-sided mask had been fitted over his head. The tears were stylized, but the face behind them was almost photographically realistic. . . .

Outside, the sun was vanishing beneath the horizon. Yet the etched figure before Keith's eyes stood out more clearly than ever. All at once, Keith realized why those features looked so familiar. They were the same eyes, nose and mouth Keith saw in the bathroom mirror every morning. It was Keith's own face looking back from this six-sided pane!

Terrified and confused, Keith backed away from the etched-glass window. Outside, the sun had vanished beneath the horizon. Dusk was falling. Yet the leaded panes were still glowing bright red, slowly pulsing as if with a life of their own.

Afraid to take his eyes off that incredible right-hand window, Keith reached behind him, searching for the doorway to the hall. But instead, his hand brushed against solid wood.

Had those doors slid shut, trapping him in here? He spun around in near-panic. But no, he'd only bumped into one of the paneled walls. The two doors were still open, just as he'd left them. Only too grateful to get out of there, he ducked through the doorway and hurried down the hall toward the front door.

As he passed the bottom of the staircase, Keith glanced out through the entryway window beside the front door—and nearly dropped in his tracks. A transparent, headless figure had stepped onto the porch, blocking his way out.

He backed away, utterly terrified, and the apparition promptly vanished. Then Keith took a second look, and understood. It was his own reflection in the entryway window!

He stepped forward again, and the headless figure promptly reappeared. One step backward, and the figure vanished. Keith looked to his right, where the day's last light was shining through the window at the foot of the stairs—illuminating Keith's shoulders and torso, but not his head.

It had all been just a trick of the light! Keith could feel his pulse slowing back to normal as he opened the front door and stepped out onto the porch. . . .

But what about the face of the Weeping Fool, back there in the six-sided room? *That* was no reflection! Keith was sure the etched face had been his own—but right now, he didn't want to go back in there to see it again.

Closing the front door behind him, Keith heard the bolt slide into place. The door was locked now; he couldn't budge the knob more than a quarter-turn. Satisfied, he stepped off the porch and headed for the path across the gully.

It was getting dark quickly now, and Jennifer had turned on the outside floodlight over the kitchen door. Then suddenly Keith had the uneasy feeling that he was being watched. He turned abruptly and stared into each of the house's curtainless windows. But there was nobody there.

He closed his fingers around the heavy bronze coin in his jacket pocket. When he finally met whoever owned this house, he'd give him back the coin—along with a reminder not to leave his front door unlocked! But in the meantime, he decided not to mention anything to Jennifer about seeing his own face in that etched-glass panel. Not until he had another chance to look at that bay window during the day. . . .

But Keith knew he wouldn't have time to come back here tomorrow. First thing Wednesday morning, he had to visit the office in Chappaqua and get caught up on bills and the phone calls recorded on the answering machine. Then he, Marc and Jason had a new job starting in Peekskill. And that evening, Jennifer would want him home early to get cleaned up, put on a tie, shine his shoes . . .

There was always a chance, of course, that David wouldn't be available on such short notice. But not much of a chance, Keith thought. When Jennifer invited him for dinner, David M. Carmichael was *always* available.

2

Wednesday, April 11, 1979

AT SIX THIRTY THAT EVENING, just as the sun was setting, Jennifer heard David Carmichael's Mercedes-Benz pull into their driveway. The antiques dealer had a long drive up the Saw Mill River Parkway to New Castle, and Jennifer was determined to cook a dinner that would make this trip worthwhile. If only David realized how much she looked forward to his visits—because he was really the only link she had to the life she had known in New York City.

Only two years before, she had been running her own interior-decorating business on the Upper East Side. It was easy for her to find quality reproductions of antique French furniture. But every so often, a client was rich enough to afford the real thing. And then she would visit the David M. Carmichael Gallery in the Fuller Building, at 41 East Fifty-seventh Street.

Jennifer never tired of looking at the chairs, bureaus and gilded bronzes that David managed to buy at auction, here and abroad. All told, Jennifer must have brought the firm of David M. Carmichael, Inc., a good two hundred thousand dollars' worth of business. But she still hadn't gotten on a first-name basis with Miss Rosewood, David's English-born secretary. Nor was she completely happy about her relationship with David himself.

Jennifer's first marriage had ended in divorce in 1974, the same year it began. After the pain and disappointment wore off, she had gone out with other men, but the relationships never lasted. David Carmichael—twelve years older than she was—was the only man in New York whom Jennifer found really interesting.

He genuinely liked her too, she could tell. There was only one problem: David was married. And not only married, but still deeply, happily in love with Eleanor Carmichael, an elegant woman in her early forties. Jennifer felt envious whenever she saw David and his wife together. Quite obviously, lifelong romantic love wasn't just something the *Ladies' Home Journal* had dreamed up to boost circulation.

Not that Jennifer saw the Carmichaels that often, of course. Eleanor and David were a couple; Jennifer was single again. And so she saw David mainly when she visited his gallery. Every six months or so, she bumped into him at a cocktail party, or at an auction at Christie's or Sotheby Parke Bernet. And once in a *great* while, they would have lunch together—a purely business lunch at a very good French restaurant. Jennifer could see that David Carmichael wasn't the kind of man who cheated on his wife, *ever*. But that only made her like him all the more.

And then she had met Keith at a Bicentennial Fourth of July cocktail party up in Pound Ridge. Relaxed and self-confident, Keith Olson was completely different from the men she'd known in Manhattan. He made his living as a carpenter and painter, but preferred to work on older houses, restoring them as authentically as possible. He wasn't as elegantly handsome as David, but he was definitely attractive, with his laughing blue eyes and sandy-brown moustache.

After three hours, he and Jennifer were still standing on the lawn, the ice melted in their drinks, talking as if they'd known each other for years. They exchanged phone numbers. And then, when the party was over, Jennifer drove back to the city.

Jennifer wanted to call Keith as soon as she walked in the door of her apartment, but she held off. Keith wasn't from Manhattan; he might take it the wrong way. Instead, he called her—the very next morning.

For six agonizing, wonderful months, she and Keith tried to convince each other that this was simply infatuation, and not anything serious. Finally they gave up and set the wedding date for May 7, 1977.

Now, nearly two years later, they still loved each other. If only Jennifer didn't feel so homesick for New York City! Summers were beautiful in New Castle—but my God, the winters took forever. There were no museums, no art galleries, only a handful of restaurants. And the only movie theaters were almost five miles away. . . .

And she wished Keith wouldn't be so jealous whenever she invited David Carmichael for dinner. What really bothered Keith, more than anything else, she knew, was that David was single again.

In November 1977, six months after Jennifer and Keith were married, David had flown to Paris for an auction at the Hôtel Druot. And Eleanor Carmichael surprised a burglar who had broken into their Riverside Drive apartment.

23

When David stepped off the Concorde at Kennedy Airport, a homicide detective was waiting to drive him back in a squad car to Columbia-Presbyterian Hospital. Eleanor lived nearly three days before succumbing to her injuries. The police caught the young drug addict responsible, and the man was now serving a fifteen-year sentence at a prison in upstate New York.

As soon as she heard the news, Jennifer had started inviting David to dinner. As the months passed, the shock and grief ebbed away, and David began to seem more like himself again. But in any case, he hadn't remarried. In Keith's mind, the man was eligible—and a threat to his own happiness. Of course he was perfectly polite whenever David came to visit. But Jennifer knew her husband well enough to sense the jealous resentment that was smoldering inside him.

Keith didn't want to say anything, but this evening, Jennifer had really gone too far. With only the three of them for dinner, she had made onion soup from scratch, followed by filet mignon, an endive salad and two bottles of French wine. Keith didn't mind lavish cooking once in a while, but this was almost embarrassing. And for dessert, Jennifer served glossy little strawberry shortcakes—or *tartes aux fraises,* as David called them.

After dinner, the three of them took their coffee cups out to the living room. Keith wished he could add something to the conversation. But David and Jennifer kept on talking about antiques and auctions, and it was hard to get a word in edgewise.

Finally there came a lull in the conversation, and Keith took advantage of it. "How are the Fowlers?" he asked. Jerry and Ruth were a happy, down-to-earth young couple he and Jennifer used to play cards with. But then Jerry Fowler had landed a job on Wall Street, and they had moved to Manhattan—where David ran into them occasionally.

"Jerry and Ruth, you mean?" David asked. "I haven't seen them lately—but I understand she's asked him for a divorce."

"The Fowlers?" Jennifer asked. "I can't believe it!"

Keith was equally stunned. "Come on! I never saw a man who was more devoted to his wife than Jerry Fowler. Why would they be splitting up?"

David looked down at the floor. "Apparently she met someone else. She asked him for a divorce so she can get married again."

"And he's going along with that?" Keith snorted. "I'll tell you, if that happened to me, I wouldn't take it lying down! Why didn't Jerry go over and shoot the man or something?"

"Who can say?" David shrugged. "The only reason I found out about this," he added, "is that one of the auction houses is cataloguing Jerry Fowler's coin collection. He's selling it as part of their property settlement."

There was a moment's pause. Keith looked at Jennifer, who was sipping her coffee. If any man tried to take her away from him, Keith honestly couldn't imagine what he'd do! He looked back at David. "Speaking of coin collections," Keith said. "Do you know much about foreign coins?"

David nodded. "I used to collect French coins, but then they all got stolen in that burglary. Why?"

"I found a coin yesterday that doesn't look American. I'm wondering if it might be worth anything."

"A lot depends on condition," David replied. "Most really valuable coins are either proof or uncirculated."

"This one looks pretty worn," Keith admitted. "But would you mind taking a look at it? It's right upstairs."

"I'd be glad to," the antiques dealer replied.

Keith leaped to his feet, almost upsetting the coffee on the end table beside his chair. Jennifer looked at him in astonishment. He was more animated than he'd been all evening.

Keith rushed to the staircase, and Jennifer could hear him going up the stairs two at a time. Then she heard him opening the closet door in their bedroom. "Honestly," she told David. "I don't have the faintest idea what he's talking about."

But David Carmichael simply smiled back at Jennifer, delighted to be seeing her again. He could never repay her for inviting him to dinner so many times in those first terrible weeks after Eleanor's death. But now—especially tonight—Jennifer seemed conscious of him in a way that seemed stronger than mere friendship. How *did* Jennifer feel about him? Her marriage, of course, stood squarely in the way of David's ever finding out. But if that relationship—or Keith himself —were ever out of the picture . . .

David Carmichael sipped his coffee and made himself stop thinking such things. It wasn't polite to entertain romantic fantasies about your host's wife. And Keith Olson was clearly the jealous type—even when there wasn't anything for him to be suspicious about.

In no time at all, Keith was back downstairs, holding a large, dark coin in his outstretched hand. "I had this in my jacket pocket," he said.

David sighed inwardly. You weren't supposed to handle a coin except by the rim, since the acid sweat of a person's fingers could tarnish a coin's surface and drastically lower its value. But the dark, pitted coin Keith was holding out· could hardly look much worse than it already did.

"Here you go," Keith said, handing the coin to David.

"Where did you find it?" Jennifer asked.

"In that house across the gully."

"You found this *yesterday?*" she asked. "You didn't tell me you went inside."

Keith nodded. "The door swung open, right in front of me, as if someone were expecting me to walk in. So I assumed somebody was home. And then I found this coin lying in the bathtub. . . ."

David took the coin between his thumb and forefinger and held it under the light of the lamp beside his chair. Underneath all the wear and corrosion, it seemed to be bronze. Then his eyes widened.

"Good Lord," he muttered.

"What's the matter?" Jennifer asked.

"Nothing," David said, "I'm just amazed. I think this coin is Roman."

"You mean it's Italian?" Keith asked.

"No, *ancient* Roman." The antiques dealer turned the coin at an angle to the light. "Did you see these letters over here above the head? C-A-E-S-A-R. The man depicted here must be one of the Roman emperors."

"Can you tell which one?" Keith asked.

David shook his head. "This coin's so worn and battered I can't make out the other letters. And to be honest, I'm no expert on ancient coinage." Once more, he tried to make out the ghostly letters circling the profile on the coin's obverse. Then he paused. What was that odd tingling sensation in his fingers?

"Keith," Jennifer laughed. "You don't just find ancient coins lying around in bathtubs!"

"Apparently Keith does," said David diplomatically.

"I think it fell from somewhere," Keith said. "I

mean, I was about to go downstairs, and then I heard this drop into the bathtub behind me."

"Perhaps there's a coin collection stored in the attic," David said. "And this fell through the bathroom ceiling?"

"I thought of that," Keith agreed. "But there weren't any holes or cracks in the plaster that the coin could have fallen through."

"You walked right in?" Jennifer asked. "Even though nobody was home?"

"But I thought somebody *was* home," Keith protested. Now he was glad he hadn't mentioned the bay windows that glowed blood-red, or the pane that seemed to be etched with his own face. It all sounded too crazy and irrational.

David rotated the old coin between his thumb and forefinger. The strange vibrations were stronger now—much stronger. "Does it ever feel funny when you hold it?" he asked Keith.

"Yes!" Keith said. "When I first picked it up, it was really warm to the touch."

The antiques dealer felt the pulsing sensation spreading up his hand. It wasn't warmth. Rather, it was a raw discomfort that was just short of actual pain.

"David?" Jennifer asked. "Did you see anyone around the new house when you drove up tonight?"

"I didn't come that way," David replied. "But on my way home tonight, I can go west and pick up the Taconic instead of the Saw Mill River Parkway."

Keith stood up and walked into the kitchen. The sun had set long ago, but there were no lights on in the house across the gully. The house at 666 Sunset Brook Lane was completely dark. Turning back to the living room, he saw the expression on David's face. The antiques dealer had turned positively green!

"David?" Jennifer asked. "Don't you feel well?"

David wasn't sure. A clammy sweat had broken out across his forehead. The vibrations from the coin were building now, and there were visual images trying to make their way into his mind.

"No, I'm perfectly all right," he said trying to pull himself back to reality; to ignore the vision that was struggling—no, *battering*—to make him acknowledge it. Seeing Jennifer's worried look, he opened his mouth to reassure her . . .

Then, all at once, it seemed to David that he was no longer in his friends' living room in New Castle. He heard hoarse cries in a foreign language. And then, as if a movie were being projected before his eyes, he saw the coin. It was bright and coppery, as fresh as the day it had been struck. A pair of iron pincers held the coin over a brazier of live coals until it too was glowing red-hot.

Then quickly, before it could cool, it was pulled from the fire—and thrust into the mouth of an eyeless thing that had once been human. Now its arms and legs were bound to an upright beam planted in the ground; and it was near death. But it still had enough breath left in its lungs for a final scream.

Vividly, unmistakably, David saw how the old coin had become so pitted and corroded. Not from years in the earth, but by being quenched in the blood of a dying man. As if in a movie close-up, he could see the coin burning its way into the victim's tongue. . . . But this was no movie!

Trying to stop the vision, David threw the coin to the floor. It rolled across the living-room carpet and came to a stop against Keith's shoe. But David's fingers still tingled painfully. And he could still see—as clearly as he could see Keith and Jennifer—a tortured victim in an amphitheater built of stone. The horrid vision was superimposed over his view of the Olsons' living room, and it wouldn't go away!

Retching, David clasped his hand over his mouth. He rose to his feet and, swaying unsteadily, hurried out of the living room.

He knew there was a bathroom here on the first floor, right off Keith's den, but he realized he would never get there in time. Instead, he ran headlong for the front door. He reached the front steps just as the first heave struck him. The dinner that Jennifer had worked so hard to prepare wound up among the rhododendrons.

Ten minutes later, the antiques dealer was lying on the Olsons' living-room couch. Keith had removed David's shoes and loosened his tie, and across his forehead Jennifer had placed a washcloth soaked in cool water. The sickening vision had faded. He was feeling somewhat better.

"Even if Keith and I aren't affected yet," Jennifer said, "it had to be something I cooked for dinner. I really want to call the doctor and make sure. . . ."

David was mortified. First he had embarrassed himself, ruining Jennifer's evening. Now she and Keith were probably going to have their stomachs pumped! But how could he explain the vivid, terrifying images that had appeared in front of his eyes? How could an old Roman coin have that kind of effect on him?

"I had the grippe yesterday," David lied. "But I didn't mention it because I was looking forward to this evening, and I didn't want to worry you. It isn't your cooking—believe me!"

Keith and Jennifer looked at each other.

"Are you sure you shouldn't spend the night here?"

Jennifer asked. "The bed in the guest room is all made up. It wouldn't be any trouble."

"But the gallery opens at ten in the morning," David said. "And I have to pick up some invoices at my apartment." He couldn't bear the thought of sleeping under the same roof as Jennifer. To know that she was right across the hall, snuggled next to her husband. . . .

At the front door, Keith helped David on with his dark overcoat, then walked back into the living room.

"If you keep going north on Sunset Brook Lane," Jennifer reminded David, "you'll drive right past that new house. The entrance to the Taconic is only a mile farther on. It's marked, so you really can't miss it."

"I remember now," David said. He'd driven that way a couple of times before. Even so, it would be another hour or so before he was back home on Riverside Drive. Out of the corner of his eye, David saw Keith returning from the living room.

The antiques dealer turned to shake his host's hand —and then recoiled. Keith was holding the old bronze coin in his right palm! Obviously it didn't affect him the way it did David.

"Is there any way I could find out which emperor this is?" Keith asked.

"There must be reference books," David stammered, backing away. "But I wouldn't know which ones to suggest. Why don't you take it to some coin dealer and let him identify it for you?"

"There aren't too many coin shops up this way," Keith replied. "There must be plenty in the city, though."

"Yes." David nodded. "Of course. . . ."

Keith thrust out the coin at the antiques dealer. "Maybe you could have one of them check this out? If it wouldn't be any trouble."

David had to get a grip on himself. He couldn't let Jennifer see his hesitation and anxiety. "No trouble at all," he said, smiling weakly. "As soon as I find out which Caesar it is, I'll send the coin back to you by registered mail."

"Oh, no rush," said Keith, handing him the coin. "Why don't you keep it till the next time we see you?"

Quickly David slipped the coin into the pocket of his overcoat. This time, it had touched his fingers for barely a second. Yet already his whole hand was tingling painfully, as if held too close to a hot fire. And from somewhere far away, David could hear the parched whispers of a man in agony. He squared his shoulders and gulped down the taste of bile rising in his throat.

"Good night, David," said Jennifer, smiling.

He shook her hand firmly. After his performance fifteen minutes ago, he didn't dare kiss her. "Good night. And thanks again. I'm only sorry I had to spoil everything for you."

"Don't be silly," Keith said. "Don't give it another thought."

"Well, I certainly am grateful." David smiled at Jennifer one last time. "The next time, you two come down to New York, and the dinner's on me."

David saw Keith and Jennifer watching from their front door. He started the Mercedes-Benz and steered out of their driveway. Then he turned left, as Jennifer had suggested, and drove north until he crossed the concrete bridge at the top of Sunset Brook Lane.

As soon as Keith and Jennifer's house was out of sight, hidden behind the trees, David steered the car over to the side of the road and turned off the headlights. He didn't want the Olsons to see that he'd

32

stopped. Then he leaped out of the car, yanked off his overcoat—with the bronze coin still in the pocket—and flung the garment into the car's back seat.

Now, at least, that damned coin was back where he couldn't brush into it by accident! Before getting back behind the wheel, he sniffed the cold spring air. Over here, on this side of the bridge, the air smelled different —dank, and heavier, somehow. Why did he feel as if he couldn't draw a deep breath? Was there dampness rising from the brook below? But there was no breeze tonight.

David climbed back into the driver's seat. Wearing only his sports jacket, he felt a bit chilly, but the Merecedes' heater was already warming up. He looked up and down the road. No other car lights were visible. Sunset Brook Lane was wholly deserted. Satisfied, David steered the green Merecedes back onto the pavement and turned on his headlights.

What the hell *had* happened to him when he'd touched that old coin? David had been handling old objects all his life. But never before had he felt that weird, almost painful vibration—much less seen and heard things that weren't there! If he was psychic or something, why had his abilities lain dormant for all these years? Or was there something special about that coin for it to evoke such a violent response in him?

He looked ahead to where Sunset Brook Lane curved to the left. Then, through the trees, he saw it—the new house Keith and Jennifer had told him about. And there was a red light flickering through one of the windows.

David took his foot off the gas pedal and slowed down for a better look. Directly ahead now, on his left, was the small back porch, built out from the back door. The scalloped clapboards reflected the glow from his headlights. And then David saw the big bay window jutting out toward the street. There was that red glow again, just behind one of the panes of glass.

Had the house caught fire? David slowed the Mercedes to a crawl and crept past the bay window in first gear. He glanced sideways, trying to see what was burning inside the vacant structure.

Only the house wasn't vacant! A figure was standing right behind the bay window's leaded glass. Bathed in red light, it was staring out at the passing Mercedes. And David was almost sure he recognized who it was.

David braked the car to a complete stop and looked back over his shoulder. But the room behind the bay window was empty now. The windows of the house were all dark, upstairs and down.

He must have only imagined it! There was no way it could have been Jennifer Olson! He had left her with Keith at her own front door only moments before. There was no way she could have made it across the gully in the dead of night. He was just thinking about her too much. . . .

David slipped the Mercedes into first gear and stepped on the gas. He was still a mile from the Taconic Parkway, and more than an hour away from his apartment on Riverside Drive.

3

Thursday, April 12, 1979

"MAYBE YOU COULD FIX THAT leak in the attic before it rains again," said Jennifer over breakfast that morning.

Keith set down his coffee cup. "Leak?" he asked.

"Remember that big rainstorm before we went on vacation? I went up to the attic to get my suitcase, and there was a trickle of water running down the chimney."

Keith and his assistants were working out in Peekskill that Thursday. So instead of eating a sandwich at work as he usually did, Keith drove home for lunch to see if he could find where the leak was.

On his way home, he passed by the house at 666. It looked just as it had on Tuesday afternoon. Only now there was an enameled metal sign hammered into the bare soil in front of the bay window:

FOR RENT
Thomas Greene,
Realtor
555-0098

Keith knew Tom Greene. Whenever a house needed to be spruced up before going on the market, Tom would recommend Keith for the job. But this new place did need work—especially on the inside, with that lousy wallboard—and Keith wondered why Tom hadn't given him a call. Well, he had been on vacation. When he got back to the office, Keith decided, he'd give Tom a ring and find out who owned this house.

Ten minutes later, Keith was up on the roof of his own house, crawling toward the chimney. Spring was here officially, but the sun kept ducking behind clouds, taking with it whatever warmth the air had accumulated. Keith wished he could have worn gloves. But for climbing around on asphalt shingles, gloves were too slippery. Keith needed his bare hands.

The roof's elevation gave him a good view of the new house across the gully. There had been a truck from the power company there that morning—evidently the electricity was getting hooked up today. And now, as Keith watched, a landscaper's van pulled up in the gravel driveway by the front porch. Two men got out and began raking the bare soil around the house and spreading what looked like fertilizer. Whoever was renting out that place sure wasn't wasting any time.

It didn't take Keith long to find the leak Jennifer had complained about. Over the winter, water had frozen under the chimney flashing, forcing the metal away from the bricks by maybe a sixteenth of an inch. But the weather today was too cold for caulking. Ideally, Keith knew, he should wait until afternoon, when the sun would fall right on the leaky spot. . . .

Then he heard a heavy engine approaching up Sunset Brook Lane. From atop the roof, Keith watched as the United Parcel truck slowed and stopped outside his driveway.

Keith rubbed his numb, chilly hands. The truck's arrival gave him a perfect excuse to get down off the roof. He backed down the shingles and lowered himself down his aluminum extension ladder. Then, when he was only six feet from the ground, Keith jumped off the rung sideways. Geronimo! He landed with a thump in the flower bed where Jennifer sowed marigolds every spring.

The United Parcel man, coming up the front path, seemed suitably impressed. "Package for Mrs. Olson," he said. "Sign here, please?"

The cardboard carton was barely a foot wide, but surprisingly heavy. The return address was some firm in Edmonds, Washington. Keith carried it into the kitchen, where Jennifer was preparing grilled cheese sandwiches. She handed Keith a cup of hot soup and began slitting open the box with a pair of poultry shears.

"What's that you ordered?" Keith asked.

"Brandied peaches. Your brother Paul loved the ones we gave him for Christmas, so I thought he'd like some more for his birthday in July."

Keith's hands were still cold, and the warm mug of soup felt good against his fingers. He glanced out the kitchen window. Across the gully, a man was using a roller on what would soon become the front lawn at 666 Sunset Brook Lane.

As Jennifer lifted jars of brandied peaches onto the table, Keith reached into the box for one of the crumpled sheets of newspaper that had protected the jars on their shipment across the country. He couldn't resist seeing what was going on in the Pacific Northwest, three thousand miles away.

The page of newsprint Keith was looking at was dated April 4. Among the furniture- and department-store ads was a two-column headline:

SLAYER OF TWO UP FOR PAROLE AFTER FIVE YEARS AT MCNEIL ISLAND

Accompanying the article was the photograph of a house that looked strangely familiar. Keith set the soup mug down on the table and picked up the paper in both hands, unfolding it as best he could. The grainy newspaper photo wasn't all that clear, but the house in it looked exactly like the one at 666 Sunset Brook Lane!

Lost in shock and amazement, Keith smoothed out the paper on the table. On closer examination, the scalloped clapboards looked the same. The gingerbread trim on the porch and eaves looked the same. And if Keith used a little imagination, he could even make out the entryway panels and fan window over the front door. The clincher would be if this house had a bay window, like the place across the gully! But the newspaper photo had been taken from an angle where the six-sided room—if there was one—was hidden on the far side of the house.

Keith read the caption under the picture:

The house at 666 Bremerton Road, as it appeared just after the murders

"Hey, Jennifer!" he said. "Take a look at this!"

She placed a grilled cheese sandwich on the table in front of him. "If you can move that newspaper—"

"But see this house in the picture? It looks exactly

like the one across the gully. It's even got the same street number!"

Jennifer stared at the picture for a moment, then glanced out the kitchen window. "I'll have to take your word for it. I haven't been over there yet."

Keith knew his wife hadn't been pleased to hear he'd entered the unlocked house on his own—snooping, she called it. Once more, he smoothed out the wrinkled page and began reading the article:

Convicted murderer James Beaufort will be granted a hearing by the Parole Board, officials at McNeil Island Federal Penitentiary confirmed today. Beaufort has already served five years of a 20-years-to-life sentence.

In 1974, he confessed to having brutally murdered Edgar Sutton and Patricia Swenson in the house he had rented for Miss Swenson's use. At his trial, he testified he had surprised her and Sutton together in the Bremerton Road residence. Convinced that Sutton was trying to talk her out of seeing him again, he killed them both in a fit of jealous rage.

In a statement to the press yesterday, Beaufort's attorney recalled his client's years of service on the Seattle City Council. The lawyer claimed that Beaufort "has behaved himself as a model prisoner and shows every sign of total rehabilitation. Moreover, he deeply regrets the crime of passion that cost two innocent people their lives nearly six years ago."

The house at 666 Bremerton Road remained vacant for years, despite attempts to rent it to others. Then last September, the two-story frame house (continued p. 18)

Keith grabbed the box and dumped all the crushed newspaper out on the floor. Then he knelt on the vinyl tiles and began unfolding the crumpled pages, one by one.

"Keith?" Jennifer asked. "What *are* you doing?"

"That's an interesting article I started," Keith said. "And I'd like to finish it."

Finally he had all the pages spread out on the kitchen floor beside him. One by one, he picked up the sheets, scanned them, and stuffed them back into the cardboard carton. Comics, sports, home-repair hints, but no page 18!

Finally, he picked up the page with the photograph on it and looked at it again. Sure, old houses sometimes resembled each other. But how often did you find two places with the same clapboards, carved wood trim, porch roof and entryway windows—three thousand miles apart? He couldn't get over it! Could the new house across the gully be the exact same structure?

He took Jennifer's poultry shears and carefully cut out the crumpled two-column article, together with the photo of the house at 666 Bremerton Road. Then he remembered Tom Greene's rental sign out in front of the new house. Certainly Tom would know who the owner was—and where the house had come from!

"Your soup's getting cold," Jennifer said.

To please her, Keith took a bite of the grilled cheese sandwich and a swallow of lukewarm soup. Then he stepped to the telephone on the kitchen wall and began dialing.

At a little past 1 P.M., just when Keith was calling Tom Greene's number, David Carmichael emerged from the private office at the back of his gallery at 41 East Fifty-seventh Street.

Miss Rosewood had noticed that her employer had come to work in a strange mood. Only once had he emerged from behind his desk, to greet an old customer

40

interested in a Louis XV *poudreuse.* But his smile was forced, his mind evidently elsewhere. Now, she saw, he had put on his dark overcoat and pigskin gloves. And was carrying the briefcase in which he kept photos of important pieces and catalogs of upcoming auctions. Ordinarily he kept the case tucked under his arm. Today, though, he was holding it in his left hand, well away from his body—as if it contained a bomb that might go off at any minute.

David glanced at his secretary with the same cheerless smile she'd seen earlier that morning. "Miss Roscwood, I should be no more than an hour."

"Very good, Mr. Carmichael. Have a pleasant lunch!"

But the antiques dealer was not going to lunch. Pushing his way out the Fuller Building's bright brass doors, he walked past a pushcart loaded with dry bagels and stale chestnuts. Then he crossed Madison Avenue and headed west. Over at Seventh Avenue and Fifty-sixth Street, the New York Sheraton was hosting a numismatic convention. According to that morning's paper, more than fifty different dealers were displaying their wares. And out of that number, David reasoned, there had to be at least one who could identify the Roman coin that Keith Olson had handed him the night before.

The dealers had set up their tables in a huge room in the basement, and before he could get in, David had to wait in line to register. The doors were guarded by a burly black policeman. Once inside, David made his way down a series of narrow aisles crammed with glass cases and thronged with dealers and collectors from a dozen different countries.

In the middle of one aisle, David stopped in front of the booth of a coin dealer from Texas. Under the plate glass of his display cases were row upon row of coins of the ancient world. All of them had been placed in square envelopes of plastic; and many, David saw, were just as worn and corroded as the one Keith had given him. Most of the coins were of bronze or silver. But here and there, David's eye saw a flash of gold. It certainly looked as if he'd come to the right booth.

Behind the counter, a pretty girl with glasses and a Navajo squash-blossom necklace smiled at the tall, well-dressed customer. "May I help you, sir?" she asked.

"I hope so," David replied. Still wearing his gloves, he fished around inside his briefcase and pulled out the old bronze coin. Even through the leather glove, he could feel the unpleasant vibrations, like the throbbing of a bee wrapped inside a towel.

"I believe this is a coin of ancient Rome," he said to the girl. "But perhaps you could tell me exactly what it is?"

He set the coin down on the glass counter, and the young woman lifted it between her thumb and forefinger. Clearly it didn't seem to affect her; she handled it as if it were no more than a subway token.

"Hm!" she said, squinting at it through her glasses. "Can you please wait here just a minute?"

"I'll be glad to," David replied.

At the rear of the booth sat a plump, bearded man. He wore glasses and a string tie and was leafing through the pages of a thick reference book. The girl approached him and showed him the coin. From his pocket the coin dealer drew a jeweler's loupe and examined it under high magnification. David saw the man's face register a small twitch of surprise. Then the dealer scrutinized the other side of the coin, turning it over carefully in his fingers. Finally he nodded to the girl and stepped over to David, holding the coin in one hand and the loupe in the other.

"Yes, sir!" the bearded man said. His Texas accent was broader than the girl's. "Your coin here is a bronze sestertius from the reign of the emperor Nero. It was struck—oh, about A.D. 64."

"I'm amazed that you can be that precise," David said.

"Well"—the dealer smiled—"it helps when you've been in business twenty years like I have." From beneath the counter he pulled a small velvet mat, and set the sestertius down on it as if the coin were a rare piece of jewelry. "You see this structure on the reverse? Here," he said, offering David the loupe. "Please have a look for yourself."

David fitted the loupe's black plastic barrel under his eyebrow. Then he lowered his head until the coin swam into focus. Under magnification, the corrosion was even more evident—but so was the original design. Between the letters *S* and *C* was an upright object that, he could now see, was composed of vertical columns.

"In A.D. 64," the Texan explained, "Nero finished building himself a triumphal arch to commemorate his victories in Parthia. That's the very same arch that appears on the reverse of your coin there. So we can date it pretty safely at around that time."

Turning the coin over, David was aware of a momentary tingling in his gloved fingers. The worn profile on the other side depicted a man with a thick, long neck and a jaw thrust aggressively forward, but the other features were worn away.

"This *is* in pretty bad shape," David admitted. "But then, I imagine it's been buried for some time."

43

"It does have a bit more corrosion than normal for a piece of this era," the coin dealer agreed. "Looks to me like it might have been in a fire of some kind. Copper alloys get that way when they've been heated."

David remembered his mental vision of the coin being heated over a brazier of red-hot coals. "But that makes no sense," he stammered. "Why would anyone want to burn a coin?"

"Oh, houses burn down," the Texan said. "Sometimes with coin collections in them. And remember the story about how Nero fiddled while Rome burned? Maybe your sestertius got buried in the ashes."

David was relieved to hear that there was a logical explanation for the coin's exposure to heat. Then what he'd envisioned probably hadn't been real after all— just some kind of terrible fantasy.

"But even so," the bearded coin dealer went on, "many collectors like to assemble a set of coins of each of the twelve Caesars. How much would you want for this?"

David Carmichael had been in the antiques business long enough to recognize that old dealer's ploy. Never make the customer an offer! Instead, ask *him* to name a price. Usually an inexperienced collector would short-change himself, asking only a fraction of the object's real wholesale value.

"This isn't my coin," David explained. "I'd have to ask the owner if he's interested in selling."

The Texas coin dealer sighed to himself. Customers *always* pretended that their coins belonged to someone else. It gave them time to think about the offer—and shop for a higher price.

"But if the owner *is* interested," David added, "can I tell him how much you'd be willing to pay?"

"Well . . ." The Texan hesitated. "Like you just said, this sestertius isn't in that good condition. Let's see, now." He drummed his pudgy fingers on the table.

"What would you resell it for, retail?" David asked.

The bearded coin dealer looked at him with some surprise. This handsome New Yorker wasn't such an amateur after all. "I could sell a coin like this one here for about one thousand dollars. I'll give your friend six hundred seventy-five."

David didn't bother to hide his amazement. How many thousand-dollar Roman coins are left lying around in bathtubs? He picked up the valuable sestertius and put it back into his briefcase.

The bearded Texan regarded David shrewdly. Perhaps this well-to-do customer wasn't willing to sell—but maybe he'd like to buy! Every collector longs to upgrade his collection, and why should this knowledgeable, well-off gentleman be any different?

"Sir?" The coin dealer held up his hand. "It so happens we're lucky enough to have another specimen of that same sestertius. Maybe even from the same dies."

"Really?" David asked.

The dealer pointed down through the thick glass of his display case. There, secure in its clear plastic envelope, was a similar bronze sestertius—but in far better condition than the one Keith had found. David couldn't help wondering what would happen if he held this other sestertius in his hand. Would it affect him the same way the first one had?

"Would you like to see it?" the coin dealer asked.

"Yes, please," David replied.

The bearded man opened the back of the case and set the plastic-encased coin down on the counter. The emperor's neck was swollen to bull-like proportions, as if he were about to explode in rage. Unlike Keith's dirty-brown discovery, this sestertius was a smooth, greenish color—and in such good condition that David could make out the capital letters surrounding the imperial profile:

NEROCLAVDIVSCAESARAVGGERPM

"As I'm sure you know," the coin dealer said, "the Romans ran all their words together, and they used abbreviations. Those letters stand for 'Nero Claudius, Caesar Augustus, Germanicus, Pontifex Maximus.' Supposedly," the Texan added, "whenever Nero was having an enemy tortured to death, he'd have a coin like this, struck with his own likeness, placed right in the mouth of the dying man. Sort of a memento for the next world, so that the victim wouldn't dare offend the emperor ever again."

David went pale. Again he recalled the image that had persisted before his eyes back in Jennifer's living room.

"Go on," the bearded Texan coaxed him. "Take a look at the reverse."

David hesitated, afraid to touch his gloved fingers to the plastic envelope. What if this coin—so much better preserved than Keith's specimen—afflicted him with an even stronger reaction?

Slowly, carefully, he picked up the plastic holder and placed it in his gloved left hand. On the reverse of the coin, Nero's triumphal arch stood out clearly, even to the four horses atop it. On either side of the arch were the letter *S C*.

"What do those letters stand for?" David asked.

"*Senatus Consulto*. Meaning that Nero ruled with the acknowledgment of the Roman Senate."

David paused, waiting for the vibrations to begin. But nothing happened. Curious now, he stripped off his glove, and placed the plastic holder directly against the palm of his left hand. But still he felt nothing—nothing at all!

This splendid sestertius filled him with a wild curiosity. Why didn't he feel anything? Perhaps the plastic interfered with the transmission of the sensation. Of course the coin dealer would never allow David to handle a rare coin like this in his bare hands. But if David *bought* the coin, he could do as he pleased with it!

The square plastic envelope was stapled to a square card bearing the coin's price—which, David saw, was expressed in letters, not numerals. Many antiques dealers used codes like that. Choosing a ten-letter word or phrase like CHARLESTON or ANTIQUERS-O, they let the first letter stand for 1, the next for 2, and so on through zero. That way, a $1,250 price tag translated into CHLN or ANQO. The customer was forced to ask the price—which let the dealer size up his client and adjust the figure accordingly.

This sestertius was priced at OEXX—a code that David didn't recognize. But if Keith's battered, worn specimen was worth a thousand dollars retail, and this one was in so much better shape. . . .

"It *is* lovely," David said. "How much is it?"

"Rather reasonable." The bearded coin dealer smiled, teasing him. "It's thirty-seven hundred."

David tried to hide his amazement. Three thousand seven hundred dollars! But after all, the sestertius *was* an antique of sorts. What the hell, he could always deduct the purchase as a business expense—and then sell it again at auction, once he had satisfied his curiosity. . . .

The coin dealer could hardly conceal his delight when David reached inside his jacket and drew out his checkbook.

"I'm a dealer myself," David said, placing one of his own DAVID M. CARMICHAEL, INC. business cards down on the glass display case. "So perhaps you could afford me some sort of professional discount?"

The Texan took a long look at David's hand-tailored suit and explained that he couldn't. Ten minutes later, David was on his way back to 41 East Fifty-seventh Street, carrying two bronze sestertii in his briefcase.

As soon as he got them home, the experiment would begin.

4

Thursday, April 12, 1979

"MR. GREENE'S OFFICE," THE SECRETARY said when Keith dialed the realtor's number.

"This is Keith Olson. I've done work for Tom before. Can I speak to him, please?"

"I'm sorry, but Mr. Greene has gone to lunch. Can he call you when he gets back?"

"Well, I'll be working in Peekskill this afternoon," Keith said. "But Tom has my home number. If he could call me at home tonight . . ."

"May I tell him what it's in reference to?"

"You sure can!" Keith looked out his kitchen window at the house across the gully. "Tell him I'm *very* interested in that house he's renting at six sixty-six Sunset Brook Lane."

Keith bolted down the rest of his sandwich and soup, kissed Jennifer and walked back out to the panel truck. On his way back to work, he stopped to take another look at the new house.

The landscaping crew had finished their work, and their van had already left. All the bare earth around the house had been raked smooth, seeded, and tamped down. The landscapers had also laid square flagstones between the front porch and the bluestone gravel driveway, and had planted a blue spruce between the front porch and the road.

Keith pulled his panel truck into the gravel driveway and got out. He wanted a close look at those etched-glass windows—and particularly that pane in which he thought he'd seen his own face on Tuesday afternoon. But the landscapers had hammered a number of little stakes into the ground at the edge of the lawn and tied a white string from stake to stake. About fifteen feet of freshly seeded ground separated Sunset Brook Lane from the bay window; and Keith didn't want to step on the new lawn in his heavy work shoes.

At this distance, though, the figures etched into the glass weren't distinct at all. Keith could barely make out the outline of the Willing Maiden, and only because he knew just where to look. Obviously the etching was like the design of a stained-glass window—intended to be viewed mainly from the inside.

During the seeding, the landscapers had left Tom Greene's metal FOR RENT sign right next to the bay window. That reminded Keith—Tom Greene usually ate very long lunches at the Millwood Inn, north of Chappaqua. Often Tom lingered at his table for an hour or more, chatting with past customers and old friends. If Keith drove down there before returning to work, he could probably catch Tom before the realtor returned to his office.

In the Washington Irving Lounge of the Millwood Inn, Tom Greene was seated in a booth against the wall, cater-corner from the bar. Finishing the last bite of his club sandwich, he leaned back happily against the booth's red leather seat. Ordinarily the dapper, balding realtor had only one drink with his lunch. But now he decided he had something to celebrate. After all, it wasn't every day that money practically crawled into his pocket.

Just now, on his way to the Millwood Inn, Tom had stopped off at the bank to deposit one thousand dollars in cash—the sum Coste had promised him for arranging all the paperwork involved in moving that two-story house to Sunset Brook Lane in New Castle. Now Coste wanted to rent the place—Tom had received the telephone call that very morning—and wanted Greene's firm to handle the listing exclusively. Yessir, it was going to be a profitable April after all. . . .

The waitress had just brought Tom Greene a second Manhattan when he saw his friend Keith Olson walk in the door. The realtor's plump face broke into a broad smile, and he waved his hand in the air to catch Keith's attention.

"God, but you look tanned!" the realtor exclaimed as Keith settled into the seat across from him. "Where have you been?"

"Grand Bahama Island," Keith said, grinning. "Just got back this Tuesday."

Tom Greene pointed to the brimming drink on the table in front of him. "Will you join me?"

"No; no thanks. I've got to get back to work this afternoon."

"Then let me buy you coffee," the realtor said. His hand shot up in the air again, and he craned his neck to see where the waitress was.

"Listen, Tom . . ." The smile dropped from Keith's

face. He liked the jaunty, cheerful old man, but today he just wasn't in the mood for small talk. "What's the story on that house you're renting across from us? The one at six sixty-six Sunset Brook Lane?"

"Story?" Tom Greene smiled genially. "The hard part was in making sure there *was* no story. See, the owner insisted on having as little publicity as possible."

"I don't understand," Keith said. The waitress approached the booth, and Tom Greene pointed to the empty coffee cup in front of Keith. "What publicity was he likely to get?"

"Well, my God!" the realtor chortled. "Whenever you move a house, an entire house, it usually makes the local news. And here was this huge, two-story structure being towed up the Hudson on a barge! They had to dock it at Ossining, and winch the whole thing off onto a flatbed trailer, and then truck it over those narrow, winding roads to your street. . . ." Tom paused. "When'd you say you got back from vacation?"

"Tuesday," Keith repeated.

"Too bad. Then you missed it all. This was all a week ago Wednesday."

The waitress returned and poured them each a cup of steaming-hot coffee. Tom Greene handed Keith the cream pitcher.

"No thanks," Keith said, "I like it black."

"Well, you see," Tom Greene continued, "we arranged the actual move after dark so that there weren't any curiosity seekers to get in the way. There was only one reporter from a local paper. He tried to take a couple of flash pictures, but I don't think they turned out."

Keith sipped the strong, hot coffee. "But why put a house that size on such a narrow tract of land?"

Tom Greene took a sip of his new drink and shrugged. "That's what Mr. Coste wanted—that particular spot, right across from your place."

"Is that the owner's name?" Keith asked. "Coste?"

Tom Greene nodded.

Keith frowned. "But all that side of the gully belongs to old Clyde Ramsey. I thought he was planning to leave his acreage to the town when he dies, so they can make it a bird sanctuary. I'm amazed he'd sell."

Tom Greene looked around the Washington Irving Lounge to see if there was anyone within earshot. Then he leaned across the table toward Keith. "The only reason Ramsey agreed," he whispered, "is because he thought he had cancer. Back in March, Clyde went for a checkup, and his chest X-ray showed the shadows of tumors in both lungs. And do you have any idea how expensive those cobalt and chemotherapy treatments are? Ramsey needed cash, and he needed it fast. See, your part of New Castle is zoned for one dwelling per acre. So when Coste called me and asked me to offer Clyde a certain amount—a very generous amount, let me tell you!—for that single acre he wanted, Clyde accepted his offer the same day."

"Jesus!" said Keith, shaking his head.

"But the good part"—Tom Greene smiled—"is that Clyde's next set of X-rays showed no trace of cancer at all! Something must have fogged the plates during his first examination. But by then, of course, Ramsey had already accepted Coste's offer—and Coste paid cash, by the way! Most of his acre runs in a narrow strip down to the brook at the bottom of the gully, but stops just short of it. Coste was very specific. He didn't want the property to be bordered by running water."

"Didn't he give you any reasons?" Keith asked.

Tom Greene shook his head, and a trace of fear crossed his face. "Coste always seems to be in something of a hurry. If I ask him unnecessary questions, he just sort of freezes me out. But I tell you, getting all those wide-load permits from the State Police was a nightmare!"

Keith stirred his coffee restlessly. "Do you know if this Mr. Coste collects old coins?" he asked.

The realtor shrugged his thin shoulders. "I haven't any idea."

"Well, what's his first name? Where's he from?"

But Tom Greene just sat there, his drink in his hand, with that strange, worried look on his face.

"Oh, come on!" Keith snorted. "Don't you have *any* information about this guy?"

"Keith, I've never met the man!" Tom Greene shook his head sadly. "All our transactions have been over the telephone. Oh, he did stop by the office once, to sign some papers . . ." He avoided Keith's gaze. "But I was out to lunch. I didn't see him."

The realtor paused. He didn't like to lie to anyone, much less to an old friend like Keith Olson. But the whole truth was simply too embarrassing to explain.

A little more than a month before, Coste had telephoned to say he wanted to visit the real estate office, deliver the money for Clyde Ramsey's land, and sign all the papers at the same time. So Tom instructed his secretary to type up everything—the deed, the formal transfer, the title search. The realtor placed them all in a manila envelope on his desk, where they would be ready for Mr. Coste's arrival the next morning.

He locked up the real estate office at five forty-five

that evening, the same as always. Or at least he thought he had. Because when he came back the next morning at nine fifteen, he found the front door unlocked. Not wide open, mind you, just ajar—so that you could hardly see it from the sidewalk.

Had there been a break-in during the night? Tom Greene hurried inside, expecting to find his office ransacked, his desk jimmied open, his files strewn all over the floor. But to his immense relief, everything was in perfect order. There was nothing missing.

Quite the contrary!

Finally he noticed the manila envelope he had left on his desk the night before. It was now sealed with Scotch tape, and looked a lot fatter and heavier than it had the previous afternoon. When he tore it open, out poured dozens and dozens of fifty- and one-hundred-dollar bills.

It took him nearly fifteen minutes to count all the money, and then another fifteen to count the bills over again and verify the amount. It was all there, down to the last dollar—enough to pay for Clyde Ramsey's acre, plus money for the closing costs and title search and Tom Greene's commission.

Stuffed behind all those bills were the documents Tom Greene's secretary had typed up. Each one was signed in the appropriate place with an elegant, if illegible, signature. Obviously Coste *had* dropped by the real estate office, first thing that morning, to sign the papers!

The aging realtor was positive that he'd locked his front door the night before. But obviously he couldn't have! Tom didn't want his secretary to think he was getting senile or absentminded. So later that afternoon, he told her that Mr. Coste had dropped by the office and signed the papers while she was out on her lunch hour. That explanation was plausible enough, and she thought nothing more about it.

Now, this very morning, Tom had collected the thousand dollars Coste had promised him for helping to arrange the house's actual move to Sunset Brook Lane. When the realtor unlocked his office door, he had found one of his office envelopes, with his own return address on it, lying in the middle of the floor. Inside were ten crisp one-hundred-dollar bills. Coste must have pushed the money through the mail slot, Tom thought. But how had the envelope managed to slide so far across the floor? And why had Coste used one of Tom Greene's own envelopes? He must have taken the stationery when he signed the papers, back in March.

Now Tom Greene watched as Keith Olson sipped the last of his coffee. Something was definitely eating at Keith, the realtor thought. Usually Keith was affable and lighthearted. Tom had never seen him lost in thought like this. . . .

"Well!" Keith cleared his throat. "Now that you're handling the rentals on Coste's house . . ."

A slow, baffled grin crept over Tom Greene's face. "Keith! How the hell did you know that?"

"I'm not blind," Keith snorted. "Your 'For Rent' sign is right out in front of the place!"

"But that can't be!" Tom Greene exclaimed. "Coste called me only this morning about my acting as the rental agent on six sixty-six! First I have to put the listing in tomorrow afternoon's paper. Then Saturday I'll drive over there and stick one of my enameled metal signs in the front lawn."

"This *is* an enameled sign," Keith insisted. "Right by the bay window, facing the street. I've seen your signs before, Tom."

The realtor sipped the last of his Manhattan, and wished he had another. Those green-and-white weatherproof signs had cost him a pretty penny, and so he kept them in a locked cabinet in his office. And no one else had a key.

"Maybe you lent Coste a sign," Keith persisted, "so that he could put it up for you?"

"Maybe," Tom Greene lied. "I just don't remember." He *must* be getting senile; there was no other explanation!

"But haven't you been to see the house yourself?"

"Oh, yes." Tom nodded. "I drove by the morning after the move, when the contractors were settling it down on the new foundation."

"Then you must have seen that place needs repairs—especially if your client intends to rent it out. You know how I love fixing up old houses, Tom. Why didn't you call me?"

"I wasn't supposed to," the realtor replied, swallowing uncomfortably.

"What do you mean?" Keith demanded. "Did Coste tell you *not* to offer me the job?"

"No, no! Quite the contrary." Tom Greene could see that Keith was puzzled and upset over the misunderstanding. *Damn you, Coste!* the realtor thought. "He did say that he wanted the house restored properly—particularly on the inside. And he must have heard of you before, because he mentioned you by name."

"Then why didn't you—"

"Coste told me not to bother calling you," Tom Greene said. "Because he wants to get in touch with you himself."

By the time Keith left the Washington Irving Lounge, he was already running an hour late. But what the hell—his assistants, Marc and Jason, could carry on without him. So rather than go straight back to Peekskill, Keith drove to the Chappaqua Library.

From a government pamphlet, "Moving Historic Buildings," he was surprised to learn that the technique of house-moving was at least two hundred years old. In 1838, a four-story brick house in New York City was moved fourteen feet, without damage to the mirrors hanging on the walls inside. In 1869, workers moved a six-story Boston hotel, also built of brick and weighing five thousand tons. In 1889, a three-story Nebraska courthouse was towed nine miles behind a railroad locomotive. And in 1975, a ten-thousand-ton Gothic cathedral in Czechoslovakia was moved to a new location half a mile away. Computers made sure the fourteenth-century structure didn't get out of alignment by more than one twenty-fifth of an inch.

By comparison, moving a two-story Victorian frame dwelling was child's play. But had a house ever been moved clear across the country before? Now Keith's curiosity was greater than ever.

Ever since Wednesday, he had been rereading that tantalizing article clipped from the Seattle newspaper. He wanted to know more about convicted killer James Beaufort, about his trial and surprise confession—and most of all, about the murder house at 666 Bremerton Road.

Keith didn't have the money for a flight to Seattle. So instead, he drove to the Olson Custom Carpentry office, where he telephoned long distance to the Seattle paper and found out the name of its managing editor. Then he sat down at his desk and typed out a letter, asking the man please to look in his paper's back files and photocopy anything and everything the paper had ever printed on the Sutton-Swenson murder case.

Reminding the editor that the crimes had been committed sometime in 1973, Keith stapled to his letter a twenty-dollar bill to reward the man for his trouble.

As his return address, Keith gave Olson Custom Carpentry in Chappaqua. Jennifer already thought he was paying too much attention to that new house across the gully—after all, it was someone else's property. If she caught him leafing through a stack of articles about a double murder that had occurred six years before, she'd probably send for the men in the white coats.

The clerk at the Chappaqua post office told him that airmail wasn't necessary. All envelopes mailed first class automatically went by airplane. But even so, the clerk admitted, mail to the Pacific Northwest could take three or four days. Keith didn't want to wait that long. He paid the extra postage and mailed his letter airmail special delivery.

On his way back to his Fifty-seventh Street gallery, David Carmichael had stopped to eat a very light lunch. But that evening, when he got home to Riverside Drive, he skipped dinner entirely. The antiques dealer deliberately left his stomach empty, because he knew what he had to do that evening. But David kept on procrastinating—he wanted to do a bit of research first.

By 11:45 P.M. his stomach was still growling, but he no longer felt hungry. He sighed and closed the one-volume *Encyclopedia of the Ancient World* and carried it back to the library. Then he returned to the living room and sat down on the couch. The lights of the brass chandelier were reflected in the polished marble coffee table in front of him.

He was almost sorry he had consulted the encyclopedia in the first place, because it had told him almost more than he wanted to know about the reign of Nero Claudius Caesar Drusus Germanicus.

The Emperor Caligula had been just as savage and cruel, but he had ruled for only four years. Nero had remained on the throne for a bloody fourteen-year reign. He had tortured and killed hundreds of people, including members of his own family and his wife, Poppaea. It was Nero who told his servants to set the fire that raged through the city for six days before it broke out anew. Nero did not fiddle while Rome burned—he sang! But no sooner were the ashes cold than Nero accused Rome's new Christian sect of having set the fire. During Nero's persecutions, the catacombs beneath Rome were packed with the bodies of martyrs. St. Paul was beheaded, and St. Peter crucified upside down.

But one fact above all had burned itself into David's memory: Nero was afraid of ghosts.

After ordering the assassination of his own mother, Agrippina, the emperor claimed that her vengeful spirit had returned to haunt him. Nero even paid a Persian necromancer to keep the murdered woman's spirit from disturbing his sleep.

Fear of ghosts! Could that explain why a bronze sestertius had been heated in a brazier and thrust into a dying man's mouth? Because what the Texas coin dealer had told David now made sense. According to the encyclopedia, pious Romans always put a small coin into the mouth of a corpse. That way, the deceased would have money to pay Charon, the boatman who ferried dead souls across the River Styx to the dark kingdom of Hades. Once they had crossed that subterranean river, the spirits could never again return to trouble the living.

David looked up at the living-room mantelpiece. There was the eighteenth-century clock he'd had repaired after Eleanor's murderer smashed it. It was nearly midnight.

David recalled that he had a full day at the gallery tomorrow. It was time for the experiment he had been postponing all evening.

He stood up and walked slowly into the bedroom. There on his dresser was his briefcase, with the two ancient Roman coins inside. Back in the living room, David placed the briefcase on the inlaid marble coffee table. Then he sat back on the couch, opened the lid, and reached for the $3,700 bronze sestertius he'd bought that afternoon.

Apprehensively, David opened the square plastic envelope and slid the heavy bronze coin out into his palm. It was mildly cold to the touch, but that was all. If there were any vibrations, they were too weak for him to detect. Apparently this well-preserved sestertius had spent a rather uneventful nineteen hundred years. Certainly it communicated none of the stomach-churning horror he had experienced when he handled the first coin.

After holding the coin for a full three minutes, he still felt nothing out of the ordinary. Then the heavy gilt-bronze clock on the mantelpiece chimed midnight.

David took a clean handkerchief and gently wiped the valuable coin so that no sweat from his hand would remain to damage its surface. Then he slid it back into its plastic envelope. Ever since the break-in two years before, David had never kept small, valuable objects like this around the apartment. First thing tomorrow morning, he would take the sestertius to the bank and put it into his safe-deposit box.

Also in the briefcase was the worn, dented sestertius that Keith had lent him. It too was fitted into a plastic envelope, which the Texas coin dealer had provided free of charge. Much as David dreaded handling it

61

again, he had to make the comparison. Opening the plastic holder, he let the ugly brown coin slide into the palm of his left hand.

Almost immediately, he felt the strong tingling in his fingers. Then he lay back on the couch and closed his eyes.

The images all came at him at once—the heat, the sight of torn flesh, the scream. David wanted to hurl the sestertius away from him. But instead, he clenched his fingers into a fist around the throbbing, burning coin. There had to be more to the coin's history than this! And if he could just bear the agony long enough, hold on to it a bit longer, perhaps other scenes would swim up before his closed eyes. And then maybe he would learn how this sestertius had gotten from ancient Rome to a bathtub in New Castle, New York. So he gritted his teeth and forced himself through the whirlpool of terror and pain.

All at once, the terrible images of blood and death began to recede. What next? David wondered. He gripped the old coin all the more tightly. Suddenly, there was a noticeable change in the air. The atmosphere in his living room seemed dank and heavy, charged with some faint animal odor.

Abruptly, quick as a flashbulb, an image of Jennifer Olson appeared behind his closed eyelids. The vision lingered just long enough for David to see that her face was completely bathed in reddish light. Her eyes were wide with panic, her mouth gasping for air.

Startled, David opened his eyes. But the room was empty, exactly as he'd left it. The old eighteenth-century clock ticked quietly on the mantelpiece, and the heavy odor was gone. Even the tingling, burning sensation in his left hand had subsided. David had been gripping the old sestertius so tightly that his fist was numb. Now, relaxing his grip, he opened his cramped fingers—and gasped in astonishment.

His hand was empty! The flesh of his palm still bore the round, white, ghostly imprint of the sestertius that he had been holding so tightly. But the ancient bronze coin itself had vanished completely.

5

Friday, April 13, 1979

OVER AN HOUR LATER, DAVID was still sitting on his living-room couch. All the lights in the apartment were ablaze. He was deathly tired, but still too puzzled and upset to go to sleep.

The imprint of the ancient bronze coin had quickly faded from his palm, but the coin's disappearance left him shaken and baffled. Could his fingers have fallen pried open without his feeling it? David desperately wanted to believe the sestertius had merely slipped from his grasp.

So first of all, he looked behind the sofa cushions. He even turned back the Aubusson carpet, just to make sure the coin hadn't rolled under there. When he still couldn't find it, he walked into the kitchen and poured himself a glass of Scotch to calm his nerves. It just wasn't possible for a coin to vanish into thin air! And there had been that heavy animal odor . . . All in all, what he had just experienced seemed like something out of the Middle Ages.

He wandered into the library, hoping that some book he had acquired over the years would help explain this. But most of David's reference books dealt strictly with the real world—with furniture, cabinetmaking and French history. He didn't have any books on religion or the supernatural.

David poured himself another Scotch and sat on the living-room couch for another half hour, thinking. By the time the clock on the mantel read one-thirty, he still hadn't solved any of the questions in his mind. But two glasses of Scotch on an empty stomach had made him slightly tipsy, and he was no longer frightened. Realizing how awfully tired he was, he changed into his pajamas and climbed into bed.

For another ten minutes or so he lay awake, listening to the sounds of traffic on the West Side Highway. The night seemed peaceful now. In a way, it was almost reassuring that the horrid bronze sestertius was no longer around to trouble him. And before David knew it, he was dreaming.

He seemed to be standing on the side of a road, somewhere out in the country. It was night. Ahead of him was a stretch of bare earth. Beyond it was empty space, where the land sloped away. And then, to David's astonishment, something began to push its way up through the rocky soil.

Clods of earth lifted, broke apart and slid down its roof. The earth was giving birth to a house! David watched in fascination as a two-story frame structure arose, complete with chimney, front porch and fresh blue paint. But instead of clapboards, the house had scales, like a reptile. And set into one wall, staring at David, was the huge, protruding compound eye of some gigantic insect.

Then blood began to seep from the raw earth around the foundation. David saw that the earth was bleeding. There came a crash of thunder. A heavy rain began to fall, trying to wash the blood away. But the house kept rising, thrusting and tearing its way out of the stony ground. The blood was flowing more quickly now, welling from the concrete foundation.

The house had risen to its full height, and the earth it had emerged from was no longer soil, but human flesh. Blood was spurting from the socket of the foundation, washing across the road to where David stood. He tried to scream, but his breath made no sound.

Years ago, whenever David had a nightmare, his wife Eleanor would hear him moaning in his sleep beside her. She would shake him by the shoulders until he was awake enough to tell her what the matter was. But now, ever since his wife's death, David had lived alone in the Riverside Drive apartment. And there was no one to wake him.

Again David tried to scream as loud as he could. But the dream-air was heavy and dank; he couldn't draw a full breath. Worse still, there seemed to be something around his neck, choking him. His voice made no sound that he could hear . . .

But suddenly, he was awake!

Or was he? In the distance, he could still hear the low grumble of thunder. But there was a loud *bang! bang! bang!* coming from somewhere right behind him.

No, this wasn't a dream. David felt the familiar pillow under his head. The pounding was coming from the wall behind the headboard of his bed. And then it stopped.

David rolled over and looked at the bedside clock. It

was shortly after four o'clock Friday morning. Switching on the bedroom lights, he got up and glanced out the window. The street below was glossy with rain. Then he heard the thunder again—soft, far away. The dream-thunder had been much closer, and more ominous. An early-spring thunderstorm must have swept over the city, and he had slept right through it.

Then David realized what the pounding meant. Only one thin wall separated his bedroom from Mr. and Mrs. Jacobs' apartment down the hall. During his nightmare, he had been trying to scream. Even if he couldn't hear himself, he had evidently succeeded. Why else would Leo Jacobs have been pounding on the wall?

David went back into the kitchen, poured himself a glass of milk and went back to bed. But he couldn't go back to sleep. Instead he lay there, sleepless and worried. What if the nightmares started up again? Would he be able to scream himself awake—or would he arouse the neighbors first?

In New Castle, Jennifer Olson awakened at the first growl of thunder. Ever since she'd been a little girl, she had been terrified of lightning. And now, hearing the approaching storm, she lay awake, immobilized with fear, wondering how long it would take for Keith to wake up.

That evening Keith had taken her to bed, and they had made love until well after midnight. Keith always slept soundly, especially after lovemaking.

Now Jennifer moved against him in the bed. She could feel his back—smooth, warm, muscular. But he didn't even stir.

Suddenly, in the predawn darkness, a brilliant flash exploded outside their bedroom window. It was followed almost immediately by a loud slam of thunder. That bolt had struck close—too close! Because of the new house across the gully, the venetian blinds were down, so Jennifer couldn't see where the bolt had struck. She couldn't stand it any longer. But Keith was still sleeping peacefully beside her. His breathing was long and slow; he was completely dead to the world.

"Keith," she said, shaking his arm. "Keith, wake up!"

He came awake quickly, just as the rain began pelting against the bedroom window. "Oh, hell . . ." he muttered. He should have fixed that leak around the chimney when he had the chance. Now it sounded as if they were in for a real downpour—and there'd be more water in the attic!

Just then, there was another bright flash and a heavy *wham!* outside the bedroom window. Jennifer gasped. Keith knew how lightning terrified her, so he turned and put his arms around her. She hugged him tightly, burying her face against his neck.

"Keith!" she whispered. "That last one sounded as if it struck something!"

"Let me go see." His bare feet hit the carpet. Naked, he padded to the window, hauled up the venetian blinds—as long as the lights were off, no one would see him—and peered out through the window glass that was spattered with raindrops. Their bedroom windows faced west; that was the direction that storms usually came from.

All at once, a bolt of lightning crashed into the chimney of the new house. The searing thunder resounded in less than a second.

Keith winced and automatically stepped back from the window. "That new house just got struck," he told Jennifer.

"Do you think it'll catch fire?" she asked.

Keith squinted into the darkness. Dim lightning

repeated in the distance, outlining the house in weak gray light. "I can't say. But there's no one living there to report it. I'd better call the police and have them make sure everything's okay."

Jennifer switched on the bedside lamp. Blinking in the sudden glare, she lifted the receiver of the telephone beside the bed. Suddenly the lamp flickered and dimmed, then came on again.

"I know the number," Keith told her, pulling a bathrobe around himself. "It's seven nine two . . ." But then he saw the puzzled look on his wife's face. Jennifer was listening into the earpiece, not bothering to dial.

"The phone's dead," she said.

"Let me see." Keith walked around the double bed and took the receiver from her. He listened for a dial tone, but there was no sound at all. He jiggled the button on the telephone cradle, but still nothing happened.

"I'll bet there's a power line down somewhere," Keith said.

A second bolt struck the chimney of the house across the gully. A shower of blue sparks slid down the side of the roof. Again the explosive thunder followed instantly.

Keith frowned. Lightning wasn't supposed to strike twice in the same place. Yet that chimney had been hit twice in the last minute or so!

High in the clouds, lightning flashed again, illuminating the house in an evil greenish light. In that prolonged instant, Keith could see that the chimney looked perfectly intact. But then he glimpsed something strange, down on the ground floor. . . .

"Keith!" said Jennifer, worry in her voice. "Come away from the window!"

"Just a minute," he replied. The bedside lamp flickered again, but Keith didn't notice. He was watching a vague crimson light inside the living room at 666 Sunset Brook Lane.

Thunder was ranging back and forth in the sky above, like the footsteps of some enormous giant searching for its prey. Keith watched as the front porch lit up with that same reddish glow. The red light had moved outside! It was between three and four feet in diameter—or at least it seemed to be. With all the rain running down the windowpane, Keith couldn't see all that clearly. He squinted, trying to see who was carrying the light. And then the glow stopped in the middle of the porch and began pulsing slowly.

Once again, Keith had the creepy sensation that he was being watched. The bedroom lamp was silhouetting him from behind, and anyone standing on the porch at 666 Sunset Brook Lane could probably see him clearly. But still Keith peered through the rainswept windowpane, trying to see that strange red light a bit more clearly. . . .

"*Keith!*" Jennifer cried.

"Okay, okay." Just as he turned from the window, a thunderous crash sounded from the front of their house, literally shaking the walls.

"Good Lord," Keith whispered. "That must have struck the roof!"

But Jennifer lifted her head, listening. Suddenly Keith heard it too.

It was the front doorbell, ringing in the vestibule downstairs. And it kept on ringing without letup, as if someone were leaning on it.

"Someone out at this time of night?" Jennifer whispered. "It must be an emergency!"

They went downstairs together. The doorbell was

still ringing when Keith unlocked the front door and yanked it open. But there was no one on the front steps. Peering farther into the darkness, he saw that a huge tree limb had fallen across the front walk.

"It must have been the maple tree that got struck," he said to Jennifer.

"Then why's the bell ringing?"

"I don't know," Keith admitted. "Maybe the bolt struck the doorbell too, and fused the wires . . ."

"Look!" Jennifer said.

Propped up against the front steps, leaning up against the doorjamb, was Keith's old spading fork. The last time he'd seen it was last October, when he'd put it away in the tool rack at the rear of the garage. Now it was wet with rain and balanced on its handle, so that one of its four prongs rested on the doorbell.

"There's your emergency!" Keith laughed. He pushed open the storm door and lifted the spading fork away from the bell. The ringing stopped instantly. "Just some kids," he snorted, "playing a joke."

"In this weather?" Jennifer asked. But Keith was looking down at the front step, a strange expression on his face. "What's the matter?" she asked.

"Nothing." Keith avoided her gaze. "I'm just wondering how anybody could have gotten into the garage. You locked it last night, didn't you?"

Ten minutes later, the storm had passed. The bedside lamp had stopped flickering, so it didn't look as if they would lose their electricity along with the telephone. But Jennifer placed a flashlight and candles by the bed, just in case. In any event, dawn was now less than two hours away.

Keith turned off the bedroom light and took another look out the window at 666 Sunset Brook Lane. There was no one standing on the porch over there. No red light, flickering or otherwise, was burning inside.

Jennifer soon drifted back to sleep. But for Keith, drowsiness just wouldn't come. For one thing, he couldn't figure out why anybody would have taken that spading fork out of their locked garage, in the middle of the night, during a thunderstorm! But what really bothered him was that the fork's handle had been wet when he lifted it off the doorbell. . . .

That water meant that the tool had been removed from their garage *after* it started raining. Whoever walked across the soaking-wet front walk should have left damp footprints on the front step. But except for the drops trickling off the spading fork, the front step under the overhang had been dry as a bone!

In the mornings, Keith usually got up about ten or fifteen minutes before Jennifer did. That way, he was able to shave before she turned on the shower and got the bathroom mirror all steamed up. But this morning, the growing daylight made Keith wake up even earlier. When he got out of bed, the clock read only five forty-five, and Jennifer didn't even stir.

Keith put on his blue jeans, work shirt and shoes and went downstairs by himself. In the kitchen, he put a pot of coffee on the stove to perk. Then he walked out the front door and dragged the fallen limb off the front walk. When things dried off, he'd get out his chain saw and cut it into firewood.

Looking up at the big sugar maple that overhung their front walk and part of the driveway, he saw where the lightning had struck. The electricity had traveled down the trunk, turning the tree's sap to steam instantly, stripping off the bark in a narrow ribbon. In the lawn, there was a series of little craters where the current had followed the maple's roots for a foot or so before dissipating in the ground.

Nasty thing, lightning, Keith thought.

Back in the kitchen, he made himself some fried eggs and toast. By then, the coffee was ready. He sat down at the breakfast table. Across the gully, the morning sun was glinting off the windowpanes of the new house. Keith looked up at the chimney. After two direct hits, why hadn't those bricks sustained any damage?

According to the clock over the stove, it was 6:05 A.M. Keith had almost finished washing his breakfast dishes when the telephone rang.

He bolted to answer it. The call would also ring on the bedroom extension upstairs, and he wanted Jennifer to sleep as long as she could. "Hello?" he said.

"Mr. Olson." It was a deep, resonant voice that Keith didn't recognize.

"Yes," he replied. "This is Keith Olson speaking. Who's this?"

"I am Coste." The voice had a strange inflection—or maybe just a hint of a foreign accent? "You like to restore old houses, I understand."

"That's right," Keith said. "Did Tom Greene mention my name to you?"

"He didn't need to." There was a brief pause. "But I believe you can . . . accomplish what I want to see carried out. You already know my house, the one directly across the stream from yours? The outside needs repairs—and fresh paint."

"Yes," Keith answered. "I know."

"Yes!" the voice replied smoothly. "And since you have already been inside, you know that the interior needs repairs as well!"

Keith was stunned. How did Coste know that he'd gone inside 666 Sunset Brook Lane? The house had been empty when he walked in; he was sure of that. Had Coste been somewhere outside, looking in through one of those uncurtained windows?

"As a matter of fact," Keith replied, flustered, "I *did* go into your house. But only because the front door was open, and I figured someone was home. I was hoping to meet you."

"All in good time," the voice said evenly.

"And upstairs in the bathroom," Keith continued, "I found this old coin. A friend of ours says it might be Roman. He's having it identified now—but I'll make sure you get it back."

Keith heard a smooth chuckle on the other end of the line. "You need not trouble yourself on that point," the voice said. "But tell me. How much do you require to prepare the inside rooms for painting and decorating?"

"To tell you the truth," Keith said. "I wasn't really paying attention the first time I was in there; I had other things on my mind. I'd have to look at your house a second time. And just how far do you want me to go? For example, that wallboard is sort of sloppily installed. Do you want me to just fill in the nail holes? Or should I go all out and replace that wallboard with some decent Sheetrock that'll let you hang heavy pictures and traverse rods?"

"My house has suffered damage in the past," the voice replied with a trace of anger. "I would like you to restore it as if you owned it yourself."

"Okay," Keith answered. "But can I ask you something? Is yours the same house that used to be out in Seattle, Washington—on Bremerton Road?"

Again there was a slight pause. "Of course you may *ask*," the voice said sharply. "When you are ready to inspect the house again, you will find the key on the front porch."

Tom Greene was right—Coste certainly didn't like to

answer questions! "But do you think it's a good idea to leave the key outside?" Keith asked. "Sure, it's pretty quiet and rural up here. But every so often we get a carload of teen-agers from Port Chester or White Plains—"

The voice was irritable and slightly superior. *"They* would not find the key, I assure you!"

Keith realized that Coste was eager to hang up, but he was still curious. "You know, your chimney got struck by lightning last night. At least twice! But from over here, it doesn't look as if there was any damage."

"There never is." It was the weary tone of a parent explaining the obvious to a child.

"Okay, one more thing," Keith said. "When I figure out my estimate on the work over there, how do I reach you? Can I have your phone number?"

"I have no direct line where you can reach me."

"Or," Keith said, "maybe I could meet you over at the house, and we—"

"Leave your price with Thomas Greene," the voice interrupted. "And he will let you know if I approve the figure."

Keith was about to say good-bye when he realized Coste had already hung up. But instead of a dial tone, the phone began emitting a low, mournful sound. Apparently the lines were still having trouble.

"Is it working?" said a voice behind him.

Keith jumped. Turning around, he saw Jennifer, wrapped in her green silk bathrobe, standing in the doorway.

"God, you startled me!" He hung up the telephone and walked over to the stove. "Want some coffee?"

"Please." Jennifer yawned. She still seemed half asleep. He handed her a fresh cup of coffee and held the chair for her as she sat down at the table.

"Who were you talking to?" she asked.

75

"Coste," Keith said. "You know, the guy who owns that house across the way? He wants me to give him an estimate on fixing up the place, inside and out."

"Is he a nice person?"

"I don't know." Keith went back to the sink and started scrubbing his remaining breakfast dishes. "We didn't talk that long."

Jennifer took a long sip of coffee; she seemed to be waking up. "Did Coste call here? When?"

"Just now," Keith replied. "The telephone rang—oh, maybe two or three minutes ago. Didn't it wake you up?"

"No." She shook her head and pushed the long chestnut hair back from her face. "I've been awake for the past ten minutes or so. The phone didn't ring, or I'd have heard it."

"But it rang down here!" Keith said.

She shrugged. "Then maybe it's only the bedroom extension that's not working. Let's see." Jennifer walked to the kitchen telephone, lifted the receiver, and held it to her ear for a moment. "Listen," she said, holding it out to him.

Keith pressed the instrument to his ear, but there was no dial tone. In fact, he could detect no sound at all. The phone was completely dead, just as the upstairs extension had been the night before, when Jennifer had tried to call the police.

"Well," he said frowning, "it was working before. I'll call the telephone company as soon as I get to work."

Keith would have liked to stop at 666 and investigate the effects of those two lightning bolts, but he was in too much of a hurry. He wanted to get to the job in Peekskill, and he didn't want to leave Jennifer completely cut off from the outside world.

He hadn't driven more than a mile when he saw a

large telephone-company truck parked beside a utility pole. In its high-rise hydraulic bucket stood a man wearing a hard hat. On the ground below, jutting into the street, was a tree limb even larger than the one that had fallen from Keith's maple tree. Another hard-hatted man was cutting it apart with a chain saw.

Keith parked his own panel truck right behind the phone-company vehicle. As he walked up, he noticed a man in the driver's seat of the truck, sipping coffee from a Styrofoam cup.

"There something wrong?" Keith asked, shouting over the whine of the chain saw.

"I'm sorry," said the driver, cupping one hand over his ear. "Say what?"

"Is there something wrong with the lines?" Keith repeated. "My telephone isn't working."

"No, sir, it isn't! That storm last night knocked out these trunk lines. Where do you live?"

"Sunset Brook Lane," Keith told him.

The driver shook his head. "Sunset Brook Lane's completely out. But we ought to have service restored by around ten o'clock."

"I don't understand," Keith shouted. "I already got one call this morning!"

"What time was that?" the driver asked him.

"Oh, around six-thirty," Keith replied. He saw doubt creep into the other man's eyes.

"Well, sir, I don't know what to tell you. All the telephones up your way have been *kaput* since about four o'clock this morning."

6

Saturday, April 14, 1979

SHORTLY BEFORE 10 A.M., KEITH finished sawing up the sugar maple limb in the front yard, and he and Jennifer sat down to a late breakfast.

Most Saturday mornings, Keith was on the road by nine to give estimates. Nearly everyone wanted to have him come by when the husband of the house was home to ask questions. Ordinarily at this time of year, there was so much work to be done that Keith had to schedule jobs for three weeks or even a month later. But during the ten days that he and Jennifer had been off on vacation, the telephone answering machine in the Chappaqua office hadn't recorded any calls. And so this Saturday morning, Keith had no appointments at all.

It was odd, he thought. He, Marc and Jason did

excellent work. His prices were reasonable, considering. But the new business just wasn't coming in.

"By the way," Keith muttered, chewing his toast. "David Carmichael hasn't called you, has he?"

"Not since he was here last," Jennifer answered, looking at him warily. All last night, and again this morning, Keith had seemed grim and preoccupied. "Why?"

"Remember that bronze coin he took with him? I wonder if he's had a chance to find out which emperor that was."

"I don't know," Jennifer said. "I'll ask him when I see him at the auction this afternoon."

Keith put down his coffee and stared at his wife. "What auction?"

"Keith, I *told* you. There's an auction at two this afternoon at Christie's, in New York. David said there'll be some old sleigh benches and quilts on sale. We talked about it on Wednesday night, and I thought it would be fun. You said you didn't mind if I went. Don't you remember?"

"Sort of," Keith grunted. David and Jennifer had been talking about antiques and auctions, and Keith really hadn't listened too carefully.

"You can come with me if you want," Jennifer added.

"No," Keith replied. "I have too many things to do around here—like stacking all that firewood behind the garage."

"I'll be back around six o'clock," Jennifer said. "We can eat at seven. Or even earlier, if you'll put the roast in the oven at five."

"Yeah, okay," said Keith, his mind elsewhere. "If David has the coin with him, can you bring it home? I really ought to give it back to Coste."

79

"Have you given him the estimate on his house yet?" Jennifer asked.

"No." Keith swallowed the last of his coffee. "That's something else I ought to do this morning."

But Keith had to face it—he was afraid of what he might see in the right-hand panel of that bay window. If it wasn't his face in that six-sided pane of glass, then he'd been letting his imagination run away with him. But what if those really *were* his features etched into the glass—what then? In either case, it was a no-win situation; and Keith was in no rush to find out.

On the other hand, it wasn't as if Olson Custom Carpentry didn't need Coste's business. By Monday morning, Keith, Marc and Jason would be finished with those dormers in Peekskill. After that, they hadn't any other jobs scheduled until May—that is, unless Coste accepted Keith's estimate and told him to begin work on 666 Sunset Brook Lane.

Impatient with himself, Keith stood up and carried his coffee cup to the sink. What was he being spooked by, after all? A few tons of old lumber, rusty plumbing, and etched glass! What was he waiting for?

"I think I'll go across the gully now," he told Jennifer. Then he ran upstairs for his outdoor jacket and clipboard.

When he came back down, Jennifer was still sitting at the breakfast table. "Is Coste meeting you over there?" she asked.

"No. But he said the key will be on the porch, and I'd have no trouble finding it. When are you leaving for New York?"

Jennifer glanced at the clock over the stove. "I'm going to drive down to the Chappaqua Station around eleven."

"Well"—Keith smiled nervously—"I certainly ought to be back before then!"

He stepped out the kitchen door and closed it behind him. Straight ahead, a hundred yards away, Coste's yellow-and-white house was bathed in the morning sunshine.

Alone in the kitchen, Jennifer looked at the kitchen clock once again. It was exactly 10:38 A.M. David had told her he'd call at ten-thirty sharp to say whether he could meet her for lunch before the auction.

Then why hadn't he called? David always prided himself on being on time. Keith might get wrapped up in his work and telephone her an hour later than he'd said he would. But David, never! It wasn't like him not to call exactly when he said he would.

Or was the telephone out of order again? Jennifer lifted the receiver and heard the dial tone. But it was ten forty and David still hadn't called. She had to dress now, or she'd miss the eleven-ten train out of Chappaqua. Had David forgotten? Or had something gone wrong?

Jennifer had assumed that Keith would be over at 666 Sunset Brook Lane for a while, at least. Even so, she didn't want her husband to walk into the kitchen while she was on the telephone with David. She climbed upstairs, picked up the bedroom extension, and dialed the number of David's gallery on Fifty-seventh Street.

Miss Rosewood answered: "David M. Carmichael, good morning!"

"Hello, this is Jennifer Olson. May I speak to David, please?"

Miss Rosewood paused for an instant. "Oh, I'm sorry. No, Mrs. Olson, Mr. Carmichael didn't come in this morning. He phoned in and told me not to expect him. And I do know he'll be attending an auction this afternoon—"

"I know that!" Jennifer said. "I was supposed to

meet him there, but he hasn't called to confirm. Did he leave any message for me?"

Miss Rosewood hesitated. Mr. Carmichael had complained that he had slept very poorly and wanted to rest up a bit. But was it possible that he had spent the night with a young lady? Mr. Carmichael was a widower, after all—and such a terribly attractive man! But the English-born secretary was careful never to speculate about her employer's private life. However innocent his reasons for not dropping by the gallery, they were surely none of Mrs. Olson's business.

"No," the Englishwoman said. "No message. I don't expect I shall hear from Mr. Carmichael until Monday. May I have him return your call next week?"

"You needn't bother," replied Jennifer, irritated at Miss Rosewood's stubborn formality. "I'll call him at home!" And before Miss Rosewood could protest, Jennifer hung up the phone.

She was a bit surprised at her own hasty temper. She vowed that the next time she spoke to Miss Rosewood, she'd apologize. Then she lifted the receiver again and dialed the number of David's apartment on Riverside Drive.

To get to 666 Sunset Brook Lane, Keith could have walked straight across the gully. But he still wanted to postpone the estimate for as long as he could. So he took the long way, around the loop of Sunset Brook Lane.

Late April was a weird time of year, Keith thought. The sun was just as strong as it would be in mid-August, but the air was still chilly. All the trees were bare. The green leaves of skunk cabbage were showing beside the brook at the bottom of the gully. Here and there, swamp maples were blooming with their little red flowers. But otherwise, it was a dead world.

Soon the yellow-and-white house came into view. Keith didn't even bother to glance at the bay window; he'd have a closer, better look at the leaded glass from inside the six-sided room.

Approaching the gravel driveway, Keith unrolled his tape measure. He had to determine the dimensions of the house in order to calculate how many gallons of paint he would need to cover the exterior.

The front porch—and the house itself—were both thirty feet wide. The new grass of the lawn hadn't sprouted yet. So Keith crept between the blue spruce and the drip line of the eaves, without doing too much damage, and determined that the house was forty-five feet deep from the front door to the kitchen wall. Finally he measured the roof's shadow and calculated that it was twenty feet from the eaves down to the concrete foundation.

Climbing up on the front porch, Keith tested the front door again. It was locked tight! The heavy brass knob hardly budged under his grip. Where was the key that Coste had promised him?

Keith looked in all the sneaky places people think of to hide their front-door keys. But there wasn't any doormat. There weren't any hooks in the corners of the entryway windows or behind any of the turned pillars supporting the porch roof. Keith even looked straight up at the porch's peeling yellow ceiling, but it wasn't there either.

Well, if he couldn't find the key, then he couldn't get inside to do the estimate! It gave him an odd satisfaction that Coste, who had been so brusque and superior over the phone, had slipped up. Sooner or later, there'd be other jobs to do. Meanwhile, Keith would call Tom Greene and tell him that maybe Coste should get somebody else. . . .

He was walking down the porch steps when something metallic bounced off the wooden boards right behind him. Keith turned around. There, lying on the porch directly in front of the door, was an old-fashioned iron house key.

This time Keith *knew* it hadn't fallen from the ceiling, because he had looked up there. Somebody must have thrown it onto the porch. He ran to the right side of the porch and looked up and down Sunset Brook Lane. But there was nobody there; he saw his own footprints in the newly seeded lawn.

The other side of the house—where the ground fell away sharply to the brook below—was the only place the key-slinger could have stood without Keith spotting him. Keith ran back across the porch and glanced up and down the gully. But again, there was no one to be seen. And there weren't any boulders or rock outcroppings large enough to hide a man.

Keith had never cared much for practical jokes. Now somebody was toying with him, trying to get his goat—and he didn't like it. Baffled and irritated, he picked up the key. It was still faintly warm to the touch. Just like that funny old coin he'd found in the bathtub upstairs!

Twisting the key in the lock, he pushed open the front door and walked down the hall to the sliding doors under the staircase. That face etched in the right-hand window was part of this whole silly game, and Keith wanted to satisfy his curiosity once and for all.

Inside the hexagonal room, the air was dry and still. But when Keith stepped up to the right-hand window that depicted the Weeping Fool, he felt a cold breeze on his face.

The single pane of glass that depicted the Fool's face had been removed from the window! And a chilly

April wind was blowing through the six-sided opening.

When Jennifer dialed David Carmichael's home telephone number, the line was busy. She tried again two minutes later. This time, David answered on the first ring.

"David? This is Jennifer."

"Jennifer!" Despite the warmth in his voice, David sounded hoarse and exhausted. "I wanted to thank you again for Wednesday night. I'm only sorry that—"

"Please, that's perfectly all right," she said. The clock over the stove read eleven forty-seven. "But are we still on for lunch today?"

"I'm afraid not. I've been having some rather disturbing . . ." Suddenly the line was heavy with crackling and static. "Can you hear me all right?" David asked.

"Yes," said Jennifer, raising her voice. "But you sound upset. Is anything the matter?"

"Not really," he replied. "I just have to—to get to the bottom of this problem, and see a doctor."

"A doctor?" Jennifer asked. She remembered David's sudden attack of nausea on Wednesday night. "Are you all right?"

"Oh, fine!" David gave an unconvincing laugh. "Nothing serious, really, just a series of bad dreams. It's nothing for either of us to get worried about."

Bad dreams? Jennifer couldn't believe that David was telling her the whole truth. "Aren't you going to the auction, then?"

"No," David replied. "I didn't sleep well last night, and I don't really feel up to it."

In that afternoon's sale, Jennifer remembered, was a rare Louis XV commode that David desperately wanted to bid on. He must be feeling quite ill to let the chance slip past him!

"I could go to the city," she suggested, "and place bids on any lots you want."

"No, please! There are other auctions coming up this spring, and believe me, I'll be at every one of them. Once I've had a talk with the doctor, we can get together and I'll explain everything."

It still bothered Jennifer that David wouldn't level with her *now*. "Remember that coin Keith lent you?" she asked. "He wanted to know if you've had it identified yet."

"Yes. I have. It's a bronze sestertius from the reign of Nero. Is Keith there now?" David asked apprehensively.

"No," Jennifer said. "He went out to do an estimate. In fact, he's—"

"Okay," David said hurriedly. "I'll bring along the sestertius the next time I see you."

"Tell me honestly," Jennifer persisted. "Is there anything wrong with you?"

"Only nightmares." David laughed. "I'll talk to you next week, okay?"

"All right," she replied, convinced he wasn't telling her the truth.

"Good-bye, then."

"Good-bye."

When she hung up the telephone, Jennifer felt puzzled and hurt. She and David had always been so open with each other. But now he seemed almost secretive. And he had actually hurried her through the conversation. . . .

Or had he been with a woman when she called? His wife had been dead for two years, after all, and of course other women would find him handsome and attractive. Despite herself, Jennifer felt jealous and confused. She loved Keith; she didn't want to be married to anyone else! But even so, she had gotten used to assuming she had David's affection all to herself.

But Jennifer and Miss Rosewood were both wrong in their speculations. The antiques dealer was completely alone in his Riverside Drive apartment.

He waited until he heard Jennifer hang up before putting down the receiver on his end. He desperately wanted to talk to her—but not today, not now. David wanted to keep the line open, on the remote chance that Dr. Fuchs-Kramer would call back.

At ten-thirty, when he was supposed to have called Jennifer, David had been on the telephone to Lenox Hill Hospital. All morning, he had been making calls to locate someone who could help him stop the sudden onslaught of terrifying nightmares.

Friday night, no sooner had he drifted off to sleep, than Thursday night's dream had begun all over again. Again, he'd seen the blue house thrusting up through the bleeding earth. Again the soil had turned to human flesh. Again David had tried to scream himself awake—and was roused, instead, by Leo Jacobs' furious pounding on the wall behind his bed.

After that second nightmare, he went into the living room and kept himself awake for an hour. He sipped warm tea and leafed through an old copy of *Connoisseur* to get his mind off the dream. Finally, around 1 A.M., he went back to bed. But around three, he had the nightmare for a third time—in all its gory detail, right from the beginning.

This time, however, David awoke to the sound of his telephone ringing, out in the living room. It was Leo Jacobs, and now David's neighbor was genuinely angry. He demanded to know why Mr. Carmichael was making such a racket at this hour of night—and threatened to call the police if David woke him up one more time.

Hanging up the phone, David was horribly embarrassed. To think that he'd awakened Mr. and Mrs. Jacobs three times in the past two nights! It was painfully clear that he was *not* able to scream himself awake. It was always some other noise—Leo Jacobs pounding on the wall, a ringing telephone—that finally roused him from the nightmare.

Afraid to go back to bed again, David carried his pillow into the living room and folded several blankets into a makeshift bedroll in the middle of the Aubusson carpet. If he started screaming in here, at least he'd be surrounded—and hopefully, muffled—by the walls of his own apartment.

David lay awake until after four o'clock Saturday morning. Then he slept—without any dreams at all. But when he awoke on the floor at 7 A.M., his neck was stiff and his back ached painfully. He simply couldn't face even half a day at his Fifty-seventh Street gallery, and he telephoned Miss Rosewood to tell her so.

When Jennifer called, he had been strongly tempted to tell her exactly what had happened since he had first handled that bronze sestertius in her living room in New Castle. But how could he explain the fleeting vision he'd had of her? *In my mind's eye, I saw you all glowing red, frightened out of your wits and panting for breath. Thought you ought to know.* Fortunately, David had bought that new, more expensive sestertius—now he could give it to Keith as a replacement. But even so, would Jennifer believe what had happened to the other coin? *That coin Keith found was worth a thousand dollars, but it simply evaporated into thin air. Sorry about that.*

How could he ever explain to Jennifer what he

88

himself didn't pretend to understand? And what about the recurrent nightmares?

David simply couldn't go on like this, with little or no sleep. . . . He had to find someone to explain it all to *him*. Someone who would be able to stop the dreams— and reassure David that he wasn't going crazy. But David didn't want a doctor who was merely a psychiatrist. He made a dozen calls before Dr. Block, a good customer who worked at Lenox Hill, referred him to Sidney Fuchs-Kramer, M.D.—a duly licensed psychiatrist with a separate degree in parapsychology.

When David called Dr. Fuchs-Kramer's number, however, his answering service picked up the phone. It was Saturday morning, of course, and the parapsychologist didn't hold office hours over the weekend. Dr. Fuchs-Kramer would not be available until Monday morning, at the earliest. David still had to face Saturday and Sunday night—and the likelihood that the dream of the terrible blue house would begin again as soon as he fell asleep!

Jennifer was still sitting in the bedroom when she heard the kitchen door slam downstairs.

"Keith!" she called out. "Is that you?"

But there was no answer. Quietly she walked to the head of the stairs and looked down. There was no one in the living room. "Keith?" she called again.

"Yeah, it's me!" His voice came from the kitchen. When Jennifer came downstairs, she found him at the breakfast table, with his clipboard and pocket calculator in front of him.

"I talked to David," she said. But Keith only grunted and jotted down some figures on his clipboard. Jennifer knew better than to bother him when he was adding up numbers.

The house at 666 Sunset Brook Lane was in worse

shape than Keith had realized. He estimated that putting the whole house back in apple-pie order would take at least two weeks of work. And for all that Sheetrock, painting and labor, he ought to charge at least $6,250. Keith whistled softly to himself. Pretty high! He ran over the figures again, but the total remained the same.

From his brief conversation with Coste on Friday morning, Keith figured that the owner was a demanding perfectionist who wouldn't tolerate sloppy workmanship. On the other hand, the mere fact that Coste had the money to move his house long-distance didn't mean he was a lavish spender. So Keith decided to lower the price by five hundred dollars. There'd still be enough money involved for him to turn a profit—if Coste approved the lower figure, that is.

Keith lifted the kitchen phone and dialed Tom Greene's number. Suddenly he noticed his wife standing in the doorway to the living room.

"Hey," he said. "I thought you were going to the city?"

Jennifer shook her head. "David isn't feeling well. He did ask me to tell you, though—the man on that coin you gave him is the emperor Nero. A sestertius, I think he said it was."

"Terrific," Keith said. "Whatever it is, I have to return it to Coste. When's David bringing it back?"

"He didn't say."

Keith was about to ask his wife why David's feeling ill prevented her from going to the city by herself. But suddenly he heard the phone being picked up on the other end of the line.

"Tom? Hi, it's Keith. You can tell your Mr. Coste that fixing up that transplanted house of his will run him fifty-seven fifty. That includes filling all the cracks and gouges on the outside before we give it two coats of exterior latex."

"Fifty-seven fifty is acceptable," Tom Greene replied.

Keith stared into the telephone. "Don't you have to ask Coste? Or did he know what the estimate was going to come to?"

"No, no." Tom laughed. "He called me early this morning, and said he'd pay up to seventy-five hundred for you to fix his house. But he wouldn't have accepted a bid for under four thousand, either. That would mean you weren't doing all the work he thinks is necessary."

Keith groaned. He could have *raised* his first estimate by a thousand dollars, and Coste would have accepted it without quibbling!

"He's also in something of a rush," Tom Greene added. "Would your guys be able to start as early as next week?"

"Sure," Keith replied. "Probably Monday afternoon, in fact."

"That's great," the realtor answered. "Coste wants you to paint the outside a dark blue. But leave the trim white. And for now, don't subcontract anybody to paint the inside."

"Why not?" Keith asked. "Does Coste want just plain Sheetrock staring at him?"

"For the time being, yes. Once he rents the place, then the new tenant can pick out the colors he wants."

"*He* wants?" Keith repeated. "Isn't that the choice of the lady of the house?"

"Not in this case," Tom Greene said. "By law, you see, I'm supposed to rent that house to any reputable party who comes along. But Coste made it very clear he doesn't want an entire family in there. He only wants to rent to a man who's single, divorced, or a widower!"

7

Monday, April 16, 1979

SITTING IN DR. FUCHS-KRAMER'S OFFICE, David suddenly realized how tired he was.

He had spent Saturday and Sunday nights on his
living room floor, terrified that the dream would begin
again—and that he would scream in his sleep and wake
up Mr. and Mrs. Jacobs. Now, after three wakeful
nights of lying on the hard floor, David was desperate.
He had been immensely grateful when Dr. Fuchs-
Kramer had agreed to see him late on Monday afternoon.

Sidney Fuchs-Kramer, M.D., was thirty-two. His
face was round and pink, and his curly blond hair was
already thinning on top. Now he adjusted his rimless
glasses and took a careful look at the handsome,
expensively dressed visitor in the chair beside his desk.

For the past three years, this midtown psychiatric

hospital had allowed Dr. Fuchs-Kramer and his assistant, Dr. Harold Werner—also a psychiatrist—to conduct parapsychological experiments. But unlike Maimonides in Brooklyn, the hospital never publicized its researches into ESP. And Dr. Fuchs-Kramer's already meager research budget was in danger of being trimmed still further. A wealthy patron like David M. Carmichael might be the answer to the parapsychologist's prayers.

"Now, then, Mr. Carmichael. What can I do for you?"

The antiques dealer cleared his throat. "I've been having some—well, unusual experiences recently. And I was hoping you could help explain them. Do you know Dr. Block, the orthopedist over at Lenox Hill?"

Dr. Fuchs-Kramer nodded.

"He's a good customer of mine; his wife bought a small writing desk from me last winter. I told him I wanted a doctor who was trained in psychiatry, who understands how the mind works. But also, a doctor who had some knowledge of ESP; who wasn't a skeptic. Someone who can comprehend exactly what's been happening to me. . . ."

"Exactly what *has* been happening?" the parapsychologist asked.

David hesitated. Where should he begin? Oh, what the hell, Dr. Fuchs-Kramer was the expert; let *him* sort it all out! "Well, last Wednesday I was up in northern Westchester, having dinner with some friends of mine . . ."

He recounted everything, from the moment he had first touched the bronze sestertius in Jennifer's living room. All the while, Dr. Fuchs-Kramer nodded to him encouragingly. David went on, describing the odor he'd suddenly smelled in his apartment—and how he had opened his hand, only to find that the ancient coin was missing.

"Let's stop there for a moment," the parapsychologist said. "And go back to last Wednesday night, when you first saw this coin. Did both Mr. and Mrs. Olson handle it too?"

"No," David said, "Jennifer never touched it. Only Keith."

"And did he seem to show any aversion, or reluctance to touching it?"

David shook his head. "Not that I can recall."

"And the other coin you bought on Thursday," Dr. Fuchs-Kramer said. "You experienced no reaction to that one whatsoever?"

"No." Reaching into his breast pocket, David withdrew the expensive bronze sestertius. He had restapled the plastic envelope so that the coin couldn't slip out accidentally.

"May I see?" The doctor took the plastic holder from David and peered at the sestertius inside. "Very pretty! And the other coin was the same type as this one?"

"Yes," David replied. "Only it wasn't in nearly as good condition."

"Okay," Dr. Fuchs-Kramer said intently. "You bought this coin from a dealer, right? And where did your friend say he got the other one?"

"He found it in a house that was recently built nearby. Keith told me he heard something fall into an empty bathtub. When he looked inside, there was this old, corroded bronze coin."

"Perhaps it was an apport," Dr. Fuchs-Kramer said.

David wasn't sure if he'd heard the doctor correctly. "An airport?"

"An *apport!*" The parapsychologist smiled reassuringly. "Apports are a fairly common occurrence in so-called haunted houses where poltergeist phenomena are being reported. The object in question is usually quite small, made of metal—a key, for example; or a coin. Some witnesses report that the apport materializes out of thin air, up near the ceiling." Dr. Fuchs-Kramer lifted his hand to illustrate. "And then the object falls *slowly* to the floor—much slower than would a normal object under the pull of gravity. Sometimes its path is a curve or zigzag, as if the apport were trying to call attention to itself. Now, then." The doctor leaned forward intently. "When your friend first picked up that coin—did he say how it felt?"

"Yes!" David nodded. "I think he said it was warm to the touch."

"Apports often are," Dr. Fuchs-Kramer stated. "And sometimes they disappear again—as you say this one did."

David still wasn't sure whether Dr. Fuchs-Kramer believed him. "But does what I'm telling you make sense, then? Is there a pattern?"

The doctor flashed a noncommittal smile. "Let's just say your account correlates very nicely with some of the professional reports I've read. Certainly the details don't sound like something a layman could imagine or dream up. I do have one question, though. Both times you held that coin—was the image of a man being tortured the *only* impression you received?"

"No," David replied. "The second time I tried it, I got a vivid picture of Jennifer Olson. She's the wife of the man who found the coin in the first place. That was just before the coin disappeared—and the same night the dreams started."

"Dreams?" Dr. Fuchs-Kramer asked.

"That's the main reason I came to you," David replied. He related his recurrent nightmare of a blue Victorian house rising out of bloody soil. "Every time,

I've tried to scream myself awake. But I haven't succeeded!"

The doctor took off his glasses and rubbed his eyes. "Let's see. You had this dream last Thursday night—and twice on the night following. How about over the weekend? Did you have any dreams on Saturday and Sunday nights?"

"I wasn't sleeping too well," David said. "If I did have any dreams, I don't remember them."

"But the nightmare about the blue house—you dreamed it three times in a row?"

"Yes," David replied. "Do you think I'll have it again?"

"I don't know." Dr. Fuchs-Kramer put his glasses back on. "Let me ask you something else. Each time you had this nightmare—did it somehow seem more vivid, more real than just an ordinary dream?"

The antiques dealer nodded.

"Mr. Carmichael . . . have you ever experienced what you thought of as a psychic event? When the phone rang, perhaps you knew who was calling. You may have had a hunch where a lost object was, or when a friend might walk in the door? Has anything like that ever happened to you?"

David shook his head. "Not that I can recall."

"What I'm wondering," the doctor went on, "is whether your repeating nightmare might be precognitive—whether it foretells the future. You see, the vividness and the repetition—three times in a row!—suggest that your subconscious may be trying to warn you about something that's going to happen."

"Warn me?" David asked. "That a blue house is really going to grow out of the ground? That's impossible!"

"Not to the sleeping mind, it isn't." Dr. Fuchs-Kramer smiled gently. "The subconscious usually communicates in shorthand, mixing up symbols and compressing its imagery. Right now, for example, I'm running tests on a factory worker who dreamed that a disembodied hand walked into his factory—on its fingers, mind you!—and turned out the fluorescent lights over his assembly line. An impossibility, right? Well, the next week, a man working on the assembly line *beside* the subject got his hand caught in the machinery. To shut off the conveyer belt, they had to turn off the power—which turned off the overhead lights as well. But it was too late. The injured man's hand was severed at the wrist."

"My God," David said.

"Do you see?" the parapsychologist asked. "The subject's dream took two elements of the coming week's accident—the worker's severed hand, and the power shutdown—and recombined them in a different sequence. Precognitive dreams often do that. They telescope separate events so that everything happens at once."

David said nothing, trying to recall the exact sequence of events in his nightmare.

"Do you recognize any of the details in your dream?" Dr. Fuchs-Kramer asked. "For example, have you ever seen a house similar to that one?"

"Yes and no," David replied. "It looks like that new house up in New Castle, where Keith found the old Roman coin. But in real life, the house is painted yellow, not blue." David paused, seeing that the doctor was thinking. "Do you think the dream *is* precognitive?"

"I'm afraid we'll just have to wait and see," said Dr. Fuchs-Kramer, smiling. "How can we tell if it really was precognition until a given event actually happens? But in the meantime, you might want us to test you for psychometric ability."

"I beg your pardon?" David said.

The parapsychologist smiled again. "The ability to hold an object—and get impressions from it—is called psychometry. Some subjects can do it rather well, and the images they receive later prove valid. My assistant is running a psychometric test right now. Would you like to watch?"

"I certainly would," David replied.

Dr. Fuchs-Kramer rose from behind his desk. "Follow me."

At about the same hour that David Carmichael left for his appointment with Dr. Fuchs-Kramer, Keith began work on the house at 666 Sunset Brook Lane.

He had spent Monday morning with Marc and Jason in Peekskill. The new shingles on the two new dormer windows Keith built hadn't matched the older, weathered shingles on the surrounding roof. Keith had solved the problem by replacing them with shingles of a light gray shade. By the time *they* started to discolor, the whole roof would need reshingling; the two dormers could be done over at the same time.

By noon, they had finished cleaning up. Keith packed their tools in his panel truck and told Marc and Jason to meet him over at 666 Sunset Brook Lane after they got through lunch.

At a few minutes before two, Keith pulled his panel truck into the gravel driveway beside the new house's front porch. He had deliberately arrived a few minutes early so that he could have a look around the place before Marc and Jason showed up.

First he examined the big bay window. The Weeping Fool's six-sided face was still missing, and Keith realized he ought to cover the hole before it rained again. Looking down, he saw a small bird lying on its side on the ground right in front of the bay window. Was it dead, or just injured?

Remembering that birds carry lice, Keith got a wide mortar trowel from the panel truck; then he tiptoed along under the drip line of the roof. The grass seed was just beginning to sprout, underneath the bay window, and he didn't want to damage the new lawn.

The bird was a sparrow. Keith scooped it up on the mortar trowel and examined it more closely. It didn't seem to have been injured; but a couple of its neck feathers were ruffled, out of place. When Keith and his brother Paul were kids, their family cat used to bring home dead birds that were similarly unmarked. Apparently they died of fear before the cat had a chance to hurt them.

Setting the sparrow back down on the ground, Keith poked at it with the tip of the trowel. The dead bird's head lolled unnaturally on the tiny shoulders. Its neck was broken. Must have flown into the bay window, Keith thought.

He flung the dead sparrow into the gully just as Marc's car pulled up on the opposite side of Sunset Brook Lane. Jason was in the passenger seat beside him. Both carpenters were in their early twenties. They did excellent work, and had been with Keith Olson since before he'd married Jennifer.

Marc looked over at the front porch and whistled. "Boy, does that house need a paint job!"

"That comes later," Keith said. He pointed to Tom Greene's FOR RENT sign over by the bay window. "The guy who owns this place wants to rent it out, so he wants the inside fixed up first."

"But why are the clapboards in such a mess?" Jason asked.

"Because the house was moved to this site," Keith

said. "It may have come all the way from the West Coast!"

Keith still had the key he'd found lying on the front porch on Saturday morning. Now he unlocked the front door and let Marc and Jason into the empty living room.

"All of this wallboard has to go," Keith said. "Jason, you love ripping out walls. You can have a great time in here!"

A cool spring breeze was blowing in the front door. Keith went into the dining alcove to push up a couple of windows; the resulting cross-breeze would carry the dust right out of the house. He was amazed that the windows slid up so easily. Old windows were notoriously sticky—and after so many miles of travel, a house could be expected to get out of plumb, which made doors and windows jam.

Jason stood in the middle of the living room, glancing from one wall to the others. "I can't figure it out," he finally said. "Didn't they use any braces?"

"What do you mean?" Keith asked.

"I once saw them move an old farmhouse," Jason said, "over in Armonk. There was a new road going through, and the farmhouse was in the way. They had to move it maybe a hundred yards across a field. But still they had to brace the inside—you know, nail two-by-fours between the beams inside the walls. You say this house was moved all the way across the country?"

"I think so," Keith said. "I'm still trying to find out."

Jason pointed to the wood paneling under the staircase. "Without interior bracing, that woodwork would have pulled itself apart before they got this place off its old foundation. And look at the ceiling. It's old plaster —and it isn't even cracked!"

"I'll bet you they *did* use bracing." Keith ran his

hand over one of the wallboard panels next to the door. "This wallboard is new," he said, "and the nailheads are still bright and shiny. The crew who moved the house must have torn out the original walls and installed braces. Then when they got the house settled here, they took down the bracing and nailed up this cruddy wallboard."

"Could be," Jason agreed.

Keith grinned. "Today's the day you get to find out. All these walls have to be done over again—properly!"

Jason started attacking the first panel of wallboard while Marc and Keith went out to the panel truck. The back of the truck was loaded with four-by-eight-foot panels of good-quality Sheetrock from the builder's supply yard. They stacked them against the wall beside the front door, one by one. Keith could hear Jason inside the house, prying the thin wallboard away from the underlying studs. Then suddenly the noises stopped, and Keith heard Jason's footsteps coming to the front door.

"Hey, Keith." Jason had a strange look on his face. "Come in here and have a look at this. You aren't going to believe it."

Keith followed him back into the living room, where Jason had ripped loose the first wallboard panel beside the front door.

In every other house Keith had ever worked in, the vertical studs inside the walls were all uniform—usually two-by-fours. But here, every single piece of wood was of a different size! Some bore traces of crude saws; others had been shaped with an axe or a chisel. One log still had its bark attached, just as it had come from the tree! And almost every piece of timber Keith could see bore unexplained scars, grooves, notches and strange brownish stains.

"You're right," he told Jason. "I don't believe it."

"Maybe somebody assembled this house out of driftwood washed up on the beach?" Marc asked.

"I don't know," Keith said. "A lot of this stuff looks as if it was scavenged from other buildings. And none of it looks bleached, the way you get with seawater."

"That beam looks like pine," Marc said, "and that" —he tapped a rough-grained plank—"is oak. But what the hell's *this?*"

Beside the front door was a thick, square beam, its bottom scorched by fire. The undamaged wood was dark and very close-grained—and again, its middle was covered with light brown stains.

"Redwood?" Keith asked. "Maybe teak? It looks tropical, somehow." But why would anyone have selected this half-charred timber for construction in the first place?

"Take a look here!" Jason put his hand on another vertical stud near the doorjamb. The wood was full of nail holes. It reminded Keith of the time Jennifer had stripped an old antique chair of its upholstery. The chair's frame was peppered with dozens and dozens of holes where upholstery tacks had been hammered in and pried out again over the years.

Of course, it made sense to reupholster a chair every so often. But how frequently did wallboard or Sheetrock have to be replaced?

"And get a load of this!" Marc pointed to where the bottom of one beam met the floorboards. "Look, Ma, no nails!"

Keith saw Marc was right. Instead of the usual six-penny nails, this house was fastened together with wooden pegs—an age-old method of construction that made for a much more solid structure than nails could achieve.

"Now I think I see why Coste's so fussy about this house," Keith said. "Think of the work it took to drill all those holes and whittle the pegs to the right size. No wonder this house came through the move in such good condition!"

Marc frowned. "Weren't they already using nails as far back as the eighteenth century?"

"There's a couple of pegs missing here." Jason ran his finger into a hole that ran through the middle of one beam. Below it was another empty hole of the exact same size.

"Could that be where the braces were attached?" Keith asked. On a hunch, he walked directly across the room to the facing wall beside the dining-room alcove. "Jason, let me have that prybar."

Keith soon had the wallboard in pieces on the floor. Behind it was another beam, aligned exactly with the one across the room. And in the middle of this beam were two more circular holes.

"See?" Keith said. "The brace must have reached from over here clear across the room."

Jason was unimpressed. "But why attach it with pegs? Why didn't they just use nails?"

"I don't know," Keith sighed. "But I'd like the rest of this wallboard torn down before you quit this evening. So let's get started!"

Dr. Fuchs-Kramer led David Carmichael to a closed room down the corridor from his office. Pulling a key ring from the pocket of his white hospital coat, he unlocked the door, switched on the light and motioned David inside.

The small windowless room contained two chairs, a cot and a console of electronic equipment. David recognized the spools of a tape recorder and a pair of earphones, among other gadgets. On top of the console was a small television set. Dr. Fuchs-Kramer walked across the room and turned it on.

When the black-and-white picture tube flickered into life, David saw a doctor in a white hospital coat who seemed about the same age as Dr. Fuchs-Kramer. Sitting across the table from him was an elderly woman with gray hair. In her left hand she was holding a large old-fashioned gold pocket watch. She had her right hand over her eyes.

"This is an experiment my assistant is running right now," the parapsychologist explained. "The woman is Enid Schwartz, who has a fairly good track record in psychometry. Enid's agreed to be videotaped while she gets her impressions; this is a closed-circuit monitor." The doctor reached over and turned up the volume so that David could hear what was going on.

"A girl and a boy . . ." Enid Schwartz whispered. She hesitated, as if groping for words. The dark-haired doctor across from her wrote down something on his note pad, but made no comment.

"Every time Enid comes over here," Dr. Fuchs-Kramer explained, "I have her psychometrize three of four different objects I've borrowed from nurses and doctors here at the hospital. Right now, for example, that watch she's holding is mine—I inherited it from my maternal grandfather. But Enid doesn't know that, and my assistant doesn't know whose it is, either. That way, if her impressions make any sense, telepathy can be ruled out."

"Yes," Enid Schwartz nodded. "A girl and a boy! The girl is older. Maybe taller, too, and she has hair that's . . . gold. Golden!"

"Sidney Golden!" Dr. Fuchs-Kramer whispered to David. "That was my grandfather's name!"

On the screen of the closed-circuit monitor, Enid Schwartz raised her right hand to her hair, as if patting an invisible wig. "The boy has curly hair," she said, "like his sister's. Only dark—his hair is dark. He loves swimming . . . ah! I see him leaping into water—no, falling. And this isn't summer! The water is cold—"

Enid Schwartz had more to say, but Dr. Fuchs-Kramer leaned forward and turned off the volume. David looked at him in surprise—the parapsychologist was clearly shaken!

"My grandfather had two children," the doctor said in a weak voice. "My mother—who was his eldest child—and then my uncle."

David was genuinely excited. "Did your uncle have dark, curly hair?"

"So I'm told," Dr. Fuchs-Kramer replied. "I never knew my uncle. You see, he drowned in the East River the winter before I was born!"

"My God," David said. "Then she was getting all that information from—just from your watch?"

"Apparently," the doctor said. "Enid says that tragic events are the easiest for her to pick up, because they generate strong negative emotions. And according to her, pain and grief and terror leave traces that joy, happiness and love can't ever erase."

The two men looked back at the silent television screen, where Enid Schwartz was setting the thick gold watch down on the table. "That's her last item for today," Dr. Fuchs-Kramer said. "They're winding up now." He switched off the monitor, then turned back to David. "Would you care to meet her?"

David and the parapsychologist arrived outside the testing room just as Dr. Fuchs-Kramer's assistant was opening the door. Enid Schwartz—a delicate, birdlike woman with luminous dark eyes—looked smaller and older than she had appeared on camera. She shook hands with David, who towered over her, and gave him a delighted smile.

"We'd like to walk Mrs. Schwartz back downstairs," Dr. Fuchs-Kramer said to David. "Would you mind waiting in my office?"

"Not at all," David replied.

The two doctors accompanied Enid Schwartz to the elevator. Just as Dr. Fuchs-Kramer pushed the DOWN button, he felt the old woman grip his arm.

"Oh, dear," Enid Schwartz whispered. "Oh dear!"

The elevator doors opened, but Dr. Fuchs-Kramer let them close again. "Enid, what's the matter?"

"I just saw it again!" Enid Schwartz exclaimed. "That wonderfully handsome gentleman with the silver hair. I forget his name?"

"Carmichael," the doctor prompted.

"Yes, Mr. Carmichael!" Enid Schwartz shut her eyes. "Just now, as we were waiting for the elevator, I saw it all again. Something's going to happen to that gentleman very soon."

This was most unusual, Dr. Fuchs-Kramer thought. Enid Schwartz generally received impressions about the past. Only rarely did she claim to have glimpses of the future.

"I don't know what exactly," the woman continued. "But I felt fear. Terrible fear! And I saw darkness, spreading toward Mr. Carmichael like a wave of black ink. In the midst of all that darkness was a red light. I don't know what it could possibly mean. But I saw it all as soon as I touched his hand."

Back in Dr. Fuchs-Kramer's office, David sat down to await the parapsychologist's return. Obviously the doctor wasn't very much interested in David's story about the ancient sestertius—but why should he be, when he had a truly gifted woman like Enid Schwartz to run experiments with? If only the bronze sestertius hadn't vanished! David would have loved to know what impressions Mrs. Schwartz received from it.

But if the coin was gone, the yellow-and-white house across from Keith and Jennifer's was still there. Perhaps David could obtain a nail or a piece of metal from the bathroom where the coin had first appeared. And if *he* could learn to psychometrize—if he did even half as well as Enid Schwartz—then maybe he could get some answers for himself.

Five minutes later, when Dr. Fuchs-Kramer walked in the door, David had made up his mind.

"Doctor, I hope I'm not keeping you . . ."

"No, no," the parapsychologist smiled. "I saw all my patients earlier today. Now that Enid's gone, I have nothing but some reports to catch up on. The rest of my afternoon's free."

"If you do have time," David said, "I'd like to take you up on your offer."

"Offer?" Dr. Fuchs-Kramer said. "I don't recall—"

David smiled. "I'd like you to test my ability to psychometrize."

8

Monday, April 16, 1979

"Mr. Carmichael?" Dr. Fuchs-Kramer said.

The antiques dealer stifled another yawn and looked back at the parapsychologist.

"Psychometry usually takes some practice. A potential subject isn't likely to get results right off the bat. And if you're feeling the least bit fatigued, this probably isn't the best time to—"

"Please," David said. "The first time I handled that old coin, up in New Castle, it was after dinner. The second time, in my apartment, it was after midnight. Being tired didn't seem to interfere with my impressions. Maybe it even enhanced them."

"Maybe," the doctor repeated. "But you've never before gotten impressions from any other objects? Only when you held that old coin?"

"That's right," David admitted.

Dr. Fuchs-Kramer removed his glasses and polished them with a handkerchief. The parapsychologist had noticed that for some reason or other, women were usually better at psychometry than men. But perhaps this Mr. Carmichael could be persuaded to contribute to the hospital's research program. And if the man wanted to waste his time, Dr. Fuchs-Kramer could probably "test" him for psychometry—and still catch up on those reports he'd been meaning to read.

"I tell you what," he said to David. "I'm going to give you one of the test objects that Enid worked with this afternoon. Let's see what images you pick up, if any. Then when you're all through—say, after a half hour or forty-five minutes—then we can go over your impressions and see how accurate you were."

"Fine with me," David said eagerly.

"Good," Dr. Fuchs-Kramer replied. "Then perhaps you'd like a room where you can be by yourself, sort of collect your thoughts?"

The parapsychologist led his visitor back down the hospital corridor to the room containing the TV monitor. "You can lie down on that cot, if you like," Dr. Fuchs-Kramer said. "Put on those earphones, and a tape recording will play that will help you relax."

Built into the electronic console were a blood-pressure cuff and a set of electrodes for measuring brain waves, but the doctor didn't intend to use them. As far as he was concerned, David Carmichael's test was merely a trial run—to humor a potential donor to his ESP research.

"You aren't going to videotape me?" David asked.

"Not for starters," Dr. Fuchs-Kramer answered. "I would like to tape-record you, though. Over here is a microphone, so that you can dictate any impressions you receive from your test object. And over here is a buzzer that rings in my office. Press it, and I'll come get you."

"You're going to lock the door, then?" David asked.

"No, just close it." Dr. Fuchs-Kramer smiled. "Don't worry, no one's going to barge in on you unexpectedly. Now let me go get you your test object."

Alone in the room, David hung his jacket on the back of the door. Then he loosened his tie, undid the top button of his shirt and lay down on the cot.

A moment later, the parapsychologist returned and handed David the earphones. They were large, soft, and padded—like the pair Eleanor had worn when she wanted to listen to the *1812 Overture* without bothering Mr. and Mrs. Jacobs.

"The tape I've prepared," the doctor said, "should put you in a relaxed, contemplative mood. When I get back to my office, I'll switch it on. Now here's your test object."

David reached out his left hand. Dr. Fuchs-Kramer gave him a little six-sided charm of bright polished silver, with the letter J engraved on it.

"I'm going to close this door when I go out," the parapsychologist said. "The tape will start running as soon as I return to my office. But take your time."

David looked at the silver charm in his left hand. "Does this belong to a woman whose name starts with a J?"

Dr. Fuchs-Kramer just smiled. "Perhaps *you* can tell *me* that. Would you like the light on or off?"

The fluorescent light in the ceiling did seem a bit harsh. "Off, I guess," David said.

The parapsychologist flicked the light switch and was silhouetted by the light from the corridor.

"One more question," David said, stifling a yawn. "Let's say I don't get any images at all. Would I be

110

more likely to get impressions if I tried to psychometrize this thing again tomorrow?"

"Probably not," Dr. Fuchs-Kramer said. "A new stimulus always seems to affect a subject most strongly. Once the stimulus becomes at all familiar, the response dampens off."

"But the second time I handled that sestertius," David said, "the images were just as vivid as the first time. How do you explain that?"

"I'm not trying to explain *anything* yet," the doctor replied. "Just remember, if you keep psychometrizing the same object, your own vibrations are likely to seep into it. You might begin picking up information on yourself, therefore, as well as on the object's owner. So don't hold on to that charm too long before you try to psychometrize it!"

"Okay," David said. "I'm ready."

"Very well," the parapsychologist replied. "Remember to buzz me when you're through."

Some light from the corridor still seeped underneath the door when the doctor closed it. David reached up in the darkness and placed the soft, heavy earphones over his head.

Again he regretted that the corroded bronze sestertius wasn't here for him to work with. But David thought he knew why the coin had vanished from his hand in the first place. He had picked up that coin specifically to get more information. In fact, he'd been getting close; he had even received a glimpse of Jennifer Olson. Perhaps someone—or something—didn't want him to learn any more. It was too wild a theory to relate to Dr. Fuchs-Kramer—but had the coin's true owner come and taken the coin away?

But suddenly David heard the gentle, recorded voice of Dr. Fuchs-Kramer coming over the earphones.

111

". . . Imagine that you are lying on a soft, grassy hill. The sun is bright, and the air is warm; and up above you there are clouds floating in the clear blue sky. . . ."

David yawned. He was feeling nothing at all from the little silver pendant he was holding in his left hand. He turned it over in his fingers. It had six sides, just like those panes of glass in the bay window of the new house on Sunset Brook Lane. The silver charm had a J on it. J for Jennifer? . . .

Dr. Fuchs-Kramer's voice droned on in the earphones. David was becoming more and more relaxed. He closed his hand around the silver charm, hoping that it would give him some vibrations, some impressions—anything at all. . . .

Within a minute, David was fast asleep.

By five o'clock that afternoon, Jason had torn down all the wallboard except for a narrow strip in the hallway that covered the back of the fireplace. They had nailed up four panels of Sheetrock, but there wasn't much point in cutting and measuring a fifth one before quitting time. So Keith called it a day.

Since they were coming back the next morning, they left all their tools inside the house. After locking the front door, Keith drove to the office in Chappaqua to check the day's mail. He was hoping there'd be a reply from the managing editor of that Seattle newspaper. He had mailed his special delivery letter on Thursday. Now it was only Monday, but even so, it wasn't too early to expect a packet of articles about the murder house at 666 Bremerton Road.

But when Keith unlocked the front door of the office, he found that only three items had been slipped through the mail slot. A bill from one of his suppliers. A newsletter on restoring old houses that he subscribed to—and a letter from the New Castle Chamber of Commerce. Nothing at all from Seattle.

It was probably too early to expect a reply, but still Keith wondered if the managing editor was off on vacation. Or maybe some kid in the mail room had opened his letter and pocketed the twenty? Disappointed, he switched on the machine that recorded telephone calls when he was out.

"Hello, Keith," said a familiar male voice. It was Tom Greene. "Mr. Coste asked me to tell you that you can expect your first installment—the two thousand payable when you start work on his house—on Wednesday. That's all. No need to call me back."

Keith kept listening, but the rest of the tape was blank. Tom Greene's had been the only call that day! Where were all the other jobs he should be getting, now that spring was here? Business had never been this slow before, not even in the dead of winter.

He was writing a company check to pay the supplier's bill when the telephone rang. Now that's more like it, he thought. He turned off the automatic recorder and picked up the receiver.

"Hello, Keith Olson here."

"Well, *finally!*" said a woman's voice. "This is Madge Sackett." Keith knew Mrs. Sackett; he'd installed a screened porch for her the summer before. "I've been calling and calling, but you're never there!"

"I just got back from vacation," Keith replied. "But this telephone has an automatic recorder. If you'd left a message—"

"I didn't get a *chance* to leave a message," Mrs. Sackett said. "I called this number at least a dozen times. And the phone just rang and rang."

"Really?" asked Keith, puzzled. "When was the last time you called?"

"This morning," Madge Sackett said.

That didn't make sense, Keith thought. The machine had recorded Tom Greene's call. Why not hers?

"I need a new trellis for my porch," the woman continued. "But I need it completed soon—in time for my clematis to start climbing it."

Keith made some fast calculations in his head. For a job like that, he could hardly charge her more than fifty dollars. "I can build you a trellis as soon as I'm through with the job I'm doing now. Maybe I could stop over tomorrow and give you an estimate?"

After he hung up, Keith stared at his office telephone. Even if it had been on the blink, that wouldn't explain why he wasn't getting any new work. Because the directory listing for Olson Custom Carpentry gave Keith's home telephone number, as well as the one here at the office. And Jennifer always took down the name and number of anyone who called. Could both telephones have been having trouble at the same time?

Well, whatever the reason, new customers simply weren't calling! That was the main reason why Keith had been able to start work on Coste's house so quickly—and why he really needed Coste's first installment of two thousand dollars.

Locking the office door on his way out, Keith Olson felt a sense of mild panic. The construction trade wasn't like selling encyclopedias—you couldn't go around knocking on people's doors to drum up business. Marc and Jason had nothing to worry about, because skilled carpenters never had any trouble getting hired. But unless some new work came along pretty soon, Keith didn't see how he could make it through the summer.

It was 5 P.M. before Dr. Fuchs-Kramer thought to look at his watch. Mr. Carmichael had been psychometrizing Joan Horowitz's silver charm for over an hour now, and he still hadn't buzzed to signal he was through. The parapsychologist smiled to himself. This wouldn't be the first time his relaxation tape had put a tired subject to sleep! He probably ought to go in and wake Mr. Carmichael up.

And then he heard the hoarse, terrified scream echoing from the room down the corridor.

In his dream, David was looking at the blue house again—only this time, there wasn't any blood flowing from the foundation. In fact, there was nice green grass coming up all around the porch. It was daylight. The sun was shining overhead. And yet the entire house was enveloped in shadow—throwing out a shroud of darkness around itself, in the same way the sun radiated light.

And then, as David watched, the house began coming apart. It was like watching an explosion in slow motion. Then the beams and clapboards rearranged themselves into scaffolds, gibbets and stakes. One long plank became the side of a guillotine. Another beam was the upright of a cross on which a man was being nailed, upside down. David saw people being beheaded, impaled and burned alive. Every stick of wood in that blue house was figuring in the torture or execution of a human being.

One stained and charred length of wood floated through the air, end over end, and planted itself in the ground—and to it was manacled the horribly mutilated man David had seen in his waking vision. The red-hot sestertius was still glowing in his mouth.

David tried to run, but his feet would not move. Coming straight at him was a shiny brass chandelier, like the one he had in the living room of his apartment. From it dangled a piece of white cloth shaped into a crude hangman's noose. The noose lifted gracefully in

115

midair and settled around his neck. He felt the fabric closing around his throat. He tried to scream, but the noose was too tight. He could make no sound at all! . . .

Dr. Fuchs-Kramer threw open the door and switched on the light. Lying on the cot was David Carmichael, his face purple; his right hand was clawing at his throat.

Then the doctor saw why. In his sleep, the man had somehow managed to tighten his necktie around his throat—so tightly that he was having trouble breathing.

Quickly the parapsychologist stepped to the cot and loosened the silk knot. David moaned and drew a deep, shuddering breath. The doctor shook his visitor by the shoulders until he was positive the man was awake.

David sat up on the cot, rubbing his neck. "I'm sorry," he muttered. "I was having another nightmare. Did I make any noise?"

"Yes," Dr. Fuchs-Kramer said. "But did you have any luck with the test object? Did you receive any impressions from the silver charm I gave you?"

"I don't think so. . . ." David's left hand was empty. The little silver charm wasn't beside him on the cot. He leaned forward, wondering if it had fallen on the floor and rolled underneath the cot. But no, it wasn't there either. . . .

"What did you do with it?" Dr. Fuchs-Kramer asked.

"Nothing. I remember I had it in my hand when your voice started coming through the earphones. Then I must have fallen asleep . . ." David shrugged, looking around the small room in bewilderment.

The doctor bit his lip in exasperation. He had promised to give Joan Horowitz back her charm as soon as Enid Schwartz was through with it.

"Could you possibly have put it in one of your pockets?"

Obediently, David stood up and turned his pants pockets inside out. All he found was a few nickels and pennies.

Dr. Fuchs-Kramer saw that David's jacket had fallen off its hook on the back of the door. When the parapsychologist stooped down and picked it off the floor, out of the breast pocket fell a square plastic coin envelope. Inside was the bronze sestertius—and tucked alongside it, Joan Horowitz's little silver charm.

The doctor shook his head. This man had *seemed* normal enough when he arrived, but now he was displaying symptoms of extreme distress. A nightmare an unconscious dramatization of some problem he couldn't face on the conscious level. Self-destructive impulses too—punishing himself by tightening that tie around his neck. And if he was a kleptomaniac to boot, that cast a whole new light on the events Carmichael had been talking about.

"Mr. Carmichael . . ." Dr. Fuchs-Kramer cleared his throat. "Let's go back to my office, please. I want to talk to you."

David was mortified to think that the doctor suspected him of being a thief. But he forced himself to look Dr. Fuchs-Kramer in the eye and listen to his explanation. According to him, all the bizarre experiences David had told him about were merely imaginary, no more than hallucinations. But when the parapsychologist fell silent, David was still puzzled. There was one detail that simply didn't make sense to him. . . .

"Why did I have such a violent reaction when I handled that sestertius up in New Castle?"

117

"Well!" Dr. Fuchs-Kramer said. "Obviously that coin had some bad associations for you. After all, who handed it to you in the first place? The husband of the woman who invited you to dinner. Now, you don't have to answer this if you don't like, but in waking life, now—do you find yourself attracted to this woman, this Mrs. Olson?"

David was silent for a moment. "Yes," he finally said.

"*Strongly* attracted?"

David nodded.

"And are you married yourself?"

"No," David answered. "My wife died two years ago."

"All right." Dr. Fuchs-Kramer nodded. "It all makes sense, then! That first coin was given to you by the husband of a woman you're sexually attracted to. Honestly, now, Mr. Carmichael—haven't you toyed with the daydream of what would happen if Mrs. Olson's husband were out of the picture?"

The antiques dealer nodded again, almost imperceptibly.

"Well, that isn't a very nice thought, is it? And so you feel guilty. And because you feel guilty, you decide to punish yourself! All these images of torture and death—possibly you were projecting onto the coin all the unacceptably violent urges that had been crossing your mind."

"Violent urges?" David asked. "I really don't think I've had any."

"Oh, I'm not saying any of this was conscious," the parapsychologist replied. "The important thing was, the *husband* gave you the coin to identify. You wouldn't mind doing *her* a favor—but him? So the very next day, you buy a coin that's similar, only in much better condition. Now, doesn't that seem rather competitive—a bit of one-upsmanship? And then, to eliminate his competition, you promptly mislaid the original coin he gave you."

"I didn't *mislay* it," David answered with some irritation. "It just—"

"Vanished?" Dr. Fuchs-Kramer smiled. "Mr. Carmichael, even a healthy mind can play tricks. Perhaps you got up off the couch in your apartment, put the coin away, came back and then promptly forgot having done so. Selective amnesia! It happens all the time."

"But there was that odor I smelled . . ." David sighed. "If the coin was an apport, as you said—couldn't it have vanished on its own?"

The parapsychologist took a deep breath. People were always unwilling to admit they had been at fault—and so they dreamed up supernatural scapegoats to take the blame. *Not me, Doc, I'm not responsible—the Devil made me do it!*

"Let's say it *did* disappear from your closed hand," the doctor said gently. "But let me tell you a true story. My assistant and I once investigated a house where pictures were flying off the walls by themselves. Loud, invisible footsteps followed us down the stairs. In the kitchen, small pebbles materialized out of thin air and clattered down onto the stove. Classical poltergeist phenomena, of the first order! And you know what we determined the underlying cause to be?"

David shook his head.

"Living in that house was a little twelve-year-old girl who was just going through puberty. She hated her new stepfather—and hated her mother for having remarried. And when the little girl went off to summer camp, all the disturbances just stopped, like that."

"You mean the girl was faking the phenomena?" David asked.

"Oh, no!" Dr. Fuchs-Kramer laced his fingers together and cracked his knuckles. "Those phenomena were completely authentic. But the combination of jealousy and awakening sexual feelings was more than the girl could cope with. By some process we don't yet understand, her emotional tensions externalized and caused the levitations and psychokinesis. In other words, when there are spontaneous psychic phenomena, usually there's an individual with conflicted emotions somewhere nearby. Do you see my point?"

"Yes," David said.

"I'm not saying you didn't undergo a genuine paranormal experience. Of course, ordinary amnesia does seem a bit more plausible. But in either case, the root cause is probably the same. Sexual tension—and probably stress as well? I imagine your antiques business can get rather hectic."

"Well," David admitted, "auctions can get tense when there are several Japanese dealers bidding against me. And I never can be sure of having enough stock to fill out the gallery."

Dr. Fuchs-Kramer drummed his fingers on the desk. "I understand that most art galleries shut down for July and August. Why don't you get out of the city and take a house for the summer? I'm sure you could afford it—and in the long run, it would probably be cheaper than going into therapy with any of the professionals I could recommend."

Half an hour later, David was back in his Riverside Drive apartment. He couldn't imagine how he had strangled himself with his own necktie. And he had no idea how that silver charm had wound up inside the plastic coin envelope—especially since Dr. Fuchs-Kramer had to pry open the staple before he could remove it!

But what if the parapsychologist was right? So far,

David couldn't verify any of his visions and nightmares. He kept on dreaming of that house as blue, when he knew perfectly well that it was yellow in real life. Selective amnesia certainly sounded more reasonable than an old bronze coin that appeared and disappeared on its own! And he certainly could do with a long rest—he hadn't taken a vacation since before Eleanor died.

He had hidden the expensive bronze sestertius in the top drawer of his bureau. But that really wasn't a safe place for such a valuable coin. David decided he'd better turn it over to Keith Olson before something happened to it too.

David picked up the telephone. Now that he'd learned the most likely reason for his bad dreams, he didn't want to let Jennifer worry unnecessarily. This was his chance—to give Keith the new coin, and to see her for one last time before he took off for the summer.

In New Castle, Jennifer Olson answered the phone on the second ring. And David could tell how happy she was to hear his voice.

9

Wednesday, April 18, 1979

"AGAIN?" KEITH STARED AT HIS wife across the breakfast table. "We had David for dinner only last week!"

Jennifer had deliberately postponed telling Keith that she'd invited David for dinner on Friday. She'd been hoping to catch Keith in a better mood. "David's going away for the summer," she said patiently. "And he wants to bring up that coin so you can return it to Mr. Coste."

"Fine," said Keith. "But why are we always feeding *him?* I mean, after all the times you've cooked him dinner, why doesn't David ever invite *us* out?"

"Actually, he did ask us down to New York this Friday," Jennifer replied. "But I know you don't like Manhattan because it takes so long to get there, and because it's expensive. David would love to treat us to a really good restaurant, but you wouldn't enjoy it because you'd be too worried about the prices on the menu. That's why I suggested he come up here instead."

Keith had to admit Jennifer was right. He *didn't* much like going out to dinner. Getting up at 6 A.M. every weekday, working until five or six, he preferred a quiet dinner at home. If Jennifer would only land herself some interior-decorating work, she'd be grateful to stay home in the evenings too. But it really irked him that she'd waited two days to tell him that David Carmichael was coming for dinner. His irritation made him eager to leave the house even earlier than usual.

When he parked the panel truck in the gravel driveway of 666 Sunset Brook Lane, Keith saw there was something wrong with the blue spruce the landscapers had planted at the side of the porch. It was about six feet tall, bushy and full. But all along the side of the tree nearest the house, the needles were starting to turn brown.

Then Keith glanced over at the big bay window, and stared in surprise. For the second time that week, there was a dead bird lying in the newly sprouted grass under the leaded windows.

Monday it had been a sparrow. Today it was a robin. Like the first bird, this one was lying on its left side, with its head at an unnatural angle to the body. Keith had heard of birds flying into picture windows—but those bay windows, with their strips of leaded glass, weren't exactly invisible. Once again, he got his mortar trowel out of the truck and heaved the bird down into the gully.

Climbing up on the front porch, he unlocked the front door and looked inside with a sense of real satisfaction. The living room looked about 300 percent better than it had on Monday afternoon! Only one narrow sliver of wallboard still had to be replaced—that long vertical piece in the hall which fitted over the back of the fireplace. Keith figured they could probably replace it with several scraps of left-over Sheetrock. So he had told Jason not to tear it out until they had finished replacing all the walls in the bedroom and dressing room upstairs.

When Marc and Jason arrived, the three of them worked upstairs for the rest of the morning, measuring, cutting and fitting new Sheetrock in the bedroom. The work went faster than Keith had figured because one entire wall was already finished in wood paneling.

By the time Keith finally thought to look at his watch, it was twelve noon. He brushed the plaster dust off his jeans and started down the stairs.

"I'll see you guys around one thirty," he said over his shoulder. "You can take off now if you want."

"You going home for lunch?" Marc called after him.

"No," Keith said. His earlier argument with Jennifer still rankled in his mind. "I want to stop by the office in Chappaqua. There may be calls on the machine, and I'm expecting something in the mail."

Marc and Jason had left their lunches in the refrigerator in the kitchen. When they came downstairs, Keith had already driven off in the panel truck. Jason stopped and eyed the narrow piece of wallboard behind the fireplace.

"There's nothing but bricks under there," Marc asserted. For the past two days, Jason had kept calling him over to look at some new variety of wood he'd discovered inside behind the wall.

"Well," Jason said, "this *does* have to come off sooner or later . . ."

While Jason went looking for his prybar, Marc took

his sandwich outside on the porch. It was unusually hot and sultry for April, and there were heavy clouds off in the west. It looked as if they might get some rain later.

"Hey, Marc!" Jason called from inside the house. "Can I borrow your flashlight?"

Marc walked back inside to find Jason standing in the hall. He had pried loose the remaining strip of wallboard and was staring at the exposed bricks at the back of the chimney.

"What is it now?" Marc asked.

"I don't know," Jason said. "There's something in here, beside the fireplace."

Marc got the flashlight from his toolbox upstairs. Jason switched it on and aimed the beam into the dark cavity beside the chimney. Next to the reddish bricks was a black metal column about six inches thick. It bore dents and hammer marks, as if it had been forged. Marc figured it was just an ordinary cast-iron pipe. But as Jason played the flashlight beam over it, Marc saw there were funny-shaped capital letters punched deep into the metal. Cast-iron foundry lettering was usually raised, not countersunk.

"What *is* that thing?" Jason asked. "Part of the plumbing?"

"I doubt it," Marc said. "All the water pipes are at the back of the house. Maybe it's a vent that comes out on top of the roof."

"Want to have a look?" Jason suggested.

"Yeah, but Keith took the truck with him. And the extension ladder's in the truck."

"We don't need a ladder," said Jason, grinning. "Have you still got that towrope in your car?"

Outside, Jason unrolled about fifty feet of heavy twine from his toolbox. He tied one end of the twine to a small rock and hurled the rock up over the top of the

125

house. Then, tying the other end to Marc's towrope, he used the twine to pull the rope up over the roof and down the other side.

Finally he tied the end of the towrope to a post at the corner of the porch, doubling the knot so that it couldn't possibly slip, then walked back around the house. The other end of Marc's towrope was dangling down beside the bay window.

"Are you sure that's such a good idea?" Marc asked. "If you climb up there, your shoes'll leave marks on the clapboards."

"The whole outside needs painting anyway," said Jason, shrugging. "What are a few more scratches going to matter?" He pulled on the rope until he was sure it was taut. Then he grabbed hold and began climbing, hand over hand.

Jason's feet skidded on the clapboards, and he heard the old wood crack under his weight. For an instant, he thought he saw a movement inside the room behind the bay window. But it was just his own reflection in the glass. About halfway up the wall, he braced his foot on the bay window's roof, and one shingle broke in half and fell to the ground. Oh, well, the owner would never know! From there, it was an easy climb to the eaves of the sloping mansard roof.

Jason paused for a moment and looked around him. The spring sun was shining brightly in the clear blue sky. But an angry dark cloud was boiling up out of the west behind him. Bracing his feet against the roof's steep slate facing, he carefully pulled himself upright until his eyes were exactly level with the bottom of the chimney, fifteen feet away.

All at once, the air became icy cold.

Had the sun gone under a cloud? Jason had a brief glimpse of the brick chimney and the strange black shape beside it, when the towrope suddenly went slack in his hands.

Unlocking the office door of Olson Custom Carpentry, Keith looked over the letters that had fallen through the mail slot. According to Tom Greene, Coste's first installment of two thousand dollars was supposed to arrive today, Wednesday. But it wasn't there, and Keith was genuinely annoyed. He probably shouldn't have started work on 666 Sunset Brook Lane until Coste had given him a check. But at the bottom of the pile of mail, underneath a builder's supply catalog, was a fat manila envelope dotted with several one-dollar stamps—and postmarked Seattle!

Keith tore open the envelope. Inside was a letter from the managing editor of the Seattle newspaper. Underneath, held together with staples and paper clips, were more than two dozen photocopied articles about James Beaufort, with headlines, photographs, the works!

The first article on top was dated October 22, 1973:

TWO FOUND SLAIN
IN BREMERTON ROAD HOME

Keith glanced a bit farther down in the pile:

WIFE ACCUSES CITY
COUNCILMAN IN
DOUBLE SLAYING

Now the police had a suspect! Accompanying the story was a photograph of James Beaufort, who had just been taken into custody. He sure didn't look like a murderer, Keith thought.

He wished he had time to read through the articles one by one, but business came first. Coste hadn't paid that two thousand dollars—and Keith wanted to mail Tom Greene a written invoice that very afternoon.

Reaching into his desk drawer, he got out an envelope with the return address of Olson Custom Carpentry printed in the upper left-hand corner. He inserted it into the typewriter and had just typed out Tom Greene's addresss when the telephone rang, startling him.

Switching off the recording machine, he picked up the receiver. "Hello," he said, "Keith Olson speaking."

"Keith!" It was Marc. "You've got to come home. Jason fell off the roof!"

"The roof!" Keith exclaimed. "What was he doing up there?"

"Looking at the iron pipe that vents beside the chimney. We found it inside the wall."

Keith remembered that 666 Sunset Brook Lane had no telephone yet. "Marc, where are you calling from?"

"Your house. Mrs. Olson just called the ambulance, and I better get back to Jason."

"How bad is he?" Keith asked.

"I don't know," Marc replied. "He's out cold, and I didn't dare move him."

"Okay," Keith said. "Go ahead. I'll be there as fast as I can."

On the way back to New Castle, Keith glimpsed an anvil-shaped cloud rising out of the west. From the static on the dashboard radio, Keith figured it was a thunderstorm. Strange weather for April!

At 666 Sunset Brook Lane, there was an ambulance blocking the gravel driveway. Keith parked his panel truck on the shoulder of the road. Marc and a white-jacketed paramedic were standing by the porch. And sitting on the porch stairs in front of them was Jason.

He didn't seem to be in pain. There wasn't any blood. When he saw Keith coming, Jason started to get up. The ambulance attendant laid a hand on his shoulder. "Take it easy."

Keith looked at his assistant apprehensively. "What the hell happened to you?" he asked.

"We found this—this huge . . . pipe, I guess," Jason answered. "By the fireplace in there—Marc can show you. We wanted to see if it ran all the way up to the roof. You took the aluminum ladder in your truck, so—"

"You climbed up there?" Keith asked.

Jason nodded. "I was standing on that sloping part of the roof when I felt the rope give way, and I fell over backward. That's all I remember. When I came to, Marc wasn't around, so I got up and went back in the house. I was just finishing lunch when the ambulance drove up."

"You might have a concussion," the ambulance attendant said. "You don't want to have anything on your stomach until the doctor takes some X-rays."

"But I'm feeling all right," Jason protested.

"Do as he says," Keith said. "My insurance'll cover this, so don't worry. I'll meet you in the hospital in half an hour."

Looking every bit as healthy as he had this morning, Jason climbed into the rear of the ambulance without assistance. As soon as the ambulance drove away, Keith turned to Marc.

"Show me where he landed."

Marc led him to the lawn beneath the bay window, where the towrope lay sprawled across the spindly new grass.

"The earth here must be fairly soft, thank God!" Keith picked up the rope and ran it through his hands. The heavy double knot at the end was still intact, in one piece. Keith tried to untie it, but Jason's weight had compressed the knot too tightly.

"This rope didn't break," Keith said. "It must have slipped off whatever he tied it to."

Marc showed Keith the corner pillar of the front porch. The rope's pressure had scraped away some of the white paint. Keith hammered at the pillar with his fist, looking for some seam or crack to open up. But the pillar—obviously a solid piece of wood—refused to budge.

Keith was completely baffled. "Where's this pipe he was talking about?"

Back inside the house, Marc picked his flashlight off the floor where Jason had left it and trained the beam into the cavity beside the chimney. "What would *you* say that thing is?" he asked Keith.

"Beats me." Picking up Jason's prybar, Keith tapped it against the dark metal column. "That sounds like solid metal. No, that's no vent! And what's this lettering?"

Marc shrugged. "Maybe the name of the foundry?"

The letters were all capitals, running up one side of the column and down the other. Keith tried to make out what they spelled, but the separate words—if they *were* words—were all run together. They must have been stamped into the iron while it was still white-hot, using almost unimaginable force. . . . Then Marc turned the flashlight beam, and Keith saw something even stranger. The letters running up the column seemed to have been filled with gold leaf!

Keith turned to Marc. "Okay," he said. "Now *I'm* curious. Will you give me a hand with the aluminum ladder?"

Off to the west, that thunderstorm seemed to have stalled somewhere over the Hudson. It didn't seem to be getting any closer. Together, Marc and Keith carried the aluminum ladder out of the panel truck and set its feet in the soil beside the bay window. Then they extended its top two rails until they rested against the edge of the mansard roof, some twenty-five feet above the ground.

Stepping up on the first rung, Keith felt the ladder's feet sink into the earth. If that ground hadn't been so soft; if Jason hadn't landed perfectly—Keith didn't want to think about it. He grabbed the ladder's rails and started climbing.

Halfway up, a blast of cold air shook the ladder. Keith looked behind him. The wind had shifted; the storm was moving in quickly now.

"Okay," he called to Marc. "One quick peek, and then I'm coming down."

He climbed up quickly, past the eaves, past the gray hexagonal slates covering the slope of the roof. The top of the roof was very nearly level. And then Keith saw what he was looking for, only fifteen feet away.

Flattened against the bricks of the chimney were the three prongs of an enormous trident. They sprang from a shaft of metal as thick as Keith's arm. The huge barbs at their tips bore faint traces of rust, and seemed to have been shaped by heavy hammer blows.

That must be cast iron, he thought—cast iron's practically immune to weathering and corrosion. And if that shaft was part of the metal column two floors below, it explained why the chimney suffered no damage during that thunderstorm early Friday morning. This giant trident would act as a lightning rod, conducting electricity straight down into the ground beneath the foundation. In fact, with this device hidden beside the chimney, 666 Sunset Brook Lane would probably *attract* lightning!

There was another gust of chilly, damp wind. Thunder growled behind him, but Keith craned his neck to get a better look. The trident's flattened blades were aligned parallel to the chimney, so that you couldn't see this thing unless you were right up here on the roof. . . .

Suddenly, Keith felt the hairs on the back of his neck begin to rise. Looking straight ahead of him, he saw the three prongs of the trident throw out a bluish glow. And then he realized what was about to happen.

"Marc!" he shouted. "Hold the ladder!" He swung his foot down to the next lower rung . . .

But it was too late. The air above him split open with a flash brighter than the sun. The lightning bolt hit the prongs of the trident, and a brilliant stream of light snaked across the slate roof toward the ladder.

Keith felt the electricity shoot through the aluminum under his hand. It all happened so fast he had no time to react. But he was barely able to climb down the rungs before his legs buckled underneath him and he had to sit down.

Marc helped him to the porch. A light rain began to fall. Keith's ears were still ringing from the crash of thunder. But already he was making calculations in his head. If that lightning rod ran from beside the chimney to the ground below, it had to be at least thirty feet long. . . .

"Are you all right?" Marc asked. "Your face is white as a sheet."

"I'll live," Keith said. "Let's go upstairs."

"What's up there?" Marc asked.

"If that iron column runs all the way up beside the chimney, then it has to pass through the wall of the master bedroom."

Marc thought for a moment. "Up behind the wood paneling, you mean?"

"Yep," Keith replied. "Let's see if we can pry it loose without doing too much damage."

But when Keith pressed on the bedroom paneling to see where the seams were, the entire wall rattled.

"That whole section is loose," Marc said. "Maybe if we pry the molding off the top . . ."

"No, wait," said Keith. "Press against it and lift!"

As he had anticipated, an entire three-foot slab of paneling slid up from its socket in the floor. He and Marc lifted it free and leaned it up against the adjoining Sheetrock wall. Behind it were the chimney and the cast-iron column.

Keith kept a healthy distance away, just in case the trident on the roof attracted another lightning bolt. But even so, he could see that both sides of the column were indented with more lettering. Up near the ceiling, one series of letters seemed to come to an end.

"Want me to put the paneling back?" Marc asked.

Keith shook his head. "Leave it off. I want to wait until the storm passes, then copy down the lettering here and downstairs. Maybe somebody else can tell us what it means." Keith listened to the gentle rain on the bedroom window. There wasn't any more thunder. It was just an ordinary shower now. That lightning bolt had seemed like an expression of bad temper—or maybe a warning?

Marc pointed to the other sections of paneling. "Do these come loose too?"

"I don't know," Keith said. "Let's see."

Together they pressed against the next panel of

interlocking hexagons and lifted it free from its narrow socket in the floor. Right behind it, stacked on iron brackets, were heavy four-inch timbers. And each one had two holes drilled through the ends.

"Hey," Marc said. "These must be the braces they used to reinforce the house while it was being moved."

Keith nodded. "And look here."

Each brace was chalked with a number, so that any idiot could tell where it was supposed to go. Once the Sheetrock or wallboard was stripped off, a single man, working alone, could probably brace this house for moving within a day or two.

But why had Coste bothered to keep these timbers— unless he planned to move the house again?

When Keith finally got home that afternoon, Jennifer met him at the door.

"How's Jason?" she asked.

"Fine, thank God! The X-rays show no broken bones, no sign of internal injuries. He's got some incredible bruises, but so would you if you'd just fallen off a roof. The doctor said there wasn't any point in keeping him for observation, so they released him. He'll probably be back at work tomorrow."

Keith took off his jacket and hung it in the hall closet. From his shirt pocket he removed the piece of paper with the letters he'd copied off the metal column. He probably ought to put it somewhere for safe-keeping. . . .

"But how are you?" Jennifer was looking at him strangely. "You look kind of harried. Is there anything wrong?"

Keith was about to tell her about his close call with the lightning, but thought better of it. Now wasn't the time to start explaining all the strange things about 666

Sunset Brook Lane. At the same time, though, Keith wished he had confided in his wife from the beginning. Now, every new detail he learned about that house seemed to drive the two of them a little further apart.

"Nope," said Keith with a smile. "Everything's just fine!"

All through dinner, he was moody and uncommunicative. Jennifer wanted to know more about Jason's accident, but her husband was definitely reluctant to talk about it. "The rope slipped," he said, without further explanation.

And so Jennifer didn't pry. She sat across the table, trying to figure out what was bothering him. When she had first met Keith, he'd been so sunny and easygoing. Now, he wasn't only bringing his worries home—he wouldn't even tell her what they were!

Part of the problem, she reflected, was that Keith was basically a loner. He found it hard to open up to people; he kept too much bottled up inside him. The only person he really confided in was his younger brother, Paul—but the two hadn't seen each other since Paul had visited them last Christmas. . . .

At Keith and Jennifer's wedding, the Reverend Paul Olson had served as both the minister and best man—and also tied a string of tin cans to the bumper of Keith's panel truck. But they hadn't seen much of Paul lately. Just last year, he had been appointed assistant rector of All Souls' Episcopal Church up in Glastonbury, Connecticut. Paul had promised to come visit them sometime in the spring. Why not now, when the flowers were about to bloom—and when Keith so obviously needed somebody he could really talk to?

"Hon?" Jennifer said. "Would you like having your brother Paul down for a couple of days next week?"

"Good idea," Keith sighed. "Are you going to write him? If you do, I'd like you to send him something."

He went upstairs and came back down with a piece of paper. On it was a strange assortment of capital letters:

ECCEINMANVTVAES . . .

"What *is* this?" Jennifer asked.

"That's what I'd like to know!" Keith said. "I copied all that off an iron pipe over in Coste's house. If Paul's still taking night courses at the seminary, he ought to know some professor there who can tell him what language this is, and what it means."

When the meal was over, Keith helped her clear away the dishes. Then he went off by himself in the den, explaining that he had to work out a design for Mrs. Sackett's new trellis. In the kitchen, Jennifer sat down with the box of blue notepaper that Keith had given her for her birthday.

Wednesday, April 18

Dear Paul,

It's hard to believe we haven't seen you since snow was on the ground. You always said you wanted to see how this place looks in spring. Now that the rhododendrons by our front door are getting ready to bloom, we were wondering if you'd like to drive down for dinner and spend the night.

We got back from Grand Bahama Island on the 10th, but recent pressures and other things have been getting Keith down. Our wedding anniversa-

ry is May 7, but I know he'd love seeing you before that, so he can get some things off his chest. Meanwhile, Keith asks if you can show this paper to someone at the seminary who might be able to tell him what the words mean. It's something he ran across in a new house he's working on, right across the gully from us.

I realize weekends aren't convenient for you, what with church services keeping you busy. So any day in the middle of next week—or the week after—would be fine with us. Just let us know.

Much love, Jennifer

She walked out on the front stoop and put the letter in the mailbox. Already in the box was another letter—an Olson Custom Carpentry envelope, addressed to Tom Greene. But it didn't have any stamp.

Jennifer took the letter out of the box and walked back into the den. Keith was bent over his clipboard, intent on the sketch of Mrs. Sackett's trellis.

"Keith," she said gently. "You have to put a stamp on a letter if you want it to get there."

"Huh?" Keith raised his head. "I didn't mail any letter."

"Didn't you?" She shrugged and handed him the envelope.

"But I didn't put this in the mailbox!" Keith exclaimed. He turned the envelope over in his hands. It was the same one he had typed up that afternoon, just before Marc called about Jason—and he had left it sitting in the office typewriter down in Chappaqua. Now whatever was inside was quite thick, and the back was tightly sealed with cellophane tape.

Puzzled, Keith tore open the envelope. A stack of

137

money fell out and spilled onto the floor beside his chair.

Jennifer helped him pick up the bills and count them. There were twenty crisp new one-hundred-dollar bills, adding up to two thousand dollars—the exact amount Coste owed him for having begun work on 666 Sunset Brook Lane.

moment it out and spilled onto the floor beside his

10

Wednesday, April 18, to
Friday, April 20, 1979

NOW THAT HE THOUGHT ABOUT it, Keith distinctly remembered having locked the office door behind him.
But he had been in a hurry, after all. In his concern
about Jason, he might not have noticed if the bolt didn't
close properly. Coste must have dropped by to pay the
bill, found the door unlocked, and used the first
envelope he laid his hands on.

There was one problem, though, Keith realized—
you couldn't lock that office door from the outside
without using a key! So Keith climbed into the panel
truck and drove back to Chappaqua again to check
things out.

The front door of Olson Custom Carpentry was
locked tight when he got there. Inside, nothing was
missing—except, of course, the envelope Keith had left
in his typewriter. Had Coste picked the lock? Did he
have a skeleton key? What bothered Keith most of all

was that right out on top of his desk were all those photocopied articles from the Seattle newspaper. Keith had left them in plain sight, never thinking to put them away. Coste couldn't have missed seeing them!

How would the owner of 666 Sunset Brook Lane feel about Keith's checking up on him—especially after Coste had gone to such trouble to avoid publicity? Hell, Keith thought, it was a free country. If he wanted to investigate the past history of houses he worked on, that was his business!

The very first thing Thursday morning, Keith called a lock-and-key shop and asked the owner to meet him at Olson Custom Carpentry. He watched as the locksmith fitted the office's front door with a brand-new lock, then started drilling a second hole, above the existing lock, to install a deadbolt.

"Can these locks be picked?" Keith asked.

"Mister," the man replied, "*any* lock can be picked. But these two locks together are going to take a man fifteen, maybe twenty minutes." He pointed to the brassy new tumblers of the deadbolt, lying in its half-opened cardboard box. "Your average burglar like we got around here won't have the time or the patience. Why's he gonna bother with your door, here, when he can break a pane in that hardware store door down the street and let himself right in?"

Before the locksmith left, he showed Keith how to work the new locks. Keith didn't have time to read the photocopied articles, so he locked them in the bottom drawer of his desk before driving back to 666 Sunset Brook Lane.

That Thursday, Jason didn't seem to be in any real discomfort. But he seemed changed, somehow— quieter, almost chastened, as if his fall had knocked some of the spirit out of him. All three of them worked

140

overtime, and by 6 P.M., the new house had all new Sheetrock both upstairs and down.

Friday they used joining compound to fill the nailholes and seams between the Sheetrock panels. Jason took more care with his work than ever before, sanding down the joining compound until even Keith couldn't detect where the nail holes had been.

By 3 P.M. Friday, they had done all they could on the interior of 666 Sunset Brook Lane. After Tom Greene found a tenant for the house, then Keith could subcontract somebody to paint the interior. So at three fifteen, Keith called it a day.

"Wear your painting clothes on Monday," he reminded Marc and Jason. "That's when we start on the outside."

David wasn't coming for dinner until six thirty. So rather than go straight home, Keith drove to the office in Chappaqua. To his delight, there were two requests for estimates on the telephone answering machine. Now, that was more like it! After Keith returned the calls, he still had plenty of time to read through those articles from the Seattle newspaper.

It was just after 4 P.M. when Keith unlocked the bottom drawer of his desk. The thick pile of photocopies was just as he had left it on Wednesday afternoon— stacked in chronological order, with the earliest news stories on top. The first one, headlined TWO FOUND SLAIN IN BREMERTON ROAD HOME, was accompanied by a news photograph of the house. But the copier machine had made the picture very dark and blurry. Was there a bay window to the left of the porch? If so, it was obscured by a bush of some kind.

Oh, well, Keith thought to himself. There would probably be other pictures. . . .

By four thirty-five, he had read through nearly all of the photocopied articles. From what he could piece together, the two bodies had been discovered in the early morning hours of October 21, 1973. A police car on its normal rounds had spotted a Cadillac, parked after hours in front of 666 Bremerton Road. When the patrolman radioed in the car's license-plate number, the station determined that the Caddy was registered to Edgar Sutton, of Tacoma.

An hour later, the car was still there—and the police officer noticed that the front door of the house was half open. He decided to investigate. Inside, in a "small ground-floor room," was Patty Lee Swenson, nineteen, her body propped against one wall. She had suffered a broken neck, a crushed windpipe and a fractured skull.

Across the room from her was Edgar Sutton, forty-eight, who died on the way to the hospital. Though Sutton's injuries were extensive, the coroner determined that he would have survived if he'd been lying flat on the floor. Instead, he had remained propped up in a sitting position. Unconscious, he had drowned in his own blood.

The damage to the bodies was so brutal that homicide detectives began looking for a team of killers. Then a week later, Mrs. Eunice Sutton Beaufort, forty-one, walked into a Tacoma police station. Claiming that her husband, a member of the Seattle City Council, had gone berserk, she asked for round-the-clock protection. Her account gave police detectives their first suspect in the case—as well as a very plausible motive.

James Beaufort, forty-three, had hired Patty Lee Swenson as a secretary right after her graduation from high school. He soon began an affair with the girl, and had helped her find the two-story house on Bremerton Road to live in, where he visited her regularly—at least three times a week.

Mrs. Beaufort had known of the affair, but assumed

that it would burn itself out. Instead, her husband asked her for a divorce so he could marry the girl. But Mrs. Beaufort flatly refused. The next day she telephoned her brother, Edgar, a Tacoma attorney, and asked him to talk some sense into Miss Swenson.

The next day after work, Sutton drove to 666 Bremerton Road in Seattle. While he was trying to persuade Patty Lee Swenson to break off her affair, James Beaufort walked in unexpectedly.

Mrs. Beaufort claimed that her husband had admitted the killings to her. But since a wife couldn't testify against her husband, Mrs. Beaufort's testimony was inadmissable in court. The district attorney's indictment had to be based solely on circumstantial evidence. At the trial, however, when Beaufort finally took the witness stand, he amazed the courtroom by confessing to the double murder.

According to Beaufort, he became enraged at finding his brother-in-law alone with Patty and beat the man unconscious. When Miss Swenson tried to restrain him, he turned on her too.

The details of his surprise testimony matched perfectly with the coroner's report—except for one crucial discrepancy. Beaufort stated that when he finally left 666 Bremerton Road, Sutton was lying on the floor. But the investigating police officer had discovered Sutton propped up in a corner of the room. In any case, the jury deliberated for only five hours before finding Beaufort guilty.

Keith was almost sure that the house at 666 Bremerton Road was the same structure that now stood at 666 Sunset Brook Lane. But to his frustration, the newspaper reporters' descriptions of the house were maddeningly vague. And every time the Seattle paper published a picture of the house, it was always the same shot, taken from the same angle. A huge shrub completely obscured the bay window behind it—if there was any bay window at all.

Six weeks after the jury's verdict, the judge handed Beaufort a sentence of twenty years to life. Two years later, the newspaper reported that Beaufort was proving to be a model prisoner at McNeil Island. The next-to-last article had appeared in September 10, 1978:

MURDER HOUSE,
SITE OF 1973 TRAGEDY,
MOVED FROM ITS FOUNDATION

Now he was getting somewhere! A story about the house was certain to mention the name of the owner. And if the owner was Coste, then Keith would know, once and for all, the identity of the structure at 666 Sunset Brook Lane.

But the bottom of the photocopied article had been torn off! The last full sentence read, "According to Spatz Realty, several offers to buy the home had been received over the past several years." The paper below hadn't been torn straight across. Rather, it looked as if somebody had ripped off tiny pieces, one at a time.

"God *damn* it," Keith said aloud. Must have been mice, he thought. But wouldn't a mouse have left some scraps around? Unless it had carried away the paper to line a nest, or something.

Each winter, Keith left a fresh mousetrap under the office filing cabinet and poison behind the radiator, just in case. Now he got up from his desk and went to look. But the trap was still set. The poison hadn't been nibbled.

Back at his desk, Keith looked at the other articles he had read. In which room of 666 Bremerton Road had Beaufort committed the killings? That "small ground-floor room" where the bodies were found—was it the hexagonal room under the stairs? Patty Lee Swenson had spent quite a lot of time in the house. Had she ever seen the etched-glass windows glowing red in the light of the setting sun? Had she—or Beaufort—ever met a man named Coste?

Now, years later, the reporters who had filed these articles would have moved on to other assignments, other newspapers. The homicide detectives who investigated the case wouldn't remember. But now that Keith thought about it, there was one person who would certainly recall the case in detail. And best of all, Keith knew exactly where to reach him! He turned to the typewriter and dashed off a hurried letter to inmate James Beaufort at McNeil Island Federal Penitentiary.

Keith walked into the Chappaqua Post Office at four fifty-five, just before it closed. And when he reached home at five fifteen, he still had plenty of time to shower and get dressed before David Carmichael arrived at six thirty.

Jennifer had planned tonight's dinner with Keith in mind, serving the ordinary meat and potatoes he would be happy to eat every other night of the week. But sitting down at the dinner table, Jennifer realized how grateful she was for David's company. For one thing, David wasn't moody. He didn't sit down for dinner with problems of molding and Sheetrock and painting still running through his head.

David had a good appetite, she saw. Whatever the antiques dealer's problem had been, his visit to the doctor had done him a world of good. He seemed more relaxed tonight, as if some heavy responsibility had been lifted from his shoulders. Jennifer wondered if she could get Keith to the same doctor—maybe even take the same prescription.

On his way to Keith and Jennifer's, David had deliberately driven past the house at 666 Sunset Brook Lane. It was definitely the same house he'd seen in his nightmares—the wooden trim, the steep slate roof, the the arrangement of windows were all identical. But the house in his dreams was always blue. The real house was definitely yellow. . . .

David didn't want to mention his horribly embarrassing visit to Dr. Fuchs-Kramer—much less the terrifying nightmare he'd had after falling asleep on the parapsychologist's cot! On Monday night, and again on Tuesday, the dream had repeated itself in every detail. Three times now, he had watched that strange blue house come apart and reassemble itself into instruments of agony and death. So when Keith began describing his work inside the place, David pricked up his ears. Was that house really composed of strange timbers of different lengths and sizes? If so, Keith would certainly have noticed it.

"Those walls you're replacing," David said idly. "What's underneath them?"

"Nothing," Keith said, swallowing a mouthful of potatoes. "I mean, we just nail the Sheetrock up against the framing—the vertical timber that forms the wall."

"What do those timbers look like?" David persisted.

Keith just stared at his dinner guest. How could David Carmichael possibly know about the incredible assortment of wood inside the walls at 666 Sunset Brook Lane?

For an instant, he considered telling David everything. But then he saw his wife, sitting right across the table. Jennifer didn't know about the strange wood inside the walls, or the thirty-foot lightning rod, or the bolt that had damn near struck him. No, if Keith

146

leveled with David now, Jennifer would learn how much he'd been holding back.

"Well, most vertical studs are two-by-fours that run from the house's foundation to the eaves. In the old days, they used horizontal lathing—thin strips of wood —as a backing for wet plaster. Today, though, Sheetrock's quicker and a lot easier."

"Yes," David said, "but . . ." He hesitated. He didn't want to have to relate his nightmare in all its lurid, violent, stomach-turning detail. Not in front of Jennifer!

And so David changed the subject.

After dinner, the three of them took their coffee cups into the living room. David reached into his pocket and handed Keith the bronze sestertius he'd brought with him from the city.

"Wait a minute!" said Keith, turning over the plastic envelope in his fingers. "This isn't the coin I gave you."

"Not the exact one, no," David replied. "But it is the same variety."

"What happened to the other one?" Keith asked.

David took a long sip of coffee. "I mislaid it," he said quietly. "Last time I saw that coin, it was in the living room, in my apartment. But for the life of me, I simply can't find it again."

Keith examined the sestertius under the lamp on the end table. "Boy," he said. "This one is sure in a lot better shape than the one I gave you."

"It's worth at least as much, too," said David with a slight cough. "When you give it back, I'm sure your Mr. Coste won't be disappointed."

There was a moment's pause. Each man had something he wanted to say to the other. But neither one knew how—or where—to begin.

"Jennifer tells me you're going away for the summer," Keith finally said.

David nodded. "I've been pushing myself pretty hard lately, having bad dreams—that kind of thing. So a doctor suggested I take off for the summer. I figured it was too late in the season to rent a beach house, but just on the off chance, I put my name on a Long Island rental agency's waiting list. Well, they called just this afternoon to say they'd had a cancellation out in Amagansett. And I'm next in line!"

"Congratulations," Keith said, feeling mildly jealous. He and Jennifer had barely scraped together enough money for their ten-day vacation on Grand Bahama. And here was David Carmichael, about to take off for a full three months!

"There's one hitch," David said. "I have to give the agency a deposit of eight hundred dollars, cash. If I don't get it to them by ten o'clock tomorrow morning, they'll bump me and rent the house to the next person in line."

"Isn't that a bit high-handed?" Jennifer asked.

"Not when you're talking about beachfront rentals," David sighed. "They can rent a place like that four times over."

"It must be nice to own a summer house," Keith said wistfully.

Jennifer looked at her husband. She could see the dream taking shape in Keith's mind: moving his carpentry business to some sunny, windswept town down by the seashore. But it would remain a dream, she knew. Keith wasn't flexible like David. He was too accustomed to New Castle to ever be happy anywhere else.

"Well!" David looked at his watch. "If I have to drive out to Amagansett by ten tomorrow, I'll have to get a really early start. So I'd better be leaving you now, I'm afraid. . . ."

At the front door, when Jennifer kissed David good-bye, Keith didn't mind. David Carmichael really wasn't a bad sort, and there were times tonight when Keith had found himself really liking the man.

He shook David's hand warmly. "Take care of yourself!"

"See you in September, I expect," David said.

Keith watched from the front door as David started the engine of his Mercedes-Benz, backed out of their blacktop driveway and drove north, up toward the loop of Sunset Brook Lane and the Taconic Parkway.

Suddenly Keith felt Jennifer's hand on the small of his back. He wheeled around and gave her a sudden bear hug that made her laugh. Maybe it was just the spring in the air, but it was wonderful to realize how much he loved this woman!

"I have to do the dishes," Jennifer protested.

Keith planted a kiss on her neck. "You can do 'em tomorrow morning," he said, grinning. "And I'll help you!"

As he drove across the concrete bridge at the head of Sunset Brook Lane, David saw the three-quarter moon in the east. He had glimpsed it before, through Jennifer's living-room window. Now it had risen higher in the sky, above the level of the trees.

Ahead, just coming into sight, was the dark silhouette of 666 Sunset Brook Lane. In the moonlight, the trees were casting their shadows across the road. But the shadow of the two-story house seemed far darker—almost solid and three-dimensional!

For an instant, David had an impulse to jam on his brakes, turn the Mercedes around and go back the way he'd come, rather than drive through the shadow that lay across the road in front of him. Oh, come on! David told himself. He hadn't been afraid of the dark since he

149

was eight years old! And this really was the quickest route back to the Taconic.

As the Mercedes entered the house's shadow, David felt a slight bump. Had his wheels run over something in the road? His headlights suddenly dimmed, then went out entirely. And the red warning lights on the dashboard all came on at once.

David moved his right foot to the brake pedal, but the car was already slowing down. What had happened to make the engine stall out that way? With what momentum he had left, he steered off the road and brought the Mercedes to a halt on the unpaved shoulder of Sunset Brook Lane.

David set his parking brake and looked around him. He was back in the moonlight again, about a hundred feet down the road from the new house. Where was he going to find a mechanic at this time of night?

Then he saw that the red warning lights on the dashboard were still glowing. At least the battery wasn't dead. Maybe the engine was just cold? David turned on the starter and stepped on the gas. To his relief, the engine started immediately, without a hitch.

On the dashboard, the red lights went off again. David made sure the gearshift was in neutral, then gunned the engine. It responded perfectly, with no hesitation.

He was about to shift into first gear when he glimpsed another flash of red—this time in the rearview mirror.

David looked up, blinking in astonishment. A bright red light was shining through the bay window of the house behind him. Then it slowly dimmed, until the bay window was dark again.

Could Keith and Jennifer have seen it too? But no, their house was on the other side of the gully. . . . Then David saw the red light beginning to shine through the entryway panels on either side of the front door. He turned in his seat to get a better look. And then the front door opened inward.

Bright crimson light spilled out across the porch, sweeping toward the Mercedes. Again the car's engine died, and the red lights on the dash glowed into life. But David, looking over his shoulder, did not notice.

His jaw dropped in amazement. Standing in the front door, enclosed in that blood-red glow, was a naked figure. David immediately recognized who it was!

And that was the last thing he remembered.

11

Saturday, April 21, 1979

WHEN KEITH CAME DOWNSTAIRS IN his bathrobe and pajamas, Jennifer was already dressed. She was sitting at the breakfast table, a cup of coffee by her elbow, scribbling words on a sheet of paper.

He and Jennifer had made love twice the night before. Afterward, he had fallen into a deep, dreamless slumber. Now he glanced at the clock over the stove. It was nearly 8:45 A.M.

"I overslept." He yawned.

"You've been working hard," replied Jennifer, not looking up. "Today's Saturday; you can afford to sleep late."

"No, I can't," Keith muttered. He poured himself a cup of coffee from the pot on the stove. "I have to make a couple of estimates this morning. The work's starting to pick up again."

"That's good," Jennifer said.

Keith sat down at the breakfast table and rubbed his eyes. "What're you doing there?"

"Working up a new interior-decorating ad for the paper." She scratched out a word with her pencil and began writing again. "That last classified didn't get me any calls at all. So I'm going to take this down to the newspaper this morning and let them run it for a week. . . ."

Keith got up and slipped half an English muffin into the toaster. Then he looked out the kitchen window. "Hey!" he said.

Jennifer lifted her head from the paper. "What is it?"

"There's a car in the driveway over at six sixty-six." Keith could see the spring sunshine glaring off the car's front bumper, but the trees in the gully were coming into leaf. He couldn't see the car clearly enough to tell what make it was.

"Maybe it's Mr. Coste?" Jennifer asked.

"Or some prospective tenant Tom Greene sent over." Keith slurped at his hot coffee. "I assume Tom has a key to that place. There has to be more than one."

"If it's Coste," Jennifer said, "then you could give him the Roman coin that David brought back last night."

"If that's Coste," Keith replied, "it won't be the last time he comes by." He glanced back at the kitchen clock. "Besides, I haven't much time. I'm due over in Pound Ridge at nine thirty sharp."

Keith was still in the shower when Jennifer pulled her blue Datsun out of the garage, past his big panel truck with OLSON CUSTOM CARPENTRY painted on its side. It was a warm, balmy April morning. Pretty soon it would be time for Keith to take the storm windows down.

She turned left onto Sunset Brook Lane, heading for the newspaper office in Ossining. As she came alongside the new house's front porch, she noticed the green Mercedes-Benz pulled up in the gravel driveway. Then she saw the familiar license plate. It was David's car!

After making a U-turn, Jennifer parked in the driveway right behind the Mercedes. There wasn't anyone behind the wheel. But what would David be doing inside the new house? Wasn't he supposed to be out at that Long Island rental office?

Jennifer got out of her car and climbed up the porch stairs. But the front door was locked tight. Puzzled, she glanced back down at the Mercedes in the driveway below. There was a silver-haired figure slumped sideways across the passenger seat!

When she pulled open the door on the driver's side, David didn't move. He must have been sitting behind the wheel and then fallen over to his right. He was still dressed in the overcoat he'd worn the night before, and one arm was wrapped around his head as if to pillow it—or protect it.

Jennifer looked at his face, where silver-gray stubble glinted in the morning light. What had happened to him?

"David," she shouted, tugging on the sleeve of his overcoat. "David, can you hear me?"

He didn't stir, and Jennifer fought back a sense of helpless panic. Then she saw his chest rise in a long, slow breath.

"David?" she repeated.

He opened his eyes, then immediately squeezed them shut again. There was bright sunshine streaming through the windshield. Slowly he pushed himself up to a sitting position, working his tongue around in his mouth. Where was he?

"Are you all right?"

He opened his eyes again and saw Jennifer leaning in the door of the car.

"Why are you parked here?" she asked. "Didn't you go home last night?"

"Home?" David asked. Automatically he patted his jacket pockets. His wallet was still there; so was his checkbook. The car keys, he saw, were still in the ignition. He stared at Jennifer in bewilderment.

"I remember driving back this way, heading for the Taconic—you know." He ran a hand over his chin. "There was a moon out. All these shadows across the road . . ."

Dimly, he recalled his car stopping . . . and then, that red light! David could feel the details slipping away from him. But Jennifer was still here! Then had—had it all really happened?

He hesitated and stared at Jennifer more closely. She was dressed, now, and she had brushed her long chestnut hair back behind her ears. That wasn't how it had been the night before. When she was enveloped in that crimson glow, her hair had been loose, falling uncombed over her soft bare shoulders. . . .

No, David thought, it must have been a dream—but at least a pleasant one for a change!

"Are you positive you feel all right?" she repeated.

David hoisted himself out of the car and stood up. After the cramped position in which he had been sleeping, his back should have been in a knot. He tensed, but instead of the pain and stiffness, his whole body felt loose and refreshed.

Smiling at Jennifer, he stretched and took a deep breath of the crisp morning air. Hammered into the new lawn beside the stairs was a green-and-white enameled metal sign:

FOR RENT
Thomas Greene,
Realtor
555-0098

Funny, Carmichael thought. He'd glimpsed that sign the night before. But then, it had been planted over by the bay windows—not here by the porch stairs.

"What about Amagansett?" Jennifer asked.

He looked back at her and blinked. "I'm sorry. What did you say?"

"Didn't you have to be out there this morning to pay your deposit on the beach house?"

Then David remembered. Glancing at his watch, he saw that his French cuff was stained with spots of blood.

"David! What did you do to your wrist?"

Right at the base of his left thumb was a deep puncture wound. But it was no longer bleeding, and it hardly felt sore at all.

"I don't know," David said. His watch read two twenty-five. That couldn't be right! He held the watch up to his ear, but he could hear no ticking at all. "What time is it?" he asked Jennifer.

"Around nine fifteen."

David had left the eight hundred dollars cash in his apartment on Riverside Drive. That meant he'd have to drive back to the Upper West Side, then on to eastern Long Island. He'd never make it!

Once again his eyes were drawn to that green-and-white FOR RENT sign beside the porch stairs.

At 10.30 A.M., Jennifer returned from the newspaper office in Ossining. On the note pad beside the kitchen telephone, Keith had penciled a note saying that he wouldn't be home until one o'clock, perhaps even later.

Jennifer brewed herself some fresh coffee and gazed out at the yellow-and-white house across the gully. Hadn't David once said it took him an hour to drive from New Castle to Riverside Drive? She glanced at the clock over the stove. It was almost ten thirty-seven now—and David had left well over an hour before.

Jennifer wondered: had David been suffering other blackouts before this? Was that the real problem he'd gone to see the doctor about? And how had he managed to cut his wrist that way? She had begged him to follow her home and have at least some toast and coffee. But David said he didn't want to be any trouble. Jennifer knew the real reason for his refusal: he didn't want to have to explain to Keith that Jennifer had found him asleep in his car. David was embarrassed enough already.

She walked to the phone and dialed David's home number. The connection went through, and she heard the telephone at the other end begin ringing. But after eight rings, there was still no answer.

Had there been heavy weekend traffic? Maybe David had stopped for breakfast along the way—or had he blacked out again and run his Mercedes off the road? To be sure that she hadn't dialed the wrong number, Jennifer hung up and dialed again.

This time, the telephone was picked up on the first ring.

"Yes?" said a male voice. Jennifer recognized a New York inflection.

157

"Hello," Jennifer said, hesitating. "Who am I speaking to, please?"

"Lieutenant DiMiglio" came the reply. "New York Police Department."

The Taconic Parkway had very little southbound traffic. Below the George Washington Bridge, the dozens of crabapple trees along the Hudson River were almost ready to bloom.

David let the garage attendant park the Mercedes for him, and walked back to his apartment. He definitely needed a shave, and his jacket and overcoat were wrinkled where he'd slept on them. First a hot shower and a late breakfast, he thought. Then he'd run out to the cleaner's and get these clothes dry-cleaned and pressed. On the way back, he'd buy a *Times* at the newsstand and start looking through the rental ads all over again.

The facade of his Riverside Drive apartment building was still in shadow. Not until afternoon did the sun swing around to the west and enter his bedroom windows. He smiled at Raul, the doorman, and took the elevator up.

When it stopped at his floor, David reached into his pocket for his house keys. But as the door slid open, he was surprised to see a uniformed policeman talking with Carl Mullins, the building superintendent. David realized that the other man beyond them, dressed in plain clothes, was a detective.

At the sound of the elevator door, Carl Mullins broke off his conversation with the police officer and turned around. "Oh, Mr. Carmichael!" he exclaimed. "It's you!"

"Of course it's me, Carl." Whatever the trouble was that had brought the police to his floor, David would hear about it from Raul sooner or later. He tried to move past Carl Mullins to get to his own apartment door, but the police officer moved to block his way.

"Just a moment, sir . . ."

Behind the officer, the door to David's apartment was standing wide open. From out here in the narrow corridor, he could glimpse the edge of the carpet in the living room.

"I'm sorry, Mr. Carmichael," the building superintendent said. "But your neighbor, Mr. Jacobs, was complaining about all this racket coming from your apartment—"

"Oh, that was the other night," David said.

"No, no," Carl Mullins said. "This morning! But when I got up here myself, all the noises had stopped. So I let myself in with the passkey, just to make sure everything was—"

"Mr. Carmichael," the uniformed officer interrupted. "When did you leave the building?"

"Last night," David answered. "Around five fifteen." But would the officer believe he had spent the night asleep in his car? Perhaps they'd want to call Jennifer to confirm it!

"It's all right if he comes inside," the detective said. "Just don't have him touch anything." David noticed that the plainclothesman was chewing gum. "By the way," he said to David, "you got a call about five, six minutes ago. A woman. She wouldn't leave her name."

"You hear him?" the cop asked. "Come on in, it's okay."

Walking into the living room, David looked around in utter disbelief. The place was a complete shambles! His Louis XV armchairs had been upended in the corner. Books had been pulled from the shelves on either side of the fireplace and scattered about the room. Every single one of the paintings had been pulled from the walls, and the fireplace poker had been used to gouge large holes into the plaster.

There was something familiar to all this chaos. To the police, it would look as if some maniac had simply torn the place apart in a fit of mindless vandalism. But David—to his horror—knew better.

David saw a flash of bright light in the bedroom. He glanced in through the open door. It was a police photographer, taking pictures. Suddenly the gum-chewing plainclothes detective was at David's elbow.

"I'm Lieutenant DiMiglio," he said. "You had trouble here before, didn't you? About two years ago?"

"My wife, Eleanor," David replied.

"The guy's wife was murdered," the detective explained to the uniformed officer.

David nodded, nearly speechless. Nearly two years before, the man who surprised Eleanor Carmichael had been after cash and jewels that he could easily pawn. He hadn't realized the apartment's furniture and antiques were themselves worth a fortune. And so, searching for David's coin collection and the antique rings and necklace he had bought Eleanor in Paris, the murderer had done thousands of dollars' worth of damage. But David had sent everything to skilled restorers and faithfully put the apartment back the way it had been before his wife died.

Now, David couldn't believe his eyes. Every detail of that original break-in had been meticulously re-created —right down to the eighteenth century mantel clock that lay smashed on the hearth. Even the broken fragments lay in the same position they'd been in on November 11, 1977.

"The man who killed my wife," David stammered. "Is he out on—"

"Naw." Lieutenant DiMiglio shook his head. "That

kid's still behind bars, doing eight to twenty. We checked that as soon as we heard about the trouble here."

"Carl?" David turned to the building superintendent. "This entire apartment is protected by a burglar-alarm system. Didn't it go off?"

"When I came in with the passkey, it sure did!" Carl smiled. "It's in okay working order. But no, it didn't go off before."

David began shaking with anger at whoever had done this. To think that this—this *someone* could go and come as he liked, ruining beautiful things! . . .

"We know robbery wasn't the motive," Lieutenant DiMiglio said.

David turned on him. "What do you mean?"

"C'mon. I'll show you."

The plainclothes detective led David into his own bedroom. Once again, the mattress was shoved off the boxspring. The curtains were torn from the valances, just as they had been on that ghastly autumn afternoon in 1977. The detective pointed to the bedroom dresser. "See there?"

Friday afternoon, David had gone to the bank and cashed a check for $800, the money he needed for one week's rental on the Amagansett house. Rather than take the money with him to New Castle, he had left the bills in the top drawer of the dresser.

Now the bills had been removed and spread out in a fan across the dresser's top. It was all there—but two hundred and fifty dollars had been placed in a separate stack from the other bills. But except for the cash atop the bureau, this room looked exactly the same as it had when David had stepped into it seventeen months before.

He sat down on the side of the box spring and shut his eyes. For a second he wondered if he was dreaming again. Was this ghastly coincidence all just a terrible nightmare? But no, this was real! This time, not even screaming could wake him.

Then David remembered. There was one detail from the original break-in that no vandal could possibly duplicate. And if *that* was missing. . . . David stood up and headed for the kitchen.

"Mr. Carmichael." Lieutenant DiMiglio reached out and touched his arm. But David moved past the detective, not to be distracted.

On November 11, 1977, the burglar had cornered Eleanor in the kitchen. The refrigerator's white enamel had been covered with her blood. Even now, David could remember the exact shape of that horrid diagonal smear. It was the kind of detail that a next-of-kin never forgets—but which nobody could possibly reproduce.

Lieutenant DiMiglio saw that Mr. Carmichael was headed for the kitchen. Okay, the detective thought. Let's see how he reacts!

David stepped onto the white-and-black-tile kitchen floor and gasped. Across the refrigerator door was the same diagonal reddish stain he remembered so well. There was one difference, though—now the blood was fresh!

The plainclothesman watched as David Carmichael came stumbling out of the kitchen, his face dead white. The look in his eyes told Lieutenant DiMiglio that the man wasn't acting. He really *had* been surprised to see the blood on the icebox.

But the detective had also noticed that deep cut on David Carmichael's left wrist—and he wondered . . .

David made his way to the bathroom, thinking he was going to be sick. But his stomach was empty. He sat down on the cool rim of the bathtub. During the original break-in, this bathroom had been left undamaged—and so it was now. It was like a tidy white storm cellar, untouched by the tornado that had raced through the rest of the apartment. Now he felt a bit better. In here, he could almost believe that none of it had ever happened, and that Eleanor was still alive.

The cut on his left wrist began to throb painfully. David got up and stepped to the medicine cabinet over the sink. He reached for a Band-Aid. Behind the left-hand mirrored door was the bottle of tranquilizers his doctor had prescribed in November, 1977. David decided he could use one now. Turning on the cold water, he reached for the drinking glass behind the cabinet's right-hand door.

To his surprise, the glass was brimming with a dark orange liquid that splashed over his hand and dripped down into the sink. It was warm and had the sharp, rank odor of animal urine—*fresh* animal urine! Gagging, David turned the water on harder and held the glass under the tap to wash the liquid away.

Then he noticed the dark round shape at the bottom of the glass. He slid it out into his hand. Almost immediately, David felt the familiar tingling vibrations. It was the corroded bronze sestertius that had vanished more than a week before!

"Mr. Carmichael?"

Looking up into the mirrored door of the medicine cabinet, David saw Carl Mullins standing behind him.

"Mr. Carmichael, I really don't understand all this. Last night and this morning, see, Raul says nobody came in who was out of the ordinary. Just our regular tenants. None of your windows was jimmied, and the cops here say your door lock wasn't picked. So what I mean is—well, this really isn't fair to Mr. and Mrs. Jacobs."

David slipped the wet sestertius into his pocket and

turned to face the superintendent. "Oh, come on, Carl! You think *I* tore this place apart, all by myself?"

The superintendent lowered his voice to a whisper. "I'm not saying that, Mr. Carmichael. But see, there's been complaints. I mean, Mr. Jacobs says he's heard you a couple nights now, yelling at the top of your lungs. And now this!" Carl Mullins shrugged helplessly toward the living room. "I mean, this is a nice, quiet, respectable building. The manager might not want to renew your lease, and—"

In the living room, the telephone rang. The detective answered it, then listened for a moment. "Mr. Carmichael, it's for you."

David pushed past Carl Mullins. The lieutenant said a woman had called before. Who could that have been—Miss Rosewood or Jennifer?

He took the receiver from the plainclothes detective and lifted it to his ear. "Hello?"

"Mr. Carmichael?" said a strange voice.

"This is he speaking," the antiques dealer replied.

"My name is Tom Greene. Hi, how are you? Listen, I'm a real estate agent up here in Chappaqua. . . ."

Real estate agent? David gazed around the ransacked living room. Everywhere he looked, he saw painful reminders of Eleanor's death, and of the loneliness, fear and frustrated rage that had haunted him ever since. No question about it. He had to get away from this apartment as soon as he could!

"I understand you're interested in the two-story house I'm representing," the man said.

"Yes," David said, his head swimming. "Yes, I am interested in renting a place for the summer. . . ."

"Well, that's excellent!" replied the man on the other end of the line. "My client, the owner, called me this morning and said you're just the tenant he'd been looking for. He'll decorate to your specifications. And you know what else he said?"

"No," David sighed. "What did he say?"

"He's willing to let you rent six-six-six Sunset Brook Lane for only two hundred fifty a month!"

12

Saturday, April 21, to
Thursday, April 26, 1979

RIGHT AFTER DINNER SATURDAY NIGHT, Keith went out
to the front step and looked in the mailbox. Now that
he had completed the inside of 666 Sunset Brook Lane,
Coste owed him another two thousand dollars. And if
another money-stuffed envelope turned up in the mailbox, he wanted to find it before Jennifer did.

Sunday night, there it was—another fat envelope
with the return address of Olson Custom Carpentry!
Obviously Coste had pilfered more than one envelope
after he picked the lock. When Keith tore it open,
inside were another twenty one-hundred-dollar bills.

But when had Coste delivered the money? Sunday
afternoon had been unusually warm, and Jennifer had
left the front door open. Keith hadn't heard any cars
stopping out on Sunset Brook Lane. Did Coste use a
bicycle? Or had he come on foot?

On Monday, Keith was eating lunch in the kitchen,

his work clothes spattered with fresh blue paint, when the phone rang. Jennifer answered it. It was David, calling to tell her that he was renting the new house across the gully from May through August. Would Jennifer be interested in decorating it for him? And once she had selected the colors and wall coverings, could Keith do the actual painting and papering—or recommend somebody who could?

Keith was completely amazed. Hadn't David been about to take a beach house on Long Island? Keith telephoned Tom Greene, who assured him that David Carmichael had indeed picked up the lease on 666 Sunset Brook Lane.

The antiques dealer was pleasant enough, but Keith wasn't wild about having him practically within earshot for the next four months! On the other hand, he could see Jennifer's delight at having an entire house to decorate from scratch. While Keith, Marc and Jason painted the outside, Jennifer spent all of Monday afternoon inside, measuring the rooms and making notes until the sun went down and it was too dark to see. That evening, she was happier than he'd seen her in months. Jennifer raved about the little six-sided room with its inlaid marble floor. Keith wanted to ask if she'd seen the windows glowing red when the sun went down. But what if she hadn't? He figured it was better to say nothing at all.

Tuesday morning at nine, Jennifer drove herself to the Chappaqua station and spent all day in New York City. That evening she came home carrying heavy books of wallpaper samples. She and David had been visiting all the designers' showrooms along Third Avenue, she said. Keith wasn't thrilled that she and David were spending so much time alone together, but he consoled himself that this was only temporary. He assured her he would subcontract the painting and papering to the Staub brothers, who could do the job right. Actually, he'd been looking forward to getting through with 666 Sunset Brook Lane once and for all. Now, between David and his wife, it looked as if he'd be hearing about that house for the rest of the summer.

Early Thursday morning, a delivery truck dropped off a large, weighty carton addressed to Jennifer. "Oh, good!" she exclaimed. "That's the wallpaper for David's bedroom."

Wallpaper? Keith thought. But ordinary paint would be easier, and less expensive.

"David wants to move in Friday, if he can," she said. "So if those men of yours could get started . . ."

Keith hadn't anticipated that David would give them only twenty-four hours' notice! But fortunately, Fred and Werner Staub were able to rearrange their schedule and start the paperhanging later that afternoon.

When the German-born painters arrived at 666 Sunset Brook Lane, Keith and his assistants were putting a second coat of deep blue paint on the clapboards. If the weather stayed sunny, Keith figured they'd finish up by the end of the day. At 12:30 P.M., Keith walked back home and phoned Tom Greene.

"We're about to start on the trim. Will you ask Coste if he'd like an ivory shade instead of the pure white that's on there now? I think off-white will look better against the blue, and it'll weather more gracefully."

Just as Keith finished lunch, Tom Greene called back to say that Coste had approved. Keith walked back across the gully to find the Staub brothers carrying the carton of wallpaper inside the house. Fred and Werner, both in their fifties, had been born in Bremen and still had mild German accents. Fred, the elder brother, was a painstaking worker but a terrible busybody, always asking questions about the people he was working for.

Keith climbed up on the ladder and resumed painting. But barely five minutes later, Fred was back outside, at the foot of Keith's ladder.

"Why are we starting with the bedroom?" he shouted up.

"Because the man who's renting this place wants to move in Friday morning," Keith called down. "And he wants one finished room to sleep in."

"Oh!" Fred said. "But I don't think he's going to like the wallpaper in that box."

"I don't care if he likes it or not," Keith snorted. "That's his problem. Your problem is to get that room papered this afternoon."

Fred shrugged and went back into the house.

An hour passed. Then about 2:30 P.M., Jason went inside to use the bathroom. When he came out, he walked over to Keith's ladder.

"Did you see the wallpaper Fred's hanging in the bedroom?" he asked.

"No," Keith said. Jennifer had wanted to show him some of the samples, but he had quickly lost interest.

"Are you sure it's the pattern Mrs. Olson wanted?" Jason said. "It looks awfully fancy to me."

"Okay," Keith said. "I'd better have a look."

When he got upstairs, he couldn't believe his eyes. Fred and Werner had already papered half the bedroom in a multicolored pattern with peonies and Chinese pheasants on a gold background! Jennifer had told him that the more colors wallpaper had, the more times it had to be printed—and the more costly it was.

"Fred," he sighed. "There has to be some mistake here. Nobody wants wallpaper this ritzy for a house he's only renting for the summer."

The middle-aged German merely shrugged. "This is all there was in the box."

Keith looked at the invoice from the wallpaper wholesaler, but all it bore was stock numbers—there was no description of the pattern. "Hold everything," he said. "I want to go check this with my wife."

"Mr. Olson?" Werner Staub said. "If you are not so sure about this paper, maybe we can start painting the dressing room outside—"

"*Wait here!*" Keith shouted. "Don't do anything more until I find out what's what!" He picked up a roll of wallpaper from the carton and hurried down the stairs.

Werner Staub looked at his brother and shrugged. Then he stepped to the curtainless window and watched as Keith strode down into the gully, heading back to his own house.

Jennifer was sitting on the pale beige living-room carpet, looking at fabric swatches, when she heard the kitchen door slam. It surprised her that Keith was home so early; usually he worked straight through until 5 P.M.

Keith walked into the living room and dropped the roll of peony-and-pheasant wallpaper on the carpet in front of her. "Look at this!" he said, pushing the roll with his shoe. "This can't be the pattern you want for the bedroom!"

"Yes it is," Jennifer said. "That's the design David approved—it's his choice."

"But *you're* decorating in that house," Keith protested. "If David wanted wallpaper, couldn't you have talked him out of it?"

Jennifer looked up at her husband. "What for?"

"What for! Because wallpaper costs much more than regular paint. And it's not as if he were planning to live there the rest of his life! When David leaves in September, he can't peel this off the wall and take it with him."

Jennifer nodded. "That's exactly the point. He isn't sure if this is the wallpaper he wants in his bedroom in

New York. So we're using that house to test our ideas for his apartment in the city. Besides, Coste is paying for the paint, wallpaper and carpeting."

"But couldn't you have steered David toward something less expensive," Keith frowned, "and saved Coste a few dollars?"

"No!" Jennifer said firmly. "Everything I've selected for the upstairs is based on that green-and-gold color scheme—right down to the canopy over the bed."

"A canopy?" Keith exclaimed. "What does David think that house is, Buckingham Palace?"

She looked back at the lavish fabric swatches lying on the plain beige carpet around her. "You have to remember, David makes his living dealing in old French furniture. Most of it's pretty ornate. So he's grown accustomed to more elegance than you or I might like."

"You mean the *whole house* is going to be done in this kind of luxury?" he asked.

"That's the idea," Jennifer said evenly. "Right now, I'm trying to figure out which fabric will work best on the dining-room chairs—assuming the walls will be Wedgwood blue. . . ."

Keith's heart sank. Without a word to him, David and Jennifer were creating a world all their own, and he felt excluded, somehow. "I just hate to see David wasting somebody else's money," he said.

"It's not a *waste*," Jennifer insisted. "David's taking all the upholstered furniture back to the city in the fall. And Coste will keep the wallpaper, draperies and carpets for whoever rents the house next."

"You know," Keith said, "if you really like this kind of wallpaper, why don't you do over *our* bedroom like this? I could give you the money as an anniversary present."

Jennifer laughed and shook her head. "We couldn't have just one room like this, all by itself. It wouldn't go with the rest of our house."

So it was all or nothing, Keith thought. "Well," he said, crestfallen. He picked up the roll of wallpaper, noticing where his fingers had left traces of blue paint. "I'd better get back to work."

Three thousand miles away, it was 12:15 P.M., Pacific Time. The prison censor at McNeil Island Federal Penitentiary looked up from his desk in the administration building. He probably had time to read and approve one more letter before it was time for lunch.

The next letter on the outgoing stack was a long one, written on four separate sheets of paper. When the censor looked at the prisoner's name on the unsealed envelope, he was mildly surprised. That Beaufort guy never had been much of a letter writer.

Back in 1974 and '75, when the Bremerton Road murders were still fresh in everyone's mind, up to fifty letters a week had come in addressed to James Beaufort. Nowadays, Beaufort received hardly any mail at all. That was why the censor remembered when the letter arrived from that Olson guy on the East Coast, asking for a description of the Bremerton Road house where Beaufort had committed the killings.

His questions seemed harmless enough, and so Beaufort had been allowed to receive Olson's letter, without any deletions.

Now here was the prisoner's reply. For a man who had once dictated all his letters, Beaufort had pretty neat handwriting. The censor uncapped his big felt-tipped pen. If any portions of Beaufort's letter had to be deleted, the pen's black ink would soak right through the prison stationery, obliterating everything on both sides.

The censor leaned back in his chair and began reading:

April 25, 1979

Dear Mr. Olson:

Thanks for your letter of April 20. I sincerely hope you are not thinking of buying or renting the house on Bremerton Road. I think my reasons for saying so will become clearer as I answer your questions.

When my secretary, Patty Lee Swenson, and I first began to realize our feelings for each other, she was still living at home with her parents. I suggested she look for an apartment of her own, and I promised to raise her salary by whatever the rent came to.

Later that week, she told me that a real estate agency had called her out of the blue to tell her about a Victorian house near the Columbia Landmark District. She had figured an entire house was more than she wanted, but the monthly rent was so astonishingly low that she was able to afford it, given her present salary. Thus the newspapers' allegation that I rented the house for her is not strictly true. I was slightly unhappy at her refusing my help, but had no real objections. She moved in about three weeks later.

The house seemed much older than the other ones built around it. A neighbor told Patty that the entire house had been moved to that site, all in one piece, about six months before she moved in. But I have no idea where this house may have been moved from originally.

666 Bremerton Road was a wood-frame building, painted yellow and white, with a wide front

porch and stained-glass panels on either side of the front door. I have seen roughly similar houses in San Francisco. There was a lilac bush planted to the left of the porch, but it withered on the side facing the house until finally half the shrub was dead.

As you came in the front door, the stairs were on your left. There was a living room to your right, and at the rear was an alcove with a fireplace and a door leading to the kitchen, at the back of the house. On the second floor were the bathroom and two bedrooms, one opening off the other. The larger one had an entire wall paneled in wood.

On the west side of the house was a small six-sided room with a large bay window. You got in there through sliding doors set under the staircase. The windows in the bay were each about five feet tall, made up of six-sided panes of glass about half a foot in diameter.

The house was furnished when Patty rented it. I used to visit her there three or four times a week. Every so often, she and I used to have log fires in the sitting room just behind the living room.

Right after that, Patty began to change. She began complaining that I didn't have the courage to divorce my wife. She was always talking about how badly she wanted to get married, until I honestly began worrying that she'd say yes to the first man who was legally able to ask her. Since she had that whole house all to herself, I started wondering if she might be seeing other men. And I had recurrent dreams that she was leaving me. In the dreams, I'd see her standing in the bay window of the Bremerton Road house, talking with some man whose face I couldn't see. I dreamed this over and over again.

It wasn't hard to see Patty wasn't happy staying home every night. So one evening after work, I took her out for dinner in Tacoma, where I figured there wasn't much chance of us being recognized.

I should have explained that my brother-in-law, Edgar Sutton, lived and worked in Tacoma. Edgar was the kind of pompous, arrogant stuffed shirt that only a lawyer can be. He always sneered at me for getting involved in city government when I could have made more money by sticking to my law practice. Ever since he'd gotten divorced in 1970, Edgar considered himself something of a ladies' man. But I always found him funny, rather than irritating.

Anyway, Patty and I were eating dinner at the back of the restaurant in Tacoma when Edgar and some woman I had never seen walked in and were seated at the very next table.

Edgar made a point of not recognizing me, which meant that he realized perfectly well what was going on. As of that moment, I had to expect that he'd eventually tell Eunice about having seen me. Patty and I talked about this at some length on the drive back to Seattle. We both agreed it would be best for me to make the first move.

I assumed Eunice would grant me a divorce once she understood how Patty and I felt about each other. Two nights later, I told Eunice everything. My wife had never deserved shabby treatment, and I didn't like having to hurt her. We had two sons, both in college in the East, who knew nothing of any of this. Eunice took it very badly indeed.

The following day at work, I grew increasingly depressed and unhappy. Patty had called in sick, saying she had the flu. So before going home to my wife, I decided to stop by 666 Bremerton Road and visit Patty, to see how she was, and to help convince myself I was doing the right thing.

You can imagine my surprise at seeing my brother-in-law's Cadillac parked in front of the house. Letting myself in with my own key, I heard Edgar's voice coming from the little room under the stairs. He was trying to talk Patty out of seeing me again, but broke off when he heard my footsteps.

Patty liked to watch the sunsets through the bay window, and must have been in there when Edgar arrived to bend her ear. As I stepped through the sliding doors, the light from the setting sun almost blinded me. I should have mentioned that on clear evenings, those bay windows caught the light in such a way that the whole room was bathed in red—a most beautiful sight, really. Also, the windows were very lightly engraved with figures of two men and a woman. Patty had told me the right-hand figure looked just like me. I could never make it out in ordinary light. But one evening when the sun was setting, she took me in there and showed me. She was right—the resemblance was uncanny.

That particular afternoon, Patty was dressed in her bathrobe. She had the flu, of course, and had probably been sleeping all day. But as soon as I saw her, I got the notion that she and Edgar had been to bed together. When I told him to get the hell out, Edgar started lecturing me about my responsibilities as a family man.

Patty walked over and put her hand on his arm. I realize now that she was trying to interrupt him, but the gesture seemed intimate, almost obscene. Then Edgar started in about how I was betraying *my trust as a member of the city council. I lost my temper and took a swing at him.*

The blow landed much harder than I had intended. I must have broken Edgar's nose. When he raised his fists to defend himself, I was overjoyed because it gave me an excuse to hit him again—and then I just kept on beating him, waiting for him to cry out and admit he'd had enough. Then I felt Patty's hands on my shoulders, trying to pull me away. That got me really enraged, that after all I'd given up for her, she'd dare lay a hand on me. So I turned and struck Patty across the face, hard. I don't recall just what happened next, until I looked up again at that right-hand window. I could have sworn it really was my own face depicted there.

The censor decided to take out that last bit. It sounded as if Beaufort were thinking of demanding a new trial, using insanity as a defense. Now, almost six years after the murders, it would be nearly impossible to prove anything one way or the other. The censor was lowering his felt-tipped pen when his eye jumped ahead to the next paragraph.

You may wonder why I confessed to first-degree murder, when I could have pleaded guilty to homicide or even to aggravated assault. But the fact is, I did premeditate Edgar's death.

It was just beginning to dawn on me that Patty was dead. I was starting to comprehend the terrible thing I'd done. But what really drove me wild was to think that if Edgar hadn't butted his nose in, none of this would have ever happened!

The red light in that room was fading quickly now, and I could see that Edgar was bleeding badly from his broken nose. So before I left the

177

room, I lifted Edgar off the floor and propped him up in a corner of the room. Since he was unconscious, I knew that he would probably choke on his own blood. But I wanted him to. And so I left him there.

Later, driving back to my apartment, I seriously thought of going back to help Edgar. But what if one of the neighbors had already called the police? I couldn't bear to think of walking in there with officers swarming all over the place. Then I thought of stopping and telephoning for an ambulance, but was afraid I'd have to identify myself. You see, I didn't want to be put in handcuffs and hauled down to the station house like some common criminal. I still wanted the dignity of my position as a city councilman. But if I had telephoned, perhaps Edgar would be alive today. I just don't know.

That is why I pleaded guilty in court. I didn't want to put the State of Washington to any more trouble on my account. And I wanted to be punished—not only for killing Patty, but for ever having doubted her in the first place. And that's why I advise you not to buy or rent the house she lived in (last I heard, it was still up for rent). Not that the place is haunted or anything, though once when I was in bed with Patty, I felt something hard fall on my back. It turned out to be an old Roman coin, and we never did figure out where it came from. But I do believe that the house acts as some kind of psychological amplifier. It put worries and doubts into Patty's head that weren't there in the first place. And it took my worst impulses and suspicions and multiplied them all out of proportion.

As you may have read, I recently refused an

offer of parole. I no longer want to live outside, because I would only be reminded of the life Patty and I could have had together—and of the hurt and damage my actions have caused. A year after my imprisonment, I let my wife divorce me. Then, the year after that, my older son committed suicide. I no longer know my younger son's whereabouts; but I understand he has changed his name.

So that makes three dead, and three other lives ruined, including my own. Maybe a parole board can overlook that, but I can't.

Very truly,
James Beaufort

Well, well, the prison censor thought. That business about premeditation sure knocked out any possibility of an insanity plea! Beaufort didn't even hint that he was seeing the prison shrink for acute depression, or that his cellmate complained of his whimpering and moaning in his sleep. He didn't mention the three times the guards had had to hustle him over to the infirmary to get his stomach pumped or his wrists sewn up.

No, there was nothing here to reflect discredit on the prison or its administration. And besides, it was time for lunch!

The censor sealed the letter in the envelope Beaufort had addressed to Mr. Keith Olson at 712 Sunset Brook Lane, New Castle, N.Y. Then, rubber-stamping the back to indicate the contents had been read and approved, he placed it on the stack of other letters that would go out on the afternoon boat to the mainland.

13

Friday, April 27, 1979

OUT IN FRONT OF HIS Riverside Drive apartment building, David Carmichael was still waiting for the movers to arrive.

He looked at his watch—which was now running again, keeping good time. It was nearly ten fifteen; the movers had said they'd be here at nine thirty. Perhaps he should go upstairs and telephone to see if their van had been delayed? But David didn't want to be alone in that apartment again—not until all the rooms had been emptied and completely redecorated.

The Saturday before, David had waited until Carl Mullins and the police finally left. Then he had thrown some clothes and toilet articles into a suitcase and checked into the Carlyle Hotel, over on Madison Avenue. Sunday, he had mailed Tom Greene his check for the first month's rental on 666 Sunset Brook Lane.

And Monday he had called Jennifer Olson to offer her the job of decorating the house—as well as his Riverside Drive apartment.

When David returned to New York in September, that apartment would have a whole new interior—as bright and cheerful as Jennifer could make it. The only furniture he was taking to New Castle was those pieces that had suffered no damage—like the canopied double bed, the dresser and the Chinese coffee table from the living room. When the other antiques came back from the restorer's, he would sell them all at auction. Meanwhile, Jennifer would be helping him try out new draperies and rugs and fabrics in the house at 666 Sunset Brook Lane.

He imagined the moving van would be coming from downtown. Shading his eyes, he looked south along Riverside Drive. But all he could see was taxis and ordinary passenger cars.

Then, suddenly, he saw the brightly painted van turning the corner of a side street two blocks away.

Over at the Upper West Side precinct house, the plainclothes detective reached over to the ringing telephone and picked up the receiver.

"Lieutenant DiMiglio here." The detective listened for a moment, chewing his gum thoughtfully. "Yeah, Type A, Negative. Thanks!"

Hanging up, he reached across his desk for the old file on Eleanor Carmichael's murder. Among the dry, brittle sheets of paper, he found the page he wanted—the report of the coroner's examination.

Lieutenant DiMiglio was right. Eleanor Carmichael's blood had been Type O, Positive. But according to the lab, the bloodstain on David M. Carmichael's refrigerator last Saturday had been Type A, Negative.

The plainclothesman had seen the deep cut on Carmichael's left wrist. Now he turned to the page in the file that gave all the data on Eleanor Carmichael's husband. Sure enough, David M. Carmichael's blood was Type A, Negative.

That hadn't been a genuine break-in. After all, the burglar alarm hadn't been tripped until the super arrived with his passkey. And Lieutenant DiMiglio had heard of nuts who reenacted the circumstances of their own rapes and muggings. A weird form of mourning, the psychologists said. But if David M. Carmichael wanted to trash his own apartment, it wasn't a real crime—nothing the city's criminal-justice system needed to get involved with.

And so Lieutenant DiMiglio assumed—quite wrongly—that he had heard the last of David M. Carmichael.

At twelve noon, Jennifer was standing in her kitchen, making sandwiches. Any minute, Keith would be trudging home across the gully from 666 Sunset Brook Lane. Usually he made his own lunch out of whole-wheat bread, luncheon meats and cheese. Today, however, Jennifer wanted to surprise him with a sandwich of prosciutto ham. Keith loved prosciutto. Maybe that would help lift him out of the mood he was in. God knows, she had tried everything else!

Obviously he didn't much care for David's moving in across the gully. But ever since their argument over David's bedroom wallpaper, Keith had been distant and formal. That, she knew, was a danger sign. When Keith was mildly annoyed, he cursed and complained and let her know it. But if something *really* bothered him, he simply withdrew. Jennifer couldn't get anywhere near him.

Jennifer was arranging slices of prosciutto on the rye bread when she heard the mail truck out front. She went out to the front step to collect the mail. Coming back into the kitchen, she saw Keith standing beside the breakfast table. From his clothes, she could smell the strong aroma of fresh paint.

"Hi, there!" she said, managing a smile.

But Keith's face was still grim. "Any letter from Paul?" he asked.

Jennifer sorted through the bills and advertisements, looking for an envelope from All Souls' Church.

"I guess not," she said.

"Damn!" Keith reached into the refrigerator for a can of beer. "You remember that piece of paper I asked you to send him?"

She nodded. "The one with all that lettering on it?"

"Right. You did put it in with your note, didn't you?"

"Of course!" Jennifer said.

"I'm beginning to wish you hadn't." Keith took a long swallow of beer. "I didn't keep a duplicate. I should have run that page through a copier, or something, in case your letter got lost in the mail."

Jennifer hesitated. "Maybe it's taken him a while to find out what the words mean."

"*Somebody* at the seminary should be able to tell him what language it is." Keith stepped to the telephone on the wall. "I think I'll give Paul a ring right now."

"Don't you want to eat first?" she asked. "I'm making you a sandwich."

Keith looked at the sliced prosciutto ham on the kitchen counter, then back at her.

"I'm really not too hungry," he said. "You shouldn't have gone to all that trouble."

Jennifer stepped to the counter and started spreading

183

mustard on the top slices of rye bread. Keith turned to her, the telephone receiver to his ear.

"You don't mind if I phone Paul now, do you?" he asked.

"Why should I?" she replied. "He's your brother!"

"Well, it was you who invited him." Keith finished dialing the number. "I don't want Paul to think we're pressuring him to come down here."

He stood there staring at the wall, waiting for the call to go through. Jennifer took a bite of her prosciutto sandwich, then set it down. She wasn't hungry either.

Keith was scowling into the telephone. Jennifer could hear the phone at the other end ringing and ringing, without being answered. Her eyes filled with tears. Was this what the rest of the summer was going to be like—with Keith sulking around the house, ignoring her? She couldn't help remembering how warm and considerate David had been during those two exhausting days of visiting showrooms along Third Avenue.

Keith slammed the telephone down in its cradle and dialed again. Not wanting him to see her cry, Jennifer hurried out of the kitchen and climbed the stairs to the bedroom. Holding her breath so that Keith couldn't hear her sobs, she heard him speaking into the phone.

"Yes, this is his brother calling. *Keith* Olson. My wife mailed him a letter, and I want to be sure he got it."

He hadn't even noticed when she left the room!

In Glastonbury, Connecticut, shortly before noon, Sergeant Philip Riley parked the police cruiser in front of All Souls' Episcopal Church.

The burly, heavyset policeman was a Methodist, and he'd never been inside an Episcopal church before. Entering the rectory, he walked down its narrow slate-floored corridor. Down at the end was a door with a nameplate that read REV. PAUL OLSON, ASSISTANT RECTOR. He knocked, and heard a voice call, "Come in!" It was the same person he'd spoken to on the telephone earlier that morning.

Paul Olson hadn't expected Sergeant Riley until later that afternoon. Rising from behind his desk to greet the policeman, he placed a magazine over the letter from Jennifer. He'd received his sister-in-law's strange and perplexing letter the week before—and had been puzzling over it ever since.

Shaking hands with the officer, Paul couldn't help noticing the object his visitor was holding in his left hand. The policeman placed the glittering silver chalice on the green blotter of the desk between them.

"Well?" the officer said. "Is that yours?"

"I'm almost sure it is," the assistant rector said. He reached out for the chalice, then hesitated. "You've already dusted it for fingerprints?"

Sergeant Riley smiled to himself—hadn't the clergyman seen him carrying the chalice in his bare hands? "We lifted a couple," he replied. "Mostly smudges, though."

"Please sit down," Paul said.

Sergeant Riley settled his navy-blue bulk into the chair beside the assistant rector's desk. Paul turned the chalice over in his hands and examined the base. It bore the imprint of the silversmith in Wallingford, Connecticut, from which the church had commissioned all its liturgical objects. "Yes," he finally said. "It's ours."

Righting the chalice again, he saw that the bowl had no dents or scratches. The chalice looked as good as the day it had disappeared. But then Paul noticed the odd reflection from within the cup. The bottom was caked with a dark brownish substance.

"Speaking of fingerprints," Sergeant Riley said.

"We'd like a chance to talk with everyone who has access to your vestry room on a regular basis. Because we have a pretty good idea who stole your chalice."

"So do I," said Paul sorrowfully. "I know who took this."

The police officer sat up straight in the chair. "Then why didn't you say so when you first reported this missing?"

"Because I didn't know at the time," the assistant rector replied. "Last Wednesday, a young woman came here to the rectory and told me what happened to our chalice. But even now, I haven't any proof."

Sergeant Riley looked Paul right in the eye. "Do you mind filling me in, Reverend?"

Paul Olson hesitated. "All right, but I don't want to mention any names."

The police sergeant looked at him across the desk, saying nothing.

"Briefly, then," Paul said. "This young woman is a college student, and her parents are members of the congregation. She told me our chalice was used in a Satanic ritual last Saturday night."

Sergeant Riley didn't bat an eyelash. "And how did she know that?"

"Because she was there! It was a blood offering, an animal sacrifice. But her boyfriend—or rather, the young man who used to be her boyfriend—told her the chalice was 'genuine.' That is, a consecrated one from a church. Then this week, her parents told her that our chalice was missing. She put two and two together and came here to see me. But she couldn't recall exactly where the ritual had been held—it was somewhere off in the country. So there wasn't much I could do to get the chalice back."

Paul Olson felt sad and discouraged. He was still amazed that Lawrence Fisher, who had organized the

Black Mass, was a member of the All Souls' Altar Guild! How had Christianity failed him? And up until last Saturday, Cindy Trumbull had accompanied him to these ceremonies. Why did young men and women like Lawrence and Cindy want to go out under the stars and invoke the age-old Enemy of God?

"You could have told *us* what she told you," the sergeant said. "And if you press charges, you can prevent it from happening again."

Paul could see the reflection of dried blood in the bottom of the chalice. Obviously it would have to be cleaned and reconsecrated. "You'll have to ask the rector," he finally said. "Taking these characters to court only gives them more publicity. It gives ideas to people who wouldn't have dreamed of such things in the first place."

Paul looked at the police officer. "Could you possibly show me where you found the chalice?"

"Sure." Sergeant Riley nodded. "If you can spare maybe a half hour. . . ."

As he was stepping into the police car, Paul heard the telephone in his office start to ring. But he didn't want to keep Sergeant Riley waiting. The rector's secretary would answer it, and if it was at all important, the party would surely call again.

About six miles outside the Glastonbury town limits, the police sergeant parked the cruiser on the grassy shoulder of the road. Paul got out and followed the officer into a deserted pasture. The stalks of last year's goldenrod stuck up in tufts through the new spring grass.

In front of an old stone wall, the grass had been trodden down flat. A large hexagon about twenty feet across had been traced on the ground with white lime. In the approximate center of the six-sided shape was a spading fork, its handle pushed deep into the earth. Its sharp black prongs pointed upward toward the clear blue sky.

Near the spading fork, lying on its left side, was a large white bird. Now hardly more than a matted lump of feathers, it had clearly been dead for several days. Right beside the bird was a wide, flat, lichen-covered rock—forming a crude altar of sorts.

"That's where your chalice was," said Sergeant Riley, tapping the rock with his shoe. Paul saw that the top of the rock bore a dark, crusty stain. In the nearby grass were thick waxy blobs where candles had been allowed to burn themselves down.

In broad daylight, Paul thought, this all looked deceptively peaceful. Birds were chirping in the nearby woods, and a small plane droned in the sky overhead. The meadow was empty now. But Saturday night, Lawrence Fisher and Cindy Trumbull had been here. And how many others?

"Reverend," Sergeant Riley said, "why the spading fork? Why would they want your chalice in the first place? I mean, is there any point to any of this, or is it just nonsense?" The policeman managed an uneasy smile. "That is, if you don't mind talking about your competition!"

Paul tried to remember the details of what Cindy had told him on Wednesday. She had been a member of this cult, or coven, until last Saturday, when she'd experienced something that frightened her out of her wits—and told Lawrence that she never wanted to see him again.

"Well," Paul began, "as for the spading fork, it's upended to mimic the cross on an altar. Its prongs point upward as a challenge to heaven, and as an insult. You see, farmers use spading forks for turning manure. So the implication is that God is so much worthless refuse."

The assistant rector pointed to the altar stone, then to a gap on the top of the nearby stone wall. "God told Moses to build his altars out of unhewn stones. But the Satanists don't build up. Instead, they tear down a wall that already exists. It's all backward, you see." Paul pushed at the stiffened bird with the toe of his shoe. From the broad bill, he saw it was the duck Cindy had told him about. "This duck was some child's pet. The whole idea, basically, is to cause as much sorrow and fear—as much negative emotion—as possible. The duck was sacrificed with a wooden knife. Its first drops of blood were spilled on the altar stone as a tribute to the Devil, who the Satanists think is the true lord and master of this earth. The rest of the blood went into our chalice—not Christ's blood, you see: a duck's blood. And then—well, the participants took their own version of unholy Communion . . ."

And right after that, Paul remembered, was what had made Cindy Trumbull decide not to attend any more rituals!

Cindy had always found the ceremonies a bit of a bore, and the sacrifices cruel and pointless. She always let some other member of the group kill the week's sacrificial animal. Last Saturday, though, Lawrence Fisher had brought two cages—one containing a rabbit and the other, the white duck. Cindy asked why he'd brought an extra animal, but Lawrence just grinned. "Damon told me to," he said.

The duck was killed with a wooden knife, as usual. But just as Lawrence began to collect its blood in the stolen chalice, Cindy felt a presence enter the hexagon. The air was suddenly dank, and the candles burned lower.

Frightened, she moved over to the cage with the white rabbit inside. It looked as if they were going to leave the rabbit alone. Cindy was glad of that, because she loved rabbits. She put her hand in the cage to stroke the animal's lovely white fur. And all at once, she smelled a rank, animal odor. The presence was right behind her now—amused, intelligent and infinitely powerful.

Something invisible closed around her arm, filling her with a breathtaking energy. The rabbit screamed—and in the dim light thrown by the candles, Cindy saw why. With one stroke of her hand, she had torn the rabbit's skin from its back!

The presence—and the exhilarating energy it had brought with it—seemed to vanish. Sobbing with fright, Cindy killed the rabbit to put it out of its misery. But to Lawrence Fisher, the whole experience had been some kind of high honor. "Don't you understand?" he asked her. "Fulfilled desire finds you the stronger!"

But Cindy didn't *want* to understand. She broke off with Lawrence that very night, vowing never to attend another ritual, ever. . . .

"You seem to know an awful lot about these Satanists," said Sergeant Riley. "You wouldn't be speaking from firsthand experience, now, would you?"

"No, no," Paul said hastily. "The young woman who came to see me told me that—"

"You talking about Cindy Trumbull?"

Paul just looked at the officer. "I told you, Sergeant, no names! All right?"

"All right!" the officer sighed. "But we're almost positive it's Cindy's boyfriend who's behind all this. Until now, we couldn't charge Fisher with anything except trespassing and cruelty to animals. See, that spading fork wasn't stolen. He charged it to his parents' account at the hardware store. But stealing your chalice, now—that's grand or petty larceny, depending on how much it cost in the first place. . . ."

The assistant rector bent down beside the blood-stained altar stone. "Give me a hand with this, will you?" he asked.

Sergeant Riley got a grip on the other side of the rock and helped Paul lift it back to its original spot atop the old stone wall. Then Paul stepped over to the spading fork and grasped it by the neck, below the prongs. Now he noticed that there were words carved into the wood. WHAT IRON IMPRISONS ran down the right side of the wooden handle. GOLD SHALL SET FREE ran up the left.

"What do you want with that thing?" the officer asked.

Paul smiled. "Our groundskeeper at the church might find a use for it." But even when he pulled with all his strength, the embedded spading fork didn't budge.

Frowning, Paul got a better grip and rocked it back and forth. Slowly, stubbornly, the fork began to wobble in the soil. But it took Paul another five minutes before he was able to work the spading fork loose.

Sergeant Riley saw the look of disbelief on the assistant rector's face. The soil of this meadow was dense clay, filled with small rocks. And yet the spading fork's unsharpened handle had been driven over fourteen inches deep in the earth.

David Carmichael reached New Castle a little before 1 P.M., a few minutes ahead of the moving van. Driving up the western spur of Sunset Brook Lane, he saw the house at 666 come into sight.

Only last Saturday, the two-story Victorian had been a faded yellow. Now it had been painted deep blue, with white trim—the exact same color as the house in his nightmares!

So that the moving van would be able to pull into the

gravel driveway, David parked his Mercedes on the street in front of the bay window. He got out of the car and gaped in astonishment. The bay window, with its six-sided panes of glass, stared straight back at him. On either side of it, the deep blue clapboards looked exactly like row upon row of scales. It all seemed horridly familiar!

He crossed Sunset Brook Lane and looked back at the house. This, he realized, was where he had been standing during his first series of nightmares. The empty void behind the house was really there—it was the gully separating the house from Keith and Jennifer's! So that much of the dream had been precognitive after all.

His heart beating faster, David unloaded his two suitcases from the Mercedes and carried them to the front porch. This was how the second series of nightmares had begun—with David standing in what he now saw was the gravel driveway.

There was a paint-spattered wooden ladder leaning up against the porch roof. A gentle breeze was blowing across the road. The fresh ivory-colored paint on the porch trim was sparkling in the bright sun. David mounted the porch steps. As he angled his suitcases through the front door, he saw two middle-aged men painting the dining alcove. They nodded to him, and David smiled back.

During the past week, he had been kicking himself for renting this house without so much as a glance inside. But now, as he carried his suitcases upstairs, he felt his reservations melting away. What marvelously high ceilings! And the bedroom, with its pheasant-and-peony wallpaper, was absolutely beautiful. David had felt guilty picking out a pattern that was so extravagant. But according to Tom Greene, Coste was happy to pay for top-quality paint and wall coverings. And the effect was certainly worth it! Even without any furniture at all, the bedroom was splendid and regal, like something out of another century.

David glanced out a bedroom window. There was Keith and Jennifer's house across the gully, barely a hundred yards away. Puzzled, David looked again. This view *did* seem familiar. And he also seemed to recall the hexagonal paneling on the wall behind him. Of course, Jennifer had shown him a rough floor plan; and they had spent two full days talking about this house. But David's knowledge ran deeper than that.

He left his suitcases in a corner of the bedroom and walked back downstairs. Under the staircase, just as he expected, were two sliding doors. Grasping the iron handles, David pulled them open, and the heavy doors rolled quietly into their sockets inside the paneling.

When he stepped into the little hexagonal room, a surge of energy went through his body. He breathed deeply, smiling. Was this what country air was supposed to do for you?

It was early afternoon. The sun was just starting to slant through the six-sided panes of glass. This was the room that Jennifer had called the conservatory. But now that David saw it, he knew he didn't want it crammed with plants. He liked it empty and symmetrical, just the way it was.

The room's three windows looked out across Sunset Brook Lane to the western hills of the Hudson River Valley. David stood gazing out at the distant horizon, until footsteps on the stairs overhead brought him out of his reverie. Through the left-hand window, he saw that the moving van had backed into the driveway. As he stepped out of the hexagonal room, David met one of the movers coming through the front door.

"Mister," the man said, "we got all these cartons marked 'Clothes.' But there won't be space in the dressing room for 'em all."

"I'm not surprised," David said, smiling. "Why don't you put the rest downstairs in the kitchen?"

"Or how about here, in this little room behind you?" the mover suggested.

"No!" David shouted. "You leave this room the way it is!"

"Okay, Mister, okay!" The mover stepped back, amazed at David's vehemence. "We'll put those boxes in the kitchen."

Keith was bitterly disappointed that his brother, Paul, had left the rectory only a minute or so before he telephoned. After hanging up, Keith had spent about fifteen minutes apologizing to Jennifer, whom he found crying in the bedroom upstairs. Then the two of them sat down to a quiet, unhappy lunch of prosciutto sandwiches. He'd been only too glad to escape from that uncomfortable, guilt-ridden kitchen and come back to work.

When he came back across the gully, the movers were carrying a disassembled bed out of the van. Keith was looking forward to seeing the things that David had brought with him. Back when he and Paul were boys, everyone went over to watch when a new family moved into the neighborhood. From the furniture and other stuff the moving men carried in, you tried to guess whether the family was strict or nice, and how many kids they had. . . . And since Keith had never seen David's Riverside Drive apartment, he was curious to see what furniture David was bringing to go with that jazzy bedroom wallpaper.

When Keith walked through the front door, he saw

David standing in the hallway. His shoes were shined, his pants crisply pressed; and there was a silk handkerchief in the breast pocket of his sports jacket. Wiping his hand on his overalls, Keith stepped forward to shake hands. But David ignored the gesture.

"Keith, come here, will you? I want to show you something."

What was eating him? Keith wondered. Without another word, David led him down the hallway and into the six-sided room.

"See that?" David pointed to the right-hand window of the bay. "How did that pane get broken?"

The face of the Weeping Fool was still missing. Keith had covered the empty space with a sheet of clear plastic, secured with masking tape.

"I don't know how that happened," Keith replied. "The window was in one piece the first time I saw it."

"Then one of your men must have done it," David said sharply.

"No," Keith said. "That pane was missing when I came here to do the estimate—before anyone actually started working."

"Well?" David frowned. "Why haven't you fixed it properly?"

"Because I'm not a glazier! And neither Marc or Jason has a soldering iron to repair leaded glass. What's the difference? You aren't going to be living here that long anyway."

"The difference," David snapped, "is that this house has suffered enough damage through carelessness and stupidity! Can't you see the incredible amount of work that's gone into those windows? Now, you tell your people to stay out of here entirely. Do you hear me?"

"I hear you," Keith said coldly. "I'm not going to come *near* this room, because I've got a new job

195

starting Monday in Pound Ridge." He stalked out of the room, David following after him. "If you want that pane replaced, take it up with your landlord!"

"You mean Tom Greene?" David asked.

"No," Keith said. "Tom Greene's only the rental agent. I'm talking about Coste—he owns this place!"

David followed Keith out onto the porch. "Keith, I apologize. I don't know what I was getting so upset about."

"Neither do I!" Keith fumed. "It's not like you'd been working in here for the past two weeks nailing up Sheetrock and climbing ladders! You've been sitting down in New York, not lifting a finger!" He started down the porch steps.

"Keith, wait!" David called. "Do you remember the sestertius I gave you? The nice-looking coin in the plastic holder?"

Keith paused on the steps and turned around. "What about it?"

"Did you give it back to Coste?"

Keith shook his head. "I've never met Coste. I gave it to Tom Greene."

"But I found the original!" David said. "If you could tell Greene, I'd like to make an exchange—"

Keith looked up at David. "Tell you what you do. Get yourself a phone installed. Lift the receiver. Look up Tom Greene's number in the book. And make the goddamned call yourself!"

"Now, listen—" David began.

"No, *you* listen," Keith shouted. "I'm not your servant, I'm your next-door neighbor. I don't like being ordered around. And when are you paying Jennifer the money you owe her?"

"The bills for the painting and wallpaper go to Tom Greene," David stammered.

"Like hell!" Keith said. "If you have the cash to rent

this place, you can damned well pay the bills you're running up, and not make my wife wait for her money."

"But Jennifer told me—"

"*I'm* telling you," Keith shouted, so loudly that the moving men by the van turned their heads. "Jennifer is *my* wife—and don't you forget it!"

14

Saturday, April 28, to
Monday, April 30, 1979

THE WEEKEND PASSED QUIETLY ENOUGH. From time to time, Jennifer looked out the window at the house across the gully at 666 Sunset Brook Lane. But David Carmichael was nowhere to be seen.

Saturday afternoon, Jennifer drove to a plant store and bought David a housewarming present—two weeping fig trees, in terra cotta pots, for the six-sided conservatory. When she pulled up beside the gravel driveway at 666 Sunset Brook Lane, David's Mercedes was gone. So Jennifer took the fig trees home and put them in a corner of the kitchen. Evidently David had gone shopping, because later that Saturday night, she saw him moving about in his brightly lit kitchen, cooking himself supper.

Sunday afternoon, she and Keith went out to the movies in Ossining. When they returned home, the weather had turned sharply warmer. A heavy mist was blowing in from the west, filling the steep ravine between the two houses.

By nightfall, the fog was so thick that Jennifer could no longer see the house across the gully. As far as she could see, David hadn't turned on any electric lights. It was as if the new house had never been there at all. For a few hours, at least, she and Keith had Sunset Brook Lane all to themselves again. Keith seemed to enjoy the misty, intimate weather. To Jennifer's relief, he seemed more like his cheerful old self.

For Sunday dinner, she made a Spanish omelette and a tossed green salad. Keith opened a bottle of white wine he'd been keeping for a special occasion. The tensions of the past week seemed finally over.

After dinner, they went through the house from room to room, setting all the clocks ahead one hour. It was the last Sunday in April, when the country switched to Daylight Saving Time. Then Keith took her into the bedroom, and they made love. He was especially gentle and tender.

Later, with her husband snoring peacefully beside her, Jennifer fell into a sound sleep.

When she woke up Monday morning, the bedside clock read six fifteen—Daylight Saving Time. Keith had awakened nearly an hour before and was already dressed for work. Now he strode over to the side of the bed and smiled down at her.

"We'll be over in Pound Ridge until Thursday at least," he said. "If you need me, I left the phone number on the pad in the kitchen."

Jennifer stretched her feet under the warm blanket. "You won't be home for lunch, then?"

"No." Keith smiled again. "But I made a sandwich out of the last of that prosciutto you bought, and I'm taking it with me." He bent down and kissed her forehead. "See you tonight!"

"'Bye, sweetheart," she murmured. Moments later, she heard his panel truck start up and pull out of the driveway. Then everything was quiet again.

Jennifer slept for another hour. When she finally got up and pulled open the venetian blinds, she was surprised to see the fog still blowing in from the west. If anything, it was even thicker than the night before.

Not bothering to put on a nightgown, Jennifer slipped into her green silk bathrobe and went downstairs to the kitchen. When her coffee and toast were done, she sat down at the table. A very light breeze was blowing outside, and the thick mist from the gully eddied past the kitchen windows.

She felt totally isolated, utterly alone. Hugging the bathrobe closer around her, she felt a bit unhappy that Keith wouldn't be back until evening. But really, she told herself, there wasn't anything to worry about. New Castle wasn't like Manhattan's Upper West Side, where David's apartment had been broken into twice in less than two years. Up here, things were rural, peaceful and safe. You didn't see many strangers except in the fall, when tourists drove up from the city to gawk at the bright autumn leaves and when deer hunters, in red jackets and caps, went stalking through the woods.

Jennifer was on her second cup of coffee, wondering what to buy Keith for their anniversary, when the doorbell rang.

She looked at the kitchen clock. It wasn't even eight o'clock yet; too early for the mailman. Pulling her green silk robe together in front, she hurried into the living room. The bell rang again—longer, more demanding.

She peered out the living-room window. Here, on

the east side of the house, the fog seemed lighter. She could see clear across the front yard. But there was no car pulled up in their driveway, or out on Sunset Brook Lane. Their front door was solid oak, with no windows that a burglar would break to gain entry. Keith hadn't gotten around to installing a peephole. So now, whoever had rung the bell was standing right on the front step, where Jennifer couldn't see who it was.

Cautiously she unlocked the door and opened it a crack.

It was David, dressed in a pearl-gray sweat suit and running shoes. For a second she almost hadn't recognized him; she had never seen David when he wasn't wearing a jacket and tie. Now he was breathing deeply, and his smiling face radiated energy. A lock of silver-gray hair had fallen down over his forehead. Jennifer thought he was almost incredibly handsome.

"I didn't know you jogged!"

"I didn't use to," he laughed. "But up here, there aren't any squash courts. So every morning, I run a mile past your house and back again."

"I haven't seen you go past," Jennifer said. "I guess we don't get up that early."

"Oh, you're always up," David smiled. "But when I see Keith's truck still in the driveway, I give your place a wide berth."

"It looks damp out there," she said. "Don't you want to come in for a minute?"

"Be glad to."

In the front hall, David paused to take off his running shoes. As he bent over to untie the laces, Jennifer saw how the sweat suit stretched against his back in an unbroken line. He probably wasn't wearing anything under the suit—just as she herself was naked under the green silk bathrobe.

201

In his stocking feet, David padded across the living-room carpet. Back in the kitchen, Jennifer gave David a warm slice of toast and poured him a cup of coffee to go with it. She felt a bit ill at ease. For the first time in more than two years, she was having breakfast with a man other than Keith.

She moved her own cup to the other side of the table and sat down. "Why have you been getting up so early?" she asked.

"Well," David smiled, "there aren't any curtains in the bedroom, so the rising sun wakes me up. And getting a lot of exercise makes me want to go to bed early. After all, there isn't much to do around here in the evenings."

"No," Jennifer agreed, "there really isn't." God, he looks handsome! she thought. "Aren't you enjoying yourself, then?"

"Oh, it's blissful," David grinned. "Nothing but running, reading, eating and sleeping. I only wish the downstairs had those new chairs and sofa you ordered."

Jennifer smiled apologetically. "Special orders always take a few weeks. But the living room should definitely be finished by the end of May."

David reached across the breakfast table and squeezed her hand. "The upstairs already looks marvelous," he said. "Do you want to come over and see it?"

His touch surprised her, and she pulled her hand away. Only one room in the house had its full complement of furniture. So when David said "the upstairs," he meant the master bedroom.

"Well," she said, "maybe this afternoon."

"Why not now?" David asked her.

"Because I'm not even dressed," she laughed. Nervously she pushed her long brown hair back from her face.

David smiled gently. "I'm not really dressed either. Besides, there's a thick fog out there this morning. No one would see you."

Was he joking? Jennifer wondered. This wasn't like him at all. Looking at him now, she saw that David had taken only one bite of his toast. He wasn't drinking his coffee. Instead, he was returning her gaze, a pleasant smile playing over his face.

Jennifer's long hair fell forward again, and she brushed it back. "I'm sorry," she said, flustered. "I should have offered you cream. Would you—"

"No, thanks," David said. "I like it black, just as you do." He smiled again. "I mean it about your seeing the upstairs—won't you come?"

"Not in my slippers, I won't," Jennifer laughed. She could imagine Keith driving home to pick up something he'd forgotten, just as she was walking down Sunset Brook Lane in her bathrobe! "Maybe you like to get up with the dawn, but I can't even *see* before nine in the morning."

David glanced at the clock over her stove and smiled. "Okay, then. In exactly one hour and five minutes—"

"*No,*" Jennifer said. "I have to take a shower and run some errands. Then I want to go to Mamaroneck and see how soon they can deliver those curtains for your bedroom. . . ."

David held her gaze until she laughed self-consciously. "Seriously," he said. "When should I look for you?"

Jennifer glanced out at the fog billowing past the window. "Is three or four o'clock all right?"

David nodded. "I think I can find time in my hectic schedule."

She stared at his happy, flirtatious smile. She had never seen this side of David before, and she wasn't sure how to deal with it.

"There's something else your house needs besides curtains," she said to change the subject. "See those weeping fig trees over by the refrigerator? I bought them for you to put in the conservatory."

"Thank you," David said. "But I sort of like that little room the way it is. I wouldn't want it to turn into a jungle."

"Neither would I," she replied. "Just two potted trees, one at either side of the room as you walk in." Crossing the kitchen, she picked up one of the trees. "They aren't heavy. If you take them with you now, I'll come over and see them this afternoon."

She accompanied him to the front door, where David put his running shoes back on. Then he picked up a weeping fig in each hand and leaned forward, kissing her on the mouth. "See you later!" he said brightly.

"That you will." She locked the door after him, then went back into the kitchen and washed out his coffee cup. She didn't want Keith to see it and start asking questions.

All at once, she was startled to see David outside the kitchen window. He smiled in at her and kept on walking past the kitchen door, the two fig trees' leaves bobbing in the air. Jennifer turned and watched him disappear into the thick fog, heading down into the gully.

On Saturday and Sunday, Keith had realized that his brother, Paul, would be busy with church services. He didn't want to bother him. But Monday morning, Keith started worrying again—had Jennifer's letter to Paul been lost in the mail? And so, when Marc and Jason took off for lunch at about twelve thirty, Keith asked the lady of the house in Pound Ridge if he could use her telephone.

"I'd like to call long distance to Connecticut," he explained. "But I'll charge it to my office number."

"Go right ahead," the woman replied. "You can use the extension in my daughter's room. She's off at boarding school this year."

Keith sat down beside a bed loaded with stuffed animals and lifted the receiver from Mickey Mouse's plastic hand.

In Glastonbury, the Reverend Paul Olson was sitting in his office in the rectory. Once again, he was trying to piece together the tiny scraps of blue notepaper spread out across the top of his desk. The ring of the telephone broke his concentration.

"All Souls' Rectory," he said into the receiver. "Paul Olson speaking."

"Hello, Reverend Speaking," said the voice on the other end of the line.

"Keith!" Paul laughed. "Hey, how are you? I was just working on that letter that Jennifer sent me!"

"Great," his brother replied. "That's just what I was calling about. Does anyone at the seminary know what language that inscription is?"

Paul glanced down at the dozens of pieces of blue paper on his desk. "Jennifer's letter is in English," he said. "I figured out that much."

"Wait a second," Keith replied. "I'm talking about a big sheet of paper I asked her to send you along with her letter."

"Oh, *that!*" Paul reached into his desk drawer and brought out the folded sheet of paper. "You mean this inscription that begins with *Ecce in manu tua?*"

"I guess that's it," Keith answered. "All in capital letters?"

"That's right," his brother said. "But I don't know Latin well enough to translate this accurately. Do you want me to show this to someone at the seminary?"

"Of course I do!" Keith said. "Didn't Jennifer say so in her letter?"

"Maybe she did, at that," Paul said with an attempt at a laugh. Frankly, he hadn't found his sister-in-law's joke very funny. "But I haven't fitted her letter together yet. Tell me, Keith, when did she get hooked on jigsaw puzzles?"

Keith hesitated. "I don't understand what you're talking about."

"Her letter!" Paul replied. "I recognized her handwriting on the envelope right away, and that's your return address—seven twelve Sunset Brook Lane. But the note inside was torn into all these incredibly tiny pieces. Didn't she show you?"

"No," Keith said, even more puzzled. "She just asked me if it was okay to invite you down to New Castle for a day or two."

"When I opened the letter," Paul went on, "the piece of paper with your Latin inscription was folded around the pile of little blue scraps. I've pieced together most of them, but some chunks of the letter seem to be missing. There's nothing here about my coming down to see you—much as I'd like to."

Keith could not understand why Jennifer would have done such a thing. "Anyway," he said, "we did hope you could come for dinner—tomorrow night or maybe Wednesday—and spend the night."

"Gee, I wish you'd have let me know sooner!" Keith could hear the disappointment in his brother's voice. "But now I have a wedding rehearsal scheduled for tomorrow night. Then on Wednesday evening, I have to visit patients in the hospital. Could we make it next week, or even the week after?"

"Well, our wedding anniversary is May seventh; that's next Monday. But come anytime you want. Meanwhile, though, can you get me a translation of what that Latin says?"

"No problem," Paul said. "Professor Whitney Sinclair teaches a seminar on early Church history. He knows Latin backward and forward. If I show him this paper tomorrow morning, he can probably read it right off. What's a good time to call you back?"

"Tomorrow? Twelve thirty," Keith said. "If I'm sure you're going to call, I'll be home at lunchtime."

"Great!" Paul said. "And by then, I can get my calendar straight and figure out when I can come see you people."

On her way back from the fabric store in Mamaroneck, Jennifer went shopping for groceries. When she finally drove over to 666 Sunset Brook Lane, it was already past 5 P.M. But with Daylight Saving Time in effect, the sun was higher in the sky, and it seemed like an hour earlier.

David met her at the front door, with his checkbook in hand. "Tell me," he said, "how much do I owe you for the painting and wallpaper?"

"Nothing," Jennifer said. "I've been sending my own bills to Tom Greene. He—or Coste, I suppose—pays me back, and then I pay the original invoices. That's how we interior decorators get our commissions."

"But Keith told me—"

"Please," Jennifer laughed. "Keith doesn't understand how these things are done."

David was almost childishly eager to show her how good his bedroom looked. She agreed it was lovely—and then walked back downstairs. There wasn't a stick of furniture on the ground floor. But David had spread out a small Oriental rug on the dining alcove's bare hardwood floor. He seated Jennifer on the rug, walked into the kitchen and came back with two glasses and an open bottle of white wine.

It was exactly like a picnic, Jennifer thought. And the dining alcove was going to be stunning! The Staub brothers had already painted the walls a light powder blue. Later that week, they would add ornamental borders of white. The final effect would resemble Wedgwood china—and all with only two coats of paint!

David clinked glasses with her. The wine tasted much better than the bottle she and Keith had shared the night before. Looking across the rug at David, she saw that being away from the city was doing him a world of good. He looked years younger—and even more incredibly handsome.

The time passed quickly. They found themselves talking about New York apartments she had decorated, of collectors and curators who had purchased his antiques. Before they knew it, the bottle of wine was empty. Outside, the sun was getting lower and lower in the sky.

When Jennifer glanced at her watch, it was nearly six o'clock. When they were on Standard Time, Keith usually got home from work about five thirty. And after working all day in Pound Ridge, he'd want an early dinner.

"I have to start supper," she said, getting to her feet.

"So soon?" David asked. "Can't you wait until seven thirty? That's when the sun goes down."

Jennifer shook her head, wondering what was so important about the sunset. "Keith should be home any second, and I don't want him to find me over here. He's jealous enough as it is!"

"But you won't believe what happens to the conservatory windows unless you see it," David said. "They glow with this intense shade of bright red. And there are figures etched into the glass that actually seem to light up on their own." He paused and smiled at Jennifer. "You're positive you don't want to stay?"

"I can't." She bent down and picked up her empty wineglass. "Did you put those fig trees in the conservatory? Let's see."

David led her into the hallway. The sliding doors under the staircase were wide open, and he stepped to one side to let Jennifer go in first.

The sun was shining straight through the leaded glass, and she raised one hand to shield her eyes against the glare. David had placed the two trees on either side of the windows. A few of their leaves brushed against the six-sided panes.

"You were right," Jennifer said. "Just two plants is plenty in here. But don't forget to water them."

"I won't," David said. "When the sun shines in through the windows, it gets really hot in here—unless I leave the doors open."

Jennifer took a deep breath. The two fig trees were adding a fresh, earthy smell to the air. And there was something deliciously private about this little six-sided room. She and David could close the doors behind them and be alone by themselves. No one—not even Keith, who knew the house so well—would ever guess where they were. . . .

She looked at David, and saw the way the sunlight was shining through his hair, turning it to gold. But then she remembered—what time was it? She looked at her watch again. It was six fifteen. Where had the time gone?

"I have to go home," she repeated. But she didn't want to leave.

David stepped aside to let her out into the hall. "I really want to thank you for all the work you're doing," he said, giving her hand a squeeze.

She turned to look at him again. "I'll come by tomorrow to see how things are coming along. Or you can come for coffee again, after you finish running."

"Why can't we do both?" David asked.

Jennifer forced herself to move toward the front door. "Thanks for the wine," she said, keeping her voice flat and casual. "And have a pleasant night in your new surroundings." Out on the porch, she leaned forward and let him kiss her. But when he was about to put his arms around her, she broke away and walked quickly down the porch stairs.

As she backed her Datsun out of the gravel driveway, David stood in the doorway, smiling at her. She had broken away, Jennifer realized, only because Keith might have been looking across the gully. She felt excited and terrified at the same time.

Driving around the bend of Sunset Brook Lane, she saw that their driveway was still empty. Keith wasn't home yet. Just as she was unlocking the front door, she heard the phone ringing in the kitchen. She threw open the door and ran through the living room to answer it.

"Hello?" she said.

"Well," said Keith's voice. "Where the hell have you been?"

"I was over with David, across the gully."

"All afternoon?" Keith asked irritably. "I've been calling you since three o'clock!"

"No," Jennifer replied. "I was over there with David for—oh, only about twenty minutes. Before that I was down in Mamaroneck, and at the supermarket—"

"Okay, okay," Keith said. "But tell me something else. Why did you tear up your letter to Paul?"

"Why did I do *what?*" Jennifer asked. She listened in amazement as Keith related his conversation with his brother earlier that afternoon.

". . . He says the envelope was still sealed when it

arrived in the mail. He's spent all week trying to piece it back together. Did you have to be so thorough?"

"Keith, I did no such thing!" Jennifer said indignantly. "I notice the sheet you asked me to send him was still in one piece. Maybe you steamed the letter open yourself and then glued it shut again."

For a moment, Keith was speechless. "Why would *I* bother to do a stupid thing like that?"

"Don't ask me!" Jennifer snapped. "Maybe you didn't want your brother to visit us after all. Or maybe it was your Mr. Coste, who leaves money in the mailbox. Why don't you ask him?"

There was a pause before Keith spoke again. "Listen, the reason I called is, I'm running late. I'll be home in maybe a half hour, around seven o'clock. I have to stop by the office on my way—"

"If you think I tore up that letter to Paul," Jennifer interrupted, "then you're out of your mind!"

"Look," Keith replied irritably. "I'm calling from a private phone, and I don't want to tie up this woman's line. We can talk about this when I get home, okay?"

Just what I need, Keith thought as he steered the panel truck toward Chappaqua. Another fight with Jennifer! His shoulder muscles were painfully sore from working on the overhead beams of a living-room ceiling, and he longed for a good hot shower. But he still couldn't resist stopping off at the office to check the mail.

It had been over two weeks since he'd written James Beaufort, and Keith hadn't checked the mail since Thursday afternoon. If Beaufort *had* written back, the letter would have had all weekend to get here.

He unlocked the two separate bolts securing the door of Olson Custom Carpentry. Spread across the floor

211

just inside were the envelopes the postman had fitted through the mail slot on Friday, Saturday and again that Monday morning. Right on top was an envelope addressed in a handwriting Keith didn't recognize. In the upper left-hand corner was the return address of McNeil Island Federal Penitentiary.

When Keith grabbed the letter off the floor, it made a soft crunch—not like the rustle of paper he might have expected. Hurrying to his desk, he switched on the overhead light. The envelope was lumpy and irregular, like a small pillow. He tore it open, and out tumbled hundreds of tiny shreds of paper.

Picking up one on the end of his finger, Keith made out part of a word, written in ball-point pen. Whoever had torn up Jennifer's note to Paul had evidently done the same to Beaufort's reply. *Maybe it was your Mr. Coste,* Jennifer had said. *Why don't you ask him?*

Keith took another look at the empty envelope. On the back was the red rubber stamp of somebody in the McNeil Penitentiary Administration. Whoever steamed the letter open had certainly done a good job.

But obviously the letter hadn't been tampered with while it was still in the post office. Coste—if it *was* Coste—would have had to wait until the letter had actually been delivered through the mail slot.

And the two new locks on the office door hadn't made any difference at all!

15

Tuesday, May 1, 1979

EVERY NIGHT SINCE HE HAD moved to 666 Sunset Brook Lane, David Carmichael had been in bed before ten o'clock. Then—as far as he could recall—he had slept straight through until dawn. But now, at three o'clock Tuesday morning, he suddenly found himself wide awake.

Why was he so terribly thirsty? Then he remembered the meatballs and spaghetti he'd made for supper. He had stirred extra black pepper and oregano into the store-bought tomato sauce.

David flung back the bedclothes and walked through the darkened dressing room to the bathroom at the head of the stairs. Turning on the light over the sink, he gulped down two glasses of water, then turned off the light again. Outside the bathroom he had paused, letting his eyes readjust to the darkness, when he saw a dim red glow shining through the window at the head of the stairs.

Was it the lights of New York City reflecting off the clouds? But then David recalled that Manhattan was more than thirty miles to the south—and this window faced due west! Curious, he stepped over and looked out.

To his horror, a bright red light was shining out of the bay window on the ground floor below. From up here, David couldn't see inside the room. But if the conservatory was on fire, the flames would soon burn through the staircase. And David would be trapped.

Thank God he hadn't brought more than a few pieces of furniture from New York! He bolted down the stairs, expecting to feel the searing heat underneath his bare feet. But the entire ground floor was completely dark. David paused at the bottom of the stairs and glanced apprehensively around him.

He distinctly remembered having watered the weeping fig trees before he went to bed—and he had left the conservatory doors wide open. If that room was on fire, then the light ought to be reflecting back into the hallway. But he couldn't see any light at all. David listened, but there was no crackle of flames. There wasn't any smell of smoke, either. Turning around, he peered out the window at the bottom of the stairs.

To his astonishment, that reddish light was still shining out of the six-sided room. It was a steady, even radiance, like the light of dying coals in a fireplace.

Then a small bird came flying out of the tree across the road. David didn't know what kind it was—the only birds he saw in the city were sparrows and pigeons. Maybe this one had been lured by the red light? David remembered reading that the Empire State Building's powerful searchlights were turned off during the spring and fall so that they didn't attract migrating birds.

The small bird flew directly toward the leaded glass windows. Then, at the last instant, it gave a frightened cry and darted away. Must have seen its own reflection in the glass, David thought. But halfway across the road, the bird veered again and flew back toward the house, red light glinting off its wings. It began fluttering back and forth in small arcs, as if trapped in an invisible cage. Then suddenly it folded its wings and swooped down toward the base of the bay window.

David tried to see what had happened to it. But then, all at once, the crimson light shining out of the hexagonal room faded and went out.

He climbed back up to the dressing room, slipped a pair of loafers on his bare feet, and walked outside to investigate. The night was surprisingly chilly, and the dewy grass moistened the cuffs of his pajamas. But he could see clearly—there was plenty of illumination falling from the window at the head of the stairs.

David stepped over to the bay window and peered in through the six-sided panes. The conservatory was empty, and completely dark. But squinting his eyes, David could see the sliding doors were closed tight. Yet he was positive he'd left them open when he went to bed!

Then he glanced down at the ground and saw the bird, lying on its left side in the new grass. Gently he picked it up in his cupped hand. The wings were pressed close to its body, and there was a small drop of blood at the corner of its beak. And it was distinctly cold to the touch. But David had seen it alive, only moments before. How could it have lost all its body heat so quickly?

He carried the bird back into the kitchen and dumped it into the garbage can. He stopped at the kitchen sink to wash his hands. Then, leaving the light burning, he walked back down the hallway to the six-sided room. He was reaching for the iron rings, about to pull the sliding doors open, when he saw his hand pass through a thin beam of dim red light.

Curious, he moved his hand and watched the crimson illumination wash over his fingers. The light was coming through a quarter-inch space between the two sliding doors.

David put his eye to the crack and looked in. The conservatory's marble floor was reflecting a bright red glow. David moved his head, trying to see where the light was coming from. But the glowing figure in the center of the room blocked his view.

Now David understood—he was dreaming again. This was the Good Dream, the one in which he cried out in pleasure instead of fear. The dream he always seemed to forget as soon as he awoke in the morning.

Eagerly he reached for the iron rings. But before he touched them, the sliding doors trembled and began moving apart of their own accord. David felt the delicious red warmth bathing his face. It was gentle, as always. And he could stare right into the center of the radiance without blinking.

The heavy doors slid into their sockets within the paneling. David watched as the diffuse glow continued to condense, taking on a familiar shape.

"Jennifer!" he called.

Over breakfast that morning, the memory of the previous evening's argument still hung in the air between Keith and Jennifer. Keith wasn't feeling terribly communicative. But still, he felt he ought to tell his wife about the shredded letter he'd opened in his office the day before.

But it definitely unnerved Keith to realize that someone was steaming open their mail. And even worse was the evidence that Coste—or whoever was

216

responsible—was able to pick two sets of locks. How could he stop this person from walking through their front door in the middle of the night?

"I have to go to New York this morning," Jennifer said abruptly, "to pick out a plate-glass mirror for David's apartment."

"Oh," Keith said. He took another bite of toast. "Is David going in with you?"

"He doesn't have to," she answered. "I already know exactly what he wants."

On his way to work that morning, Keith stopped off in Chappaqua again. He had figured his letters couldn't possibly be tampered with if he picked up all his mail directly at the post office.

Several people were waiting in line ahead of him, and Keith had plenty of time to contemplate the photographs of wanted criminals that were posted under plate glass. The fat, white-haired clerk behind the counter wore a handlebar moustache, and his shirt pocket was crammed full of ball-point pens.

"I'd like to rent a post-office box," Keith told him.

The white-haired clerk just shook his head. "The only ones left are the big drawer-sized lockboxes."

"You mean all the smaller ones are taken?" Keith asked.

"That's right," the clerk said. "We got too many little boys sending off for magazines their moms wouldn't like them to get at home." The man winked. "And too many wives renting a box so they can get letters they don't want Hubby to know about!"

Keith quit work early that morning, leaving Pound Ridge at eleven thirty so that he'd be home in plenty of time for his brother's telephone call. On the way, he stopped at 666 Sunset Brook Lane to see how the painting was coming along. The Staub brothers' truck was still in the driveway. But David Carmichael's green Mercedes was gone.

Inside, Werner and Fred Staub were putting a second coat of blue-gray paint on the hallway. The sliding doors under the stairs were wide open. Keith looked in at the two weeping figs that Jennifer had given David. They didn't seem to be doing too well.

"Where'd Mr. Carmichael go?" Keith asked Werner Staub.

"He left about nine this morning," the painter answered. "Said he was going to New York. But he didn't say when he'd be back."

In the kitchen at 712 Sunset Brook Lane, Keith made himself a bologna sandwich. But he really wasn't hungry. Why had David rushed off to New York on the same morning Jennifer decided to go in? For a while, he thought about driving down to Chappaqua to see if her Datsun was really parked at the train station. But that wouldn't prove anything. She could have met David in New York. Or if he'd picked her up in his Mercedes, they could have driven anywhere at all.

Keith realized he had no reason to be so suspicious. Jennifer had never lied to him before—so why shouldn't he believe her now? If David had decided to drive to town, it was probably just a coincidence. . . .

But there had been too many goddamned coincidences lately! Impatiently, Keith glanced at the clock over the stove. It was nearly 12:45 P.M., almost time for Keith to start back to the job in Pound Ridge. Had Paul gotten delayed or something?

Keith got up, tossed his empty beer can into the garbage and glanced out the window. Across the gully, the Staub brothers' truck was still the only vehicle in the driveway. And the swamp maples down by the brook were really leafing out. Pretty soon, Keith wouldn't be able to see David Carmichael's house at all.

Suddenly the phone rang, and he hurried across the room to answer it.

"Hi, Keith!" It was Paul. "I meant to call you earlier, but Professor Sinclair really took his time. According to him, you have two different inscriptions there."

That made sense, Keith thought. There had been a different series of letters on each side of the cast-iron column. Thinking they were halves of a single message, Keith had run the two together.

"Did he tell you what they mean?" Keith asked.

"He sure did, and let me tell you, he was most impressed! He wants me to ask you where you found them."

"Easy," Keith said. "I copied them off a lightning rod."

"Oh, come on!" Paul exclaimed. "We have lightning rods here on the roof of the rectory. You can't fit long inscriptions on a piece of metal only six inches long."

"This lightning rod I'm talking about," Keith said, "is more like thirty feet long! It sticks up beside the chimney of the new house across the gully from us. But half the lettering is sealed up behind the Sheetrock in the hall, so I can't invite your professor to come have a look. But tell me—what do the inscriptions say?"

"Okay." Paul took a deep breath. "One is from the Vulgate translation of the Bible. See, the Old Testament was originally written in Hebrew. Saint Jerome translated it into Latin toward the end of the fourth century. The inscription's from the Book of Job. God gives Satan permission to inflict all kinds of havoc on Job, but not to actually kill him. That's your first inscription—chapter two, verse six: *Ecce, in manu tua est verum, tamen animam illius serva.* 'Behold, he is in thine hand; but spare his life.' "

"I see," Keith said. "How about the other one?"

"Sinclair says its Latin of the very early Christian era, back when the language was actually being spoken in the streets and not used only for liturgical purposes. He's not sure whether it's from one of the early Church Fathers, or perhaps from a book of the Apocrypha—"

Keith laughed impatiently. "But what does it *say?*"

Paul cleared his throat. *"Hominibus deus vitam donavit, ergo illam jactare potest homo solus.* It means, 'God gave men the gift of life; therefore only man can throw the gift away.' In other words, human life is so sacred that the devil can't touch it. Only human beings—who are given life in the first place—have the power to throw it away, through murder or suicide. So Satan doesn't kill people—*people* kill people!"

"Whoa," Keith said. "You mean those inscriptions actually refer to Satan by name?"

"No," Paul laughed. "It's just that I've got the Devil on my mind these days. We just had to reconsecrate our chalice after a Satanic coven borrowed it for a ritual."

"Good Lord!" Keith said. "When was this?"

"Oh, it was stolen a week ago Friday. But we got paid back, in a way. Our groundskeeper's really happy with the spading fork they used in the ceremony."

"A spading fork?" Keith asked. He remembered the night of the storm, when his own spading fork had been removed from the garage and propped against his doorbell.

"Yes," Paul said. "They had stuck it in the ground with the prongs up, and there were words carved on the handle."

"Wait a minute!" Keith exclaimed. "How were those words carved?"

"With a penknife, I guess."

"No, I mean how were the letters arranged? Did they read up one side of the handle, and then back down the other?"

"That's right," Paul replied. "How did you know?"

"Because that lightning rod I told you about—the inscriptions were punched into its shaft the same exact way!" Keith hesitated. "Look, Paul, I know this call's on your nickel. But do you have a few extra minutes?"

"Sure. What's the matter?"

It was such a tremendous relief to finally be able to talk to someone! Keith sat down at the breakfast table and told Paul about the afternoon he had seen his own face in the window at 666 Sunset Brook Lane. He explained about the bronze sestertius, and the stormy night he had glimpsed that strange red light on the porch of the empty house. He added what he'd learned from the Seattle newspaper, the theft of his office stationery—and finally, the shredded letter from James Beaufort that he'd opened the day before.

"Well," he concluded. "Go ahead and say it. You probably think I'm crazy."

"Of course not," Paul said. He had heard Keith's urgency and conviction. "I believe you."

Embarrassed now, Keith looked at the clock over the stove. "Hey, we've been on this line for almost half an hour. But Jennifer *did* invite you. And I'd really like to see you again. Can you make it down next week? Please?"

"What's wrong with this Thursday?" Paul asked. "The day after tomorrow?"

"But I thought this week was bad for you," Keith said.

"You're the only brother I've got," Paul laughed. "I'll *make* time."

221

"Great!" Keith smiled. "We can have David Carmichael over for dinner too. He's an antiques dealer who's living in that house across the gully."

"Has he noticed anything strange happening over there?" Paul asked.

"I don't talk to him much," Keith admitted. "Maybe he has. But we'll see you for Thursday dinner, then—around seven o'clock?"

"God willing," Paul said. "Take care of yourself, Keith."

"You too," Keith said. "Good-bye."

In the All Souls' rectory, Paul Olson hung up the telephone and stared at the chaos of blue notepaper littering the top of his desk. What Keith had just told him sounded impossibly bizarre. But Paul knew his older brother was too practical and level-headed to let his imagination run away with him. And now Paul was genuinely concerned for Keith *and* Jennifer—because some details of Keith's account seemed to match with what Cindy Trumbull had told him.

According to Cindy, you could trust the Satanists to do things exactly backward. The motto of the Roman Catholic Church was *Ex oriente lux*—Out of the East, light. In early times, every church was aligned so that the congregation faced the east. And on Easter morning, Christians around the world celebrated sunrise services. . . .

Lawrence Fisher's coven, on the other hand, celebrated not the rising, but the setting sun. For a Sabbath, they preferred a night of complete darkness, when the moon was down and none of God's lights shone in the heavens. Now Paul thought of that strange six-sided room where Keith had seen the windows glowing blood-red—how interesting that those windows faced the west—the direction where the sun died!

But what was the significance of the words carved into the handle of that spading fork? And, for that matter, what about the Latin inscriptions that Whitney Sinclair had translated that morning?

Paul Olson reached into his desk for the address book where he kept the telephone numbers of members of the Altar Guild. He now realized what he had to do—certainly before he saw Keith and Jennifer for dinner on Thursday.

It was time he had a little chat with Lawrence Fisher!

16

Wednesday, May 2, 1979

TRAFFIC LEAVING THE CITY WAS very light. And so, at 8:15 A.M., David Carmichael pulled his Mercedes into the driveway of 666 Sunset Brook Lane.

Two days later, he had stripped off his clothes and looked at himself in the full-length mirror behind his dressing-room door. He decided he'd been away from the squash court for too long. He definitely needed some exercise to tighten his stomach and firm up his shoulder muscles. But there weren't many squash courts up here in northern Westchester. What he really needed was a rowing machine.

Monday morning, the phone-company truck arrived to install a telephone. David then called a locksmith, who came right over and changed the locks on the doors and installed a security chain on the kitchen door in the back.

Now, finally, David felt perfectly safe in his new house. While waiting for Jennifer to stop by, he began calling sporting-goods stores in the Yellow Pages. But none of them sold rowing machines. After a dozen fruitless calls, David gave up and decided to drive into the city the next day.

Tuesday morning, he found the kind of machine he wanted in an exercise-equipment store on Manhattan's West Forty-eighth Street. It cost David several hundred dollars—but after all, he was paying thousands so that Jennifer could see her ideas transformed into reality at 666 Sunset Brook Lane. What was the point if he was going to neglect his own appearance?

He tied the machine onto the luggage rack of the Mercedes and drove uptown. At 41 East Fifty-seventh Street, he told Miss Rosewood that he planned to close for the summer but would keep paying her salary until the gallery reopened in September. He spent the rest of the afternoon going over bills and correspondence that had piled up. But his mind wandered. He kept wondering what Jennifer Olson was doing back on Sunset Brook Lane.

David didn't want to drive back to New Castle in the dark. He still remembered the Friday night when he had blacked out on his way home from Keith and Jennifer's. So he had an early dinner, spent the night at the Carlyle Hotel, and checked out at six thirty the next morning. He entered the town limits of New Castle shortly before eight o'clock.

Lifting the rowing machine off the luggage rack, he carried it upstairs to the dressing room, where it would be easy to reach. And after he'd worked up a good sweat, the bathtub was only a few steps away.

All he had to do now, he figured, was be patient. He had watched Keith's truck drive off in the mornings and return in the evenings, and he knew how many empty hours Jennifer Olson had on her hands. It was only a matter of time before she began spending them in bed with him.

He was about to change into his sweat suit for his morning's two-mile run when he remembered those weeping figs Jennifer had given him. Maybe they needed some water.

The sliding doors of the hexagonal room were wide open, as he'd left them on Tuesday morning. But both trees were wilted! Their leaves—which had been fresh and glossy only the day before—now hung limply from the branches.

David couldn't understand it. The soil in both pots was still damp to the touch. Sure, this room heated up if the doors were closed—but they'd been open since he'd left for New York. How could both trees be in such bad shape after only twenty-four hours?

David carried one of the fig trees out to the Mercedes. Last time he was shopping for groceries in Millwood, he had seen a florist's. They'd probably be able to tell him what the problem was.

The inside of the store reminded David of a funeral parlor—the same flowery smells, the same dim lighting. The short, bulky woman behind the counter took one look at the withered fig tree. *"Ficus benjamina,"* she pronounced. "Let me have a look at it!" She grabbed the pot out of David's hands and marched it off to the rear of the store.

She was back scarcely a minute later, holding the fig tree in one hand and its pot—still filled with moist soil —in the other. "You have any mice in your house?" she asked.

"Maybe." David shrugged his shoulders. "I really

226

don't know. I just moved into the house where I'm staying."

"Could be mice," the woman said. "See here?"

She thrust the tree's damp roots toward him. David saw that beneath the level of the soil, the bark on every root had been stripped away.

"Something must have burrowed into the pot," the woman declared. "A tree isn't going to survive without bark on its roots, you understand."

"But isn't there anything I can do?" David asked. "If I plant it in special soil or something, won't the roots grow back?"

The woman frowned. "With *Ficus,* you can usually root cuttings in sand—you know, with a plastic bag over the top. But that's not going to work in this case."

"Why not?" David asked.

"'Cause you have to take cuttings off a *live* tree." She shook her head. "And this tree of yours has been dead for—oh, at least a week now!"

When David got back to 666 Sunset Brook Lane, he threw the other dead fig tree into the gully. But how was he going to explain this to Jennifer?

After lunch, he tried out the rowing machine. At first it was easy, but after five minutes, he could feel the strain in his back and shoulders. After another five minutes, he quit, sweaty and exhausted. Too bad this house didn't have a sauna, like his racquet club in the city.

He was about to step into the bathtub when he remembered how the afternoon sun slanted through the conservatory's bay window. If he closed the sliding doors behind him, would the room heat up? He no longer had the weeping figs to worry about. It was worth a try. . . .

Wrapping a towel around his waist, he went downstairs to the six-sided room. At first he felt self-conscious in front of those ground-floor windows. But beneath each window was about two feet of wooden paneling. When David sat down on the floor, he was completely hidden from any cars passing on Sunset Brook Lane.

The inlaid marble floor was already warm from the sun. A spring breeze was tugging at the plastic that Keith had taped in place of the missing pane of glass. Within minutes, David could feel a dry heat building in the room. His muscles began to relax. Feeling drowsy, he closed his eyes against the glare—and seemed to lose all track of time.

Suddenly he found himself bathed in bright red light. According to the watch on his wrist, it was seven thirty. Had he fallen asleep? David rose up on one knee and peered out the leaded glass windows.

The sun was just slipping down behind the horizon. The three windows were glowing a deep crimson, just as David had seen them do before. But now he noticed something else: the light in the room actually seemed to be pulsing!

Once again, he saw that each window was etched with a different figure. A smiling man, a dancing woman—and a fellow with a six-sided plastic patch where his face ought to be.

Then David heard the telephone ring upstairs. The noise was slightly muffled by the two sliding doors behind him. Could that be Jennifer calling? Snatching his towel off the floor, David pushed open the sliding doors and ran upstairs. He picked up the receiver on the fourth ring.

"Hello!" he panted.

"Good evening, Mr. Carmichael!" said a deep,

resonant voice. "This is Coste. Are you enjoying your stay?"

"Oh, yes!" David said, glad to speak to the house's owner at last. "Yes. I only hope you don't think that I spent too much of your money on the bedroom wallpaper."

"Indeed not."

David frowned. How did Coste know the value of the wallpaper? He must have come by one day while David was out—before he had the locks changed. . . .

"Now, then," the voice continued. "You told Thomas Greene that you have my sestertius. I would not care to lose that coin."

"I can give you the sestertius anytime you want," David said.

"Good. But be careful. That coin is extremely valuable, and there have been several burglaries here in town. A thief, who enters people's homes while they are asleep, and takes objects of value. And what he cannot steal, he damages or destroys. . . ."

Uncomfortable memories of his Riverside Drive apartment flashed through David's mind.

"Put my coin in a very safe place, Mr. Carmichael. I shall visit you tomorrow evening—let us say eight thirty."

Earlier that same afternoon, Jennifer had heard her phone ring in the kitchen. Thinking it might be David, she ran upstairs to answer it. But it was Keith, calling from Pound Ridge.

"Tomorrow," he reminded her, "you're going to be cooking for both Paul and David. Want to go out for dinner tonight?"

Keith made reservations at a restaurant overlooking the Hudson, north of Ossining. They arrived at seven thirty while the sunset was still reflecting in the water. The restaurant itself was an old nineteenth-century mansion with high ceilings and a fireplace in each room. Their table was right next to the window, and Keith ordered a bottle of red wine.

Jennifer had every reason to feel happy. Tuesday, in New York, she had found the perfect plate-glass mirror for David's apartment. That week, her new classified ad in the paper had brought in three responses. Tonight was a soft, magical spring evening. Her lamb chops were delicious—and Keith was in a wonderful mood once again. . . .

Then why did she feel so terribly ill at ease?

Part of the reason, she knew, had to do with David Carmichael. When he had first asked her to decorate 666 Sunset Brook Lane, she had been filled with enthusiasm—and determined to design interiors that *Architectural Digest* would want to photograph. But now she found herself wondering if Keith was right. Perhaps it *was* a waste. Because come Labor Day, the house across the gully would be empty again—and David would be back in Manhattan.

What bothered her even more, though, was that she and David were so strongly attracted to each other. Back when they had met only once a month, if that, it had been easy to dismiss their affection as ordinary friendship. But now with Keith off at work for most of the day, and David barely a hundred yards from her kitchen door . . .

Jennifer Olson sipped her wine and looked across the table at her husband. Keith looked handsome; he had trimmed his moustache right before they left for the restaurant. But he seemed to be drinking more lately; and she wasn't surprised when he ordered a second bottle of red wine to wash down his T-bone steak.

Finally the meal was over. Keith figured out the tip

and held her coat, and they walked out into the asphalt parking lot. In Manhattan, Jennifer had always loved to window-shop on her way home to her apartment. Here, all she had to look forward to was six miles of winding country road.

She was quiet as Keith got behind the wheel and drove the car home. He could be so wonderfully thoughtful and cheerful—when he wanted to be. But David was *always* pleasant! It would be so easy to drift into an affair with him; to simply relax and allow it to happen. But how would Keith react if he even suspected such a thing?

As they drove up the western spur of Sunset Brook Lane, Jennifer looked across the gully. There were the lights of their own house, gleaming through the trees. Dead ahead was the two-story bulk of the new house. David's green Mercedes was parked in the gravel driveway, but the house was completely dark.

As they drove past, Jennifer thought she saw a glimmer of reddish light in one of the downstairs windows. But when she looked again, it was gone. Probably the Datsun's taillights reflecting in the glass . . .

"It's only nine thirty," Keith said to her. "Do you suppose there's anything wrong with David's electricity?"

"I don't think so," she replied. "David goes to bed very early, you know."

Keith was silent until they had crossed the narrow concrete bridge at the loop of Sunset Brook Lane.

"How do you know that?" he asked.

"David told me. He was out jogging Monday morning, and he stopped in for a cup of coffee."

"Oh," Keith said. "Thanks for telling me these things."

While he parked the Datsun in the garage, Jennifer

231

unlocked the front door and went upstairs. She was changing into her green silk robe when the dressing-room lights suddenly went out. Startled, she turned around. Keith was standing in the bedroom doorway, silhouetted by the light from the hall.

She always relished the slow, gentle way he made love to her. Now he undressed her in total silence and placed her robe and lingerie neatly on the dressing-room chair. Lifting her in his arms, he carried her to the bedroom and lowered her onto the fresh sheets she had put on the mattress that very morning.

The bedroom window was open a few inches. Jennifer heard the spring peepers calling by the brook that ran down the bottom of the gully. He kissed her and stretched out alongside her on the bed. He was slipping his hands under her back when suddenly he froze. A loud scream echoed through the night air.

Keith pulled away from her and sat up. "What the hell was *that?*"

"Maybe a 'possum?" Then she heard it again—a long shriek of pain and fear.

"That's no animal!" Keith said. And then Jennifer realized that the sound was coming from across the gully, at 666 Sunset Brook Lane.

In the dream, David was confused and terrified. What had started as the Good Dream was turning into a horrible nightmare.

As usual, he was in the hall outside the six-sided room. The doors slid open, and inside, waiting for him, was Jennifer—her long chestnut hair hanging below her shoulders, her naked body glowing with beautiful blood-red light.

That was how the Good Dream always began. She was holding him in her arms when David heard a knocking on the front door, out in the living room behind him. Once, twice—a total of six knocks. Then he heard heavy footsteps coming down the hall. David knew it was Keith Olson. But Jennifer was holding him too tightly—he couldn't turn around!

Suddenly he felt Keith's arms close around his chest, pulling him away from Jennifer. But they weren't Keith's hands. The fingers were blue in color and covered with scales, like a lizard's. The muscles in the forearms were thick and incredibly powerful. And the long, sharp nails were tearing at the skin of David's chest, drawing blood.

He tried to breathe, but the two arms were tightening around his chest in a crushing bear hug. He tried to speak, but he could not; cry out, but could not. He felt his ribs cracking under the brutal pressure. Again he tried to scream, but his lungs seemed empty. The air hissed uselessly out of his throat. He couldn't make a sound. And meanwhile, the crushing pain was getting worse and worse.

Then something grasped his left shoulder. Suddenly David realized he was lying on his back. A strong hand was shaking him, and someone was striking at his face.

"Wake up," a deep voice said. "Wake up, damn you!"

David opened his eyes. Directly over him was a glowing disk of light—so bright it blinded him. Then the disk flattened and fell to one side. And David recognized the dark figure bending over him. It was Keith! This was no dream, this was real!

David lashed out in panic. But Keith reacted instantly, pinning David's right wrist. He lifted the flashlight like a club, ready to bring it down on David's head.

"No!" gasped David, his heart pounding. "Don't!"

233

"What's the matter with you?" Keith asked, letting go of David's right arm. "What's wrong with you, you son of a bitch?"

"I was dreaming," David exclaimed. "It's all right."

"All right?" Keith straightened up, backing away from the bed. "You throw another punch at me, and I'll break your arm!"

David sat up in bed and looked around him. He had flung off his sheets and blankets in his sleep. And the air was quite cold. He looked at Keith, silhouetted in the light from the dressing room. In the dream, Keith had been dressed in overalls and a work shirt. Now he was wearing gray slacks and a sports jacket—with no shirt underneath it.

"I walked all the way over here in the dark," Keith said, "because I heard you yelling. And now you try to hit me!"

"I was having a nightmare," David repeated. "You were in it, you and . . ." He stopped himself. Better not mention Jennifer—Keith was mad enough already!

"You have these nightmares often?" Keith asked.

"Yes—recently," David replied.

"And then what happens?" Keith persisted. "You just keep on screaming until somebody comes and wakes you up?"

David nodded. Naked except for his boxer shorts, he stepped onto the bedroom floor and reached for the bathrobe on the chair nearby.

"Well," Keith said. "Do us a favor, will you? Keep your goddamned windows shut! That way, if you start screaming in the middle of the night, you aren't going to wake us up."

But now David remembered—the night had been chilly, and before going to sleep, he had closed all three bedroom windows. But Keith was right. The windows across the room were wide open at the top—all three of them!

Keith turned and walked out into the dressing room.

"I'm terribly sorry," David said as he slipped his arms into the white terry-cloth bathrobe. "I'll come with you."

"I know my way!" Keith said. "Don't you remember?—it was me who installed all the new Sheetrock in this house."

"I'm really sorry," David said again.

"So am I!" Keith shot back.

David stood there in his bare feet, listening as Keith made his way down the stairs. A moment later, he heard the front door slam shut. Stepping to the open bedroom windows, David saw the lights of Keith and Jennifer's house shining through the trees. Then he saw Keith's flashlight beam bobbing down the trail across the gully.

David shut the bedroom windows. Then he remembered something else. Before going to bed, he'd locked the front and back doors. And both locks had been changed. So how had Keith managed to get inside?

David figured he'd better go down and find out. He picked up the small flashlight he kept on top of his dresser. Directly underneath it, in the top drawer of the bureau, was where he had hidden Coste's bronze sestertius. Now, to reassure himself, before going downstairs, David pulled out the drawer and slid his hand under the pile of clean socks, feeling for the square plastic envelope.

It wasn't there!

David pulled the entire drawer out of the bureau and emptied it out on the bed. There were a dozen matched pairs of calf-length socks—but no coin.

He was positive he'd left the sestertius in this top

drawer. But then, he also recalled closing the bedroom windows and locking the doors downstairs. Was his memory slipping?

David pulled every drawer from his dresser, one by one, and sorted through their contents on the bed. But the sestertius wasn't there either. And Coste would be coming by at eight thirty tomorrow night. If the corroded bronze coin hadn't turned up by then, what would David say to him?

At 10:35 P.M., David put on a pair of slippers and went downstairs to check the front door. It was unlocked, of course. David turned the key in the lock until he heard the bolt slide into place inside the jamb. Then he walked down the hall to the kitchen.

The back door was unlocked too. And the brass security chain was dangling from its anchor plate on the wall. Obviously the door had been opened from *inside* the kitchen! What the hell was going on?

Too upset to go back to sleep, David stood at the kitchen counter and tried to think where else that sestertius could possibly be. Gazing out his kitchen window, he watched the lights on Keith and Jennifer's second floor go out, one by one, until their house was all dark.

David realized it would be easier to look for that coin by the light of day. So, switching off the kitchen light, he walked back upstairs. He made sure that all three bedroom windows were locked—so that they couldn't possibly slide open again. Then he cleaned all the socks and clothes off his bed, crawled back between the covers, and turned off the light.

And then he heard a sharp scratching sound from somewhere on the ground floor.

David sat up in the darkened bedroom, holding his breath, listening. There it was again—a raw noise like metal being rubbed against glass. In New York City,

David knew, burglars often used glass cutters to enter a building. And 666 Sunset Brook Lane had nearly a dozen ground-floor windows!

David slipped on his bathrobe again, retrieved the flashlight and tiptoed downstairs in the dark. The intermittent scraping noises were coming from the conservatory. But why would anyone want to break in through all that leading? There were much easier windows in the living room.

As soon as David reached the doorway under the stairs, the noises suddenly stopped. He switched on his flashlight. But the six-sided room was empty. He aimed the beam out through the leaded-glass windows. There wasn't anybody standing outside on the new grass.

Then where had those noises been coming from? David lowered the flashlight and swept its beam across the marble floor. There in one corner lay a crumpled piece of clear plastic.

When David bent over and picked it up, the attached masking tape stuck to his fingers. It was the hexagonal patch that Keith had put over the gap in the right-hand window.

David pointed the flashlight at the spot, and its beam reflected off shiny new metal. Fresh solder gleamed against the dark lead that held the window together.

The missing pane of glass had been replaced!

17

Thursday, May 3, 1979

"HELLO, REVEREND," SAID THE YOUNG man, stepping into Paul Olson's office in the rectory of All Souls' Episcopal Church.

The clock on the office wall read five forty. As he greeted his visitor, Paul remembered that he was due at Keith and Jennifer's at seven. The drive from Glastonbury to New Castle took at least an hour. But Lawrence Fisher couldn't have made it any earlier. He worked from nine to five for an insurance company—a job he'd landed after graduating from college the year before.

Now Lawrence Fisher settled himself in the same chair where Sergeant Riley had been sitting two days before. The young insurance broker was only twenty-three, but he looked older. Tall and thin, he always wore conservative three-piece suits.

Now he smiled at the assistant rector. "You wanted

to ask me why I took the chalice," he said evenly. "Isn't that right?"

Paul was taken aback by Lawrence's utter frankness. "Yes," he finally replied. "I would like to know why you took it."

"We needed it for a ceremony," Lawrence answered.

"What's the matter?" Paul asked. "Can't your coven —or whatever you call it—afford utensils of your own?"

"Coven is correct," the young man replied. "Naturally we have our own chalice that we use for most Sabbaths. But last Saturday was a Welcoming for the Archangel. And for his Welcoming, the Archangel requires a consecrated chalice stolen from a Christian church."

"A Welcoming for the Archangel?" Paul asked. "What do you mean?"

"If you remember the Book of Job," said Lawrence, "the Archangel Satan declares that he is forever ranging to and fro in the earth. Recently, we in the coven have dreamed that the Archangel is drawing near to us—to establish a new place of residence, you might say. We felt his presence more strongly than before. And so a Welcoming was in order."

"Well," Paul said. "Assuming your Satan wanted a consecrated chalice, why didn't he come get it himself? If he's so powerful, why'd he need you to swipe it for him?"

"It would cause the Archangel unspeakable agony to touch any object in the possession of a minister of God," said Lawrence.

"Unless it's been stolen?" Paul asked.

Lawrence nodded quite seriously. "Yes—or unless the clergyman hands it over personally, of his own free will." Lawrence smiled slightly. "But there's an unfortunate shortage of ordained ministers who obey the Archangel."

Paul still couldn't believe this same polite, soft-spoken young man had served in the Altar Guild for the past year, never missing a single Sunday! "Okay," he said. "You held this Welcoming ceremony. Did your guest of honor show up?"

"We all felt his power!" Lawrence smiled like a devout worshiper who has just taken Communion. "After the chalice was filled, I grasped the spading fork and pushed its handle so deep in the soil that later, we couldn't pull it out. But I didn't do that myself, you see—it wasn't my strength. It was the Archangel himself using my muscles, acting through me!"

Paul tried to mask his disbelief. "But you didn't *see* anything, did you?"

The young man shook his head sadly. "The Archangel shows himself very seldom—only when he wants to command obedience. Only a few people living have ever seen him revealed in his true form."

"Well, then, Lawrence." The assistant rector folded his hands on the desk. "Is this going to happen again?"

Lawrence smiled pleasantly. "Will the coven meet again this Saturday? Of course. Another blood offering? Naturally. But will I steal your chalice again? Certainly not! You see, when I took it, I had to betray the trust you placed in me. Also, I had to be sure that you would learn that I had stolen it; that I was responsible. My betrayal—and accepting the consequences in advance—added to the significance of the Welcoming. But if I took it again, what trust would I betray? Stealing the same chalice twice would be like serving leftovers to a guest of honor—as you put it."

"You *wanted* me to learn you took it?" Paul repeated. "Then did you—"

"Ask Cindy to come and tell you?" Lawrence shook

his head. "No, Cindy came to see you on her own, I'm afraid. But she only told you everything she *knows*. That's another reason I came here today, Reverend—to explain to you what Cindy never could understand." Lawrence leaned back comfortably in the chair. "So please feel free. Ask me anything you like!"

Paul was irritated enough to call Lawrence's bluff. "Okay, here's a puzzler: That spading fork you used in the ceremony. On the handle was carved, 'What iron imprisons, gold shall set free.' What does that mean? And do you have to sacrifice those animals?"

"First things first." Lawrence smiled. "According to legend, the Archangel forged a huge trident and aimed it at Heaven—and vowed that one day he will ultimately return to claim his celestial throne. Down the right side of the trident he stamped the Rule of Iron that Heaven had imposed on him—and up the left side, he inscribed the Rule of Gold he is using to fulfill his desires regardless."

Paul shook his head in bewilderment. "What's a Rule of Iron?"

"Iron Rules," Lawrence said, "are prohibitions imposed by man or God—laws and restrictions that keep us from doing what we want. Our coven has an Iron Rule of Silence, for example. If we want to do something, we're not supposed to dilute our determination by talking about it beforehand. And we don't brag about it afterward, either! At the least, we'd make people jealous. At the worst, they'd call the police!"

"If you're bound by a rule of silence," Paul said, "then why are you sitting here now, telling me all this?"

"Because I want to!" Lawrence said brightly. "And because there are Rules of Gold as well as Rules of Iron!"

Paul shook his head again. "I don't understand."

"But that's the whole point of the motto you saw on

241

the spading fork—for every Rule of Iron that binds us, there's a Rule of Gold to set us free. And the strongest one is the Gold Rule of Fulfilled Desire."

Paul remembered what Lawrence had told Cindy Trumbull after she killed the rabbit.

"'Fulfilled desire finds us the stronger.' Is that it?"

Lawrence nodded eagerly. "Only you left out the comma. 'Fulfilled desire finds *us,* the stronger.' Satisfy one desire, see, and you can devote all your energy to a new goal—you're automatically stronger! And by fulfilling our desires, we grow more powerful—always more powerful—with every Sabbath."

"But what has that got to do with the Rules of Iron?"

"Because," Lawrence said quietly, "any follower of the Archangel vows to accept *all* consequences for his actions. We all agree to that when we join the coven—and it's a good incentive. If you have accepted the pains of hell, you have to become strong enough to bear them. *But,*" Lawrence said, "once you *are* strong enough, there isn't any law of God or man that you have to obey. That's why we worship the Archangel, of course—to get what we want, here on Earth. And as long as we're strong enough to deal with the consequences, we can do exactly as we please!"

"Really?" Paul looked his visitor straight in the eye. "And what if it pleased you to commit murder?"

Lawrence looked away, avoiding his gaze. "Let's say I wanted to kill—oh, some young woman who betrayed our coven by speaking to an outsider without permission—"

"Are you talking about Cindy?" asked Paul, enraged.

But Lawrence Fisher held up one hand. "Please! I haven't finished answering your last question! If I committed murder, I'd have to admit it. I'd have to be clever enough to concoct an airtight defense at my trial,

242

and be strong enough to escape her family's revenge. But I'm not that strong or clever—yet! And so I'm not planning to kill anybody."

"*Yet?*" Paul asked. "Meanwhile, you only kill ducks and rabbits."

"But they have no souls!" Lawrence said. "One of the great Christian saints made that point, and who are we not to take him at his word? Besides, didn't God Himself accept animal sacrifices from the ancient Hebrews? Reverend, everything we believe is right there in the Bible!"

"But what's the *point?*" Paul asked. "What good can it possibly do to make an animal suffer?"

"You must understand," Lawrence said. "Ever since his fall from Heaven, the Archangel has existed in a state of torment and pain. And so the more pain and fear our rituals create, the more he feels at home. The more a creature's torment approaches his own, the more pleasing to his eyes. Ideally," Lawrence added, "the Archangel's throne on earth would be built entirely of wood that's been anointed with the blood of dying men. In the Middle Ages, such a throne was actually rumored to exist. But no one I've spoken to has ever seen it."

With an extra hour of daylight, Keith didn't mind working later on outside jobs like the one in Pound Ridge. But his brother Paul was due at 7 P.M., so Keith finally quit work at six o'clock sharp. That gave him a full hour to drive back to New Castle, shower and shave.

Keith was whistling as he climbed into the panel truck and started the engine. The best thing about Daylight Saving Time was that the sun was higher in the sky at quitting time. It didn't shine right in his eyes during the drive home.

Just south of Mount Kisco, the road ran under an old railroad bridge that had been built back in the '30s. It was a clear spring afternoon, with a few hazy clouds. Sunset was still more than an hour away. And yet the shadows under that railroad overpass looked darker than Keith had ever seen. In fact, the air in there seemed to be filled with gray smoke.

Out of some inner caution, Keith eased up on the gas pedal as he entered the tunnel. It wasn't smoke in the air, because he'd have smelled it. Instead, the air smelled musty, dank—an odor that Keith thought was eerily familiar.

He was in the middle of the dark tunnel when the red oil light on the dashboard came on. Keith heard the engine falter. Surprised, he shifted down into second gear, then let up on the clutch. But the jump-start didn't work. Keith allowed the heavy vehicle to coast out from under the railroad bridge and steered it over onto the shoulder of the road.

Of all evenings, this had to happen tonight, when his brother was coming for dinner! Keith climbed out and lifted the truck's hood. When he grounded the battery terminal with his screwdriver, there was a healthy spark. There didn't seem to be anything wrong with the coil, ignition or spark plugs, either.

After twenty minutes of tinkering, Keith finally gave up. The sun was getting low enough that he couldn't really see what he was doing. But the panel truck was full of hundreds of dollars' worth of tools and equipment. He couldn't leave it parked here by the side of the road. He'd have to call for a tow truck. But most gas stations, he knew, would already have closed for the evening.

He removed the keys from the ignition, locked all the doors and started walking back the way he'd come. There had been a roadside tavern a mile or two back

down the road, and they'd be sure to have a telephone.

In the rectory of All Souls' Episcopal Church, Paul
Olson stole another look at his office clock. It was now
6:25 P.M. To reach Keith and Jennifer's house by seven
o'clock, he should have been on the road nearly half an
hour ago. But despite himself, Paul was utterly fasci-
nated by his conversation with Lawrence Fisher.

"What you've seen in the movies isn't so," Lawrence
said. "Covens never kidnap people for ritual murder. If
the Archangel wants a human sacrifice, he always
selects his own victim—as well as the sacriphant to do
the killing. According to tradition, the sacriphant is
given a coin of the emperor Nero to pay him for his
trouble—the same coin that's been paid to every sacriphant down through the centuries."

Paul's eyes widened. Keith had said something about
finding an old Roman coin! "Why Nero?" he asked.

"Because Nero was the greatest sacriphant of all! It
was he who killed Saint Peter and Saint Paul, at the
Archangel's direction. Ordinarily, though, the only
victim the Archangel deems acceptable is the sacriphant's own friend or lover." Lawrence smiled again.
"That's why none of us in the coven worry too much
about his selecting *us* for sacrifice. We really don't love
each other all that much!"

Paul wondered: had Cindy Trumbull loved Lawrence
Fisher. She had dated him for nearly a year, and her
mother had been positive Cindy was about to become
engaged. Fortunately, Mrs. Trumbull had never
learned how the young couple had been spending their
Saturday nights. . . .

"As for Cindy," said Lawrence, as if reading Paul's
thoughts, "she broke an Iron Rule by speaking to you
without our coven's permission. Therefore, she is

bound to face the consequences—but not from us! You see, we leave it to the Archangel to settle our scores for us. Satan has power over this entire earth—over our fortunes, our jobs, our possessions, even our health. The only thing the Archangel is forbidden to do is to take a human life. That was the Rule of Iron that God handed down in the Book of Job—'Behold, he is in thine hand, only spare his life.'"

Paul recalled the Vulgate verse that Keith had copied off a "lightning rod" in the neighboring house—and the assistant rector's blood ran cold.

Lawrence smiled. "But it's Rules of Gold that provide the way around the Rules of Iron. And the Archangel has a Rule of Gold, too!"

"What's the Arch—I mean Satan's—Rule of Gold?" Paul stammered. "The Rule of Fulfilled Desire?"

The young man shook his head sadly. "His forces are not yet numerous enough to defy Heaven. Someday they will be. But for now, the Archangel employs a more ordinary Rule of Gold. Isn't it obvious to you?"

Impatiently, Paul glanced at the clock on the office wall. It was nearly a quarter to seven.

"Don't you read the newspapers?" Lawrence asked. "People kill their loved ones all the time. So even if the Archangel can't take a man's life, then he can persuade some other human being—a sacriphant—to do it for him."

God gave men the gift of life. That was the other inscription Keith had copied off the iron column. *Therefore, only man can throw the gift away.* The assistant rector rose from his desk, his head spinning.

"Lawrence, I'll have to cut this short. I'm expected for dinner tonight over in Westchester County, and—"

"That's all right," said Lawrence, also standing up. "But just remember, Reverend—if you would like to

246

be among us this coming Saturday, we will be glad to have you."

Paul stared at his visitor in disbelief. Was this why Lawrence had been so eager to tell him all about Satanic worship?

Lawrence was positively grinning! "I sensed your curiosity now, even as we spoke. The others have voted to let me talk with you. We think you, as an ordained minister, will be invaluable to our coven."

"I'm not interested in joining your bunch of fanatics!" Paul shouted. "And you aren't going to recruit me—you of all people!" He threw open his office door. "As for your being in the Altar Guild, I want your resignation on my desk tomorrow! Now get out of this rectory."

Lawrence stepped out into the corridor—but waited while Paul locked the office door behind him. "You are in a rush, aren't you?" Lawrence asked. "Damon said it was important to delay you by about forty minutes."

Paul strode off down the corridor. His white Chevy Vega was outside in the church parking lot, all ready to roll. "Who's this Damon?" he asked.

"Each of us in the coven has a voice to tell us what's going to happen, and what the Archangel would have us do." Lawrence Fisher quickened his pace to keep up with the assistant rector. "My voice calls itself Damon."

Paul halted and turned on Lawrence. "All right, then! If this voice of yours knows what's going to happen, then ask him this—who has my brother invited for dinner tonight? Besides me."

"You shouldn't sneer at me," Lawrence said. He followed Paul into the parking lot before he spoke again. "You're going to be with a policeman for the rest of the night!"

Paul halted next to the white Vega. His overnight bag was already packed and in the back seat. "The man who's coming for dinner is an antiques dealer," he laughed. "Not a policeman. So tell Damon that he's not exactly batting a thousand."

For the first time in the year he had known Lawrence Fisher, Paul saw anger spread over the young man's face.

"If you don't like our prophecy, Father," Lawrence spat out, "then here's another. When you see your brother tonight, you will remember the sight for the rest of your life!"

Over the years, Keith must have driven past Thatcher's Tavern hundreds of times. But he'd never been inside. When he finally walked through the door, it was a few minutes past seven o'clock.

Inside, there were a few older men seated around the bar. Keith asked the bartender for a dollar in change, then headed for the phone booth in the corner. Leafing through the stained, ragged Yellow Pages, he located a towing service that was open all night and wasn't too far away—located a couple of miles to the north, up toward Mount Kisco.

He dialed the number and instructed the tow-truck driver to pick him up in Thatcher's parking lot. Then Keith hung up, pushed another dime into the slot and called Jennifer.

"Where are you?" He could hear the worry in her voice. "It's nearly seven fifteen!"

"Don't I know it!" said Keith, glancing at his watch. "The truck broke down on my way home. I'm here at Thatcher's Tavern, on the other side of the railroad tracks."

"Do you want me to drive over there and pick you up?"

"Wish you could," Keith sighed, "but I have to wait for the tow truck."

There was a pause. "When do you think you're going to be home?"

Keith looked at his watch again. "Eight o'clock, eight thirty? I really don't know. Can I say hello to Paul?"

"Paul's not here yet. He just called from a gas station on the Merritt Parkway and said he's going to be about forty-five minutes late."

"Okay," Keith said. "When he does get there, hand him a drink and tell him I'll be home as soon as I can. You can tell David the same thing."

Jennifer hesitated. "I didn't invite David," she said. "He's never met your brother Paul. And you did act as if we were having David over too often."

Keith groaned. "Well, this is one night I *do* want David over for dinner! I'd like Paul to ask him some questions about that house he's renting." Suddenly he saw a flash of yellow light through the tavern window. A tow truck, a flashing light rotating on its roof, was pulling into the parking lot.

"Why should Paul care about that house across the gully?" Jennifer asked. "Is there something wrong you haven't told me about?"

"Look," Keith said. "I'm calling from a pay phone, and the tow truck is here. The faster I get moving, the faster I'm going to be home. So please—just call up David and ask him over. All right?"

"All right," Jennifer said. "But how are you going to get home?"

Keith sighed. "You'll have to drive me, I'm afraid. I'll call you as soon as I get to the garage."

When she got off the telephone with Keith, Jennifer picked up the receiver again and dialed David's number. But there was no answer—the phone just kept ringing.

After six rings, she hung up. If he wasn't home, that made everything much easier. She wanted to keep David and Keith apart as much as she could. And she definitely didn't want Paul to see her and David together! David might be able to hide his true feelings in front of Keith, but Keith's brother was a minister—and too good a judge of human nature.

She crossed the kitchen and peered out the window. Through the trees she could make out David's green Mercedes parked in the gravel driveway of 666 Sunset Brook Lane. Then he *was* home! Could he be taking a bath? But his telephone was in the dressing room, only a few steps away. And he said he jogged in the mornings, not at sunset. . . .

Again Jennifer recalled that Saturday morning, two weeks before, when she had found David slumped across the front seat of his car. Now he was all alone in that house. What if he had suffered another blackout and fallen downstairs? He might not be able to reach the phone!

She had a sudden impulse to drive over and make sure he was all right. If he was out running, she'd probably meet him on the road. Besides, she'd been meaning to speak with David alone, face to face. What she had to explain to him wasn't the kind of thing she could say over the telephone. And with Paul running late; with Keith tied up at the garage—perhaps now was as safe a time as any.

Jennifer had been expecting Paul at seven o'clock, so she was already dressed for dinner. For a moment she considered changing out of her good shoes. But she wouldn't be over at 666 Sunset Brook Lane for more than a couple of minutes. If Keith was going to call from the garage, that gave her the perfect excuse to come right back after talking to David—and then Keith would never know.

The tow truck drove under the railroad bridge and parked on the side of the road, directly in front of Keith's panel truck.

"Okay!" Keith opened the door and started to climb down from the cab. "Can I help you hook the tow chains to the front of my truck?"

"Not so fast," the driver said. "I'd like to take a look under your hood first."

"But I already did!" Keith protested. "The engine won't turn over, no matter what. Let's tow it to your garage, and then my wife can drive me home. We've got people coming over for dinner."

"Mister," the driver said, "if I can get that truck started, you can drive *yourself* home. Plus it'll cost you a lot less. Can I have the ignition key?"

Keith handed over his key ring and climbed down from the cab of the tow truck. He watched as the driver slid behind the wheel of the Olson Custom Carpentry vehicle. All at once, the panel truck's engine roared into life.

Keith stared up at the driver in astonishment. "What the hell did you do?" he asked.

"Just turned the key in the ignition," the driver replied. "Why don't you try driving it home? I'll follow behind you in case anything else goes wrong."

Jennifer eased her Datsun out of the garage and decided to leave the overhead door open. That way, after she picked up Keith, she could drive straight back in.

The clock on her dashboard read seven twenty-seven. The sun would be setting any minute now. But within ten minutes, probably less, she'd be through with David and back in her kitchen—ready for Keith's call from the garage.

The night before, Jennifer remembered, he had been in such a wonderfully tender, romantic mood. Then David's nightmare had ruined everything. When Keith had come back to their house, he was too angry to want to make love. Jennifer had finally drifted off to sleep. But several times during the night, she had been awakened again by Keith's restless tossing and turning in the bed beside her.

The next morning, after Keith had driven off to Pound Ridge, Jennifer poured herself more coffee and stayed in the kitchen, thinking. David had always seemed cheerful and confident. But now Jennifer realized that he must have been terribly affected by Eleanor's death. As a widower, David had been mourning her for nearly two years. Now, finally, he was coming out of it—and it was only natural that he was getting interested in women again. And it was even more natural for him to turn to her, since they'd known each other for such a long time.

But that sudden nausea the night he came for dinner, the mysterious problem he had to see a doctor about, the blackout that Friday night—and now this screaming nightmare that Keith had told her about last night! It all indicated that David Carmichael was a seriously troubled man. Was he really strong enough to handle the guilt and tension of an affair with her?

Jennifer also realized she wasn't being fair to Keith. His moodiness had really started on the afternoon they had returned from the Bahamas to find Coste's house sitting across the gully. And of course he had been jealous and resentful lately—why wouldn't he be, with David vacationing practically in their backyard? But despite everything, Keith had put his own feelings aside and let her decorate David's house and apartment. Obviously he wasn't keen on the idea—but he never complained, because he knew how much the work meant to her. And because he loved her too much. . . .

She had been divorced once before, and she didn't want to go through that again. Her marriage with Keith deserved more of a chance than she'd been giving it—without outside pressures, and without competition.

Steering the Datsun around Sunset Brook Lane, Jennifer drew a deep breath. She was rehearsing in her mind what she had to say. She parked beside David's Mercedes in the gravel driveway.

Across the road, the sun was almost down to the horizon. When she climbed the porch steps, she saw that the front door was ajar. It swung inward at her push, the hinges making no sound at all.

The living room was still completely empty, just as she'd seen it on Monday afternoon. The sun, low in the west, was shining through the window at the bottom of the stairs. Shutting the front door behind her, Jennifer glanced up to the second-floor bathroom. She couldn't hear any water running. And no one seemed to be moving around inside.

"David?" she called. But there was no answer. Could he be in the kitchen? She started down the bare hallway, her footsteps echoing through the empty living room.

Only a few moments before, David had heard the sound of his telephone ringing upstairs. My God, he thought, it's probably Coste! David shoved open the heavy sliding doors and bolted up the stairs. But before he reached the phone, it had stopped ringing. He picked up the receiver and heard only a dial tone.

What was he going to do? That morning, he had searched the entire house, upstairs and down, without finding Coste's bronze sestertius. And now Coste would be here in a little more than an hour. And of course he'd want to keep the sestertius for which David had paid $3,700!

David tucked the towel back around his waist—the damned thing was always slipping loose—and walked back downstairs. Returning to the six-sided conservatory, he closed the sliding doors behind him. The sun was almost down, but the heat in here was still warm and relaxing.

Maybe if he thought hard enough, he could figure out what had happened to that bronze coin. Could it have been stolen? Last night David had discovered the ground-floor doors unlocked, and all his bedroom windows open. But the only people he knew had been inside the house were the Staub brothers—and Keith, of course. And nothing else had been missing. Only the sestertius. . . .

All at once, through the closed doors, he heard someone walk in the front door. Then Jennifer called his name. Was he hearing things? He opened his eyes and saw the leaded windows in front of him, stained with that familiar crimson glow.

The figure in the right-hand window had a face again, but his features still weren't clear. It would take another minute or two before the window's red tint deepened enough and those etched lines really became visible.

Then he heard Jennifer's footsteps coming down the hall. He remembered what Dr. Fuchs-Kramer had said about precognitive dreams—that their details were often mixed up, in a kind of shorthand. Well, now this room was bathed in red light. And here was Jennifer, coming to see him. Now, of course, it was David who had no clothes on. The Good Dream had been the other way around—but then, how exact did a precognitive dream need to be?

David got to his feet and wrapped the towel more tightly around his waist.

"Jennifer!" he called out. "I'm in here!"

When Keith came in sight of his own driveway, he waved his hand out the panel truck's window, signaling to the tow truck behind him. Looking in the rearview mirror, he saw the tow-truck driver make a U-turn and head back toward Mount Kisco.

Keith steered his panel truck to the very edge of the driveway, so that his brother Paul would have plenty of room to park alongside. Then he saw that the garage door was open. Jennifer's car was gone. She must have needed something from the store, he thought.

On the front step, he saw there was an envelope stuffed in the mailbox. There wasn't any stamp or address written on the front. Something else from Coste? Keith wondered. But Coste didn't owe him any more money.

Puzzled, he turned the envelope over. There on the back, in engraved letters, was the return address:

DAVID M. CARMICHAEL
1411 RIVERSIDE DRIVE
NEW YORK, NEW YORK 10025

Keith tore it open. The envelope was stuffed with crisp one-hundred-dollar bills. Then he recalled—of course! David owed *Jennifer* money for the work she'd been doing for him. But sticking between the bills was a torn scrap of blue paper. Picking it out, Keith immedi-

255

ately recognized the color of the notepaper he'd given his wife for her birthday. On it was her signature: *Much love, Jennifer.*

Had she been writing love notes to David? Or was this scrap of blue paper part of the note Jennifer had mailed to Paul? That would explain a lot of things! Whoever had picked the office locks in Chappaqua and steamed open their mail had to have plenty of time on his hands—and be rich enough to pay his debts with hundred-dollar bills. No, it wasn't Coste who had torn up Jennifer's invitation and Beaufort's letter from McNeil Island. It was David M. Carmichael!

Keith was annoyed to find that Jennifer had left the front door unlocked. Really angry now, he stormed into the kitchen. Had Jennifer left any note on the pad beside the telephone? No, she hadn't! Then, out of the corner of his eye, he saw a glint of red light through the kitchen window.

It was the setting sun, reflecting off the roof of a blue Datsun parked next to David's green Mercedes in the driveway of 666 Sunset Brook Lane. Keith peered between the branches of the swamp maples. The trees were coming into leaf rapidly, but he could see that it was definitely Jennifer's car.

What the hell was she doing over there, with Paul due to arrive any second? And why hadn't she noticed the envelope David had stuffed in the mailbox? What in hell was going on between those two?

Keith walked out the kitchen door, slammed it behind him and started down the trail into the gully. It was time to put a stop to this nonsense once and for all.

18

Thursday, May 3, 1979

IT WAS EXACTLY 7:43 P.M. when Paul Olson drove into Keith and Jennifer's driveway. He'd been exceeding the speed limit all the way down the Merritt Parkway—and thinking over the details of what Lawrence Fisher had told him. He was genuinely worried for his brother and sister-in-law, and glad that his phone call had found Jennifer in the house. But now as he drove up Sunset Brook Lane, he didn't see any new construction. Where was this new house Keith had been talking about?

It had been a long, tiring day, and Paul was looking forward to this evening. He parked his car beside the truck with OLSON CUSTOM CARPENTRY lettered on its side. The truck's engine was still making quiet ticking noises as it cooled down. Evidently Keith had gotten home only minutes before. But then Paul saw the empty garage, its overhead door still open. Then Jennifer had gone out for something or other.

He carried his overnight bag to the front step and pushed the doorbell. It rang inside, but no footsteps came to the door. The sun had set a few minutes before, but there weren't any lights on anywhere in the house.

Weren't they expecting him? Paul tried the doorknob and found that the front door was unlocked. He pushed the door open and stepped into the house.

"Keith!" he called out. But there was no answer. "Jennifer!" Apparently both of them had gone off on errands.

In the kitchen, Paul opened his overnight bag and took out the bottle of red wine he'd brought for dinner. It might be a good idea to open it so that the wine could breathe. He was looking through the kitchen drawers for a corkscrew when he saw an enormous shadow looming against the sky outside the window.

There was the house Keith had described to him! It sure hadn't been there last Christmas. And there were two foreign cars parked to the left of the front porch. In the twilight, the western sky behind the house was ribbed with purple clouds. Could there really be the prongs of a thirty-foot trident hidden beside the chimney? And was its shaft really inscribed with a Rule of Iron and a Rule of Gold?

He felt a strong urge to drive over to the house and take a closer look at it. But the sun was already set, and it was getting dark out. Besides, What's-his-name—the new tenant over there—was probably dressing for dinner. He wouldn't appreciate Paul's snooping around in his backyard.

As he finished opening the wine, the assistant rector felt uneasy. He had the nagging sensation that something was terribly, dreadfully wrong. But what could he do? Certainly Keith and Jennifer would be back any second. Otherwise, they wouldn't have left the front door unlocked so that he could get in.

To make himself calm down, he walked back into the living room and picked up a copy of *Architectural Digest* from the coffee table. Then he sat down in a comfortable green-and-yellow armchair facing the front door, and switched on the lamp behind it.

He looked out the living-room window to the driveway outside. His sister-in-law's car was nowhere in sight. He lowered his eyes and opened the magazine.

Why did he feel so suddenly, unaccountably exhausted?

The conservatory doors were heavier than Jennifer had remembered. It took her full strength to push them apart—and inside, the crimson light was enough to take her breath away.

Then she saw David, with only a bath towel wrapped around his waist. He was standing against one of the paneled walls, as if he'd known she was coming. But why didn't he have anything on?

"Well, hello!" he exclaimed with a broad smile.

"Hello . . ." she replied. His torso was lean and beautifully muscled. But then, he ran in the mornings and played squash at that racquet club in the city. . . . She forced herself to look away from him. Outside the windows, the entire world seemed to be blood-red.

"You look lovely," David said.

Jennifer hesitated. "Keith doesn't know I came here," she began awkwardly. "He wanted me to invite you over for dinner tonight, to meet his brother, Paul. But I didn't want . . ."

Abruptly, she forgot what she was about to say. The air in the conservatory was stiflingly warm—and heavy, as if it were about to solidify around her.

"What didn't you want?" David asked.

She saw the way the red light shadowed the muscles of his arms. Again she forced her eyes away. Where were the two fig trees she'd given him?

"I want you to understand one thing," she said. "I think of you as a very close friend . . ."

"I should certainly hope so!" replied David, smiling.

And then she noticed the nearly life-size figures etched in each of the three windows. On the left there was a man, a woman in the center, and on the right, a second man. Even from here, Jennifer could see that the right-hand figure's face didn't seem to match his body.

"Do you want some more wine?" David asked. "I saw how you liked the bottle we had Monday. I bought a whole case."

"No," Jennifer said. "I . . ." Why was it so hard to concentrate? "The point is," she stammered, "I really can't go on decorating your apartment on Riverside Drive. Keith resents all the work I've been doing for you here in this house. I don't want to go to New York and be alone with you, day after day. Because it bothers him, and—"

"Smart idea," David said. He took a step toward her. "Why make your husband suspicious if you don't have to?"

"There are several wonderful decorators I used to know, and I can give you their names . . ." The heat was making her dizzy, and she felt perspiration breaking out on her forehead. "Please don't take this the wrong way," she said. "But I have to ask you a very large favor."

"Yes?" He was right next to her now, glowing with red light. She could feel his gaze on her, shrewd and alert.

"I know the expenses you've run up in decorating

this place," she said. "But David, it isn't working out right, having you so close by. It's not fair to Keith. He's terribly jealous of you, because you and I knew each other when we lived in the city. And what with your moving in here for the summer—and now last night, when you were screaming in your sleep . . ."

She stole a quick glance at him. David was still smiling, and his eyes had an odd, dreamy look. Wasn't he listening to what she was saying?

"Oh, forget about Keith!" David murmured. "How about you, Jennifer? What do *you* want?"

Looking at him, she felt a frightening surge of desire. "David," she said, "I want you to leave here!" She stepped back, and then she saw the surprise and pain in his eyes. "Seriously, there have to be plenty of other places you could go for the summer . . ." But then she heard something.

Heavy footsteps were climbing up the steps of the front porch—and she was almost sure she recognized them as Keith's! If he walked into the conservatory and saw David half-naked like this, there'd be no way she could possibly explain!

David was opening his mouth to speak to her. But without another word, she turned and rushed from the room. She reached the hallway just as the front door swung inward.

"Keith!" she exclaimed. After the dry heat of the conservatory, the living-room air felt cool on her face. She kept on walking toward him, managing a smile.

"What the hell are you doing over here?" he asked.

"Talking with David," she answered quickly. "It's too bad, but he can't make it for dinner tonight."

"Did you have to drive over here to find that out?"

"I called him on the telephone," Jennifer protested. "I let it ring and ring but he didn't answer. I was afraid something might have happened to him, so . . ." She

261

could feel that her blouse was damp with perspiration. "How did you get home from the garage?"

Keith looked up the staircase, ignoring her question. "Where's David now?"

She had to get Keith out of here! In desperation, she looked out the living-room window at her own house across the gully. In the driveway was Keith's panel truck—and beside it, Paul's Chevy Vega!

"Look," she exclaimed, pointing to the window. "Your brother's arrived!"

But Keith pushed past her and headed for the hall. When Jennifer turned, she saw that blood-red light was pouring through the doorway under the stairs.

"Keith!" she called, hurrying after him. "Paul's waiting for us. Let's go home, please!"

The red light set Keith's face aglow as he stepped between the sliding doors. Then he halted. Looking past him, Jennifer saw David standing in the middle of the room. He was tucking the bath towel back around his waist.

She saw the surprise on her husband's face. Slowly David looked up and met Keith's stare. "Don't get upset," he said with a bitter smile. "Evidently your wife prefers you after all."

Keith stepped forward and hit David hard, in the stomach. Jennifer heard the blow land. But David didn't react at all. He just stood there, staring back at Keith with an expression of dazed astonishment.

"Keith . . ." Jennifer said. She watched, horrified, as Keith stepped closer and aimed two savage punches at David's face, backing him against the left-hand wall. She saw David's head snap back against the wooden paneling. He wasn't even trying to defend himself! The red light in the room nearly camouflaged the blood running from his mouth.

"Keith!" she repeated. She had to stop him before

David got seriously hurt. But Keith ignored her, drawing back his fist again.

Then she saw the small, round object fall from the ceiling over Keith's head. Zigzagging down through the air, as if in slow motion, it struck the marble floor with a hard, metallic sound.

Surprised, Keith looked down. The coin rolled across the floor and struck the paneling beneath the leaded glass windows.

Ignoring Keith, David bent over and picked it up. When he straightened up again, Jennifer saw that his eyes were dark and furious.

"You had this in your pocket, didn't you?" David asked. "You broke in here last night and stole this right out of my bureau drawer!"

"No," said Keith, shaking his head. He stood his ground, his fists raised warily.

Jennifer blinked in disbelief. All at once, the red light seemed to be flowing inward from the three windows, condensing around David. His left hand closed into a fist around the coin. His bruised features were transforming themselves into a mask of cold fury. Then Keith quickly stepped forward, ducking in low, and aimed another punch at David.

Jennifer had never seen anyone move so fast. David blocked Keith's swing with one hand and then, before Keith could pull back, seized his wrist. There was an odd loud cracking sound, and Keith backed away, his wrist bent at a strange angle. David had broken his arm!

"Keith!" Jennifer cried. He was sidestepping toward the doorway, backing against the wall. But David stepped in front of him, blocking his path.

"Coward!" David whispered. "Come here!"

Keith shook his head.

"Come here!" With one incredibly swift motion,

David seized him by the scruff of the neck, forcing him to his knees on the marble floor.

Keith was striking out with his good hand, but David didn't seem to feel the blows. Slowly he brought his other hand down on the back of Keith's head.

Jennifer heard her husband shriek—a high, terrified sound. Without thinking, she rushed forward, hammering at David to make him break his hold.

Slowly, David turned to look at her—not even blinking as she struck at his face. For an instant, she saw his eyes. They had a look of bitter hate that she had never seen before. And then she glimpsed something coming toward her—a crimson blur. His fist struck her on the breastbone, above the solar plexus.

The strength of his blow knocked her clear across the room. She hit her head against the paneling under the right-hand window. And when she tried to breathe, an astonishing pain flared in her chest.

Jennifer had had the wind knocked out of her before, but this was infinitely worse. Had David broken her ribs? Slowly she pulled herself up on the window ledge and looked through the blood-red glass. Outside, the sun had vanished completely. Yet the six-sided panes were glowing even more brightly than before! And now she could make out the face of the figure in the right-hand window. . . .

An unmistakable likeness of David Carmichael, silver hair and all, was looking down at her from the six-sided pane of glass!

She stood up. But trying to fill her lungs caused such excruciating pain that her knees buckled again. Keith was flat on the floor now. David was crouched over him, his back to Jennifer—ignoring her. And Keith wasn't screaming anymore. What had David done to him?

Then she remembered the sight of Paul's car in their

driveway across the gully. The front door was unlocked; he'd have let himself in. And there was a telephone in David's dressing room at the head of the stairs. If she could just get out of this blood-red room without David's seeing her . . .

But even the shallowest breath was agonizing. Jennifer knew she'd faint if she tried to stand up. So on hands and knees, she crawled toward the sliding doors.

No! Stop her! The deep voice came from directly over Jennifer's head. *She must not leave this room!*

Who had said that? She looked up, her head swimming.

The light in the room was pulsing now, as if in time to a gigantic heartbeat. And David was standing over her. The towel had slipped from his waist. He was naked.

"Jennifer?" he asked. His face was contorted with fright and concern, just as it was in his etched-glass portrait in the window. "I didn't mean to hurt you," he said, stretching out his hand.

She shrank from his touch—and then struck out at him, blindly. Everything was glowing red—her hands, the floor, the air itself. But only a few feet away was the hall, freshly painted in the gray-blue color she had picked to match the dining room.

Her hands pulled her forward. She was across the threshold. Then David stepped over her, straddling her body with his bare legs. He grasped the iron rings of the two sliding doors and slammed them together as hard as he could.

Paul Olson awoke with a start. For an instant, he didn't know where he was. Then he felt the magazine, still propped open across his lap—right where it had been before he dozed off.

But it was almost pitch dark in here in Keith and Jennifer's living room. He stood up and groped for the switch on the wall. The familiar living room blazed into light. But what about the lamp he'd been reading by? Had the bulb burned out or something?

He pressed the button of his digital watch. The numerals glowed: 8:14! He'd been drowsing for nearly half an hour. And Keith and Jennifer *still* weren't home?

Maybe they'd had a flat tire. But then, where was the antiques dealer Keith had invited? David—that was his name, David Carmichael. He should have been here before this. Or was Paul supposed to meet them all over there, at the new house?

Of course—there had been two cars in the driveway! But then, why hadn't Keith and Jennifer noticed his car in *their* driveway and given him a telephone call?

He walked out the front door and closed it behind him, making sure he didn't lock himself out. But before backing his car out of the driveway, he hesitated. Paul believed in life eternal, in God's infinite mercy. But he had to admit that right now, he was worried—even frightened.

Last Christmas, along with the brandied peaches, Jennifer had given him a plain silver cross on a silver chain. Paul always wore it under his shirt because it was a personal gift and—well, because he didn't want to look *too* clerical. But now he found the chain behind his neck and pulled out the cross so that it lay atop his black shirt.

When he pulled into the driveway of the new house, his headlights lit up Jennifer's blue Datsun B-210, parked next to a green Mercedes. He parked his own car behind it and stepped out. Straight across the gully, he saw the light he'd left burning in Jennifer's kitchen.

Towering above him was the two-story Victorian structure that his brother had been working on. There were lights on upstairs. But the ground floor was almost dark, except for one dim light shining through a window at the rear of the house.

The front door was standing wide open. Even so, before stepping inside, Paul knocked on the jamb. But there was no answer. To his left, a flight of stairs led up to the second floor. Ahead, at the end of a narrow hallway, a bulb was burning in what looked like the kitchen. But the living room in front of Paul was completely empty of furniture. There was the clean, snappy smell of fresh paint in the air. Hadn't the new tenant moved in yet?

Then Paul heard a muffled sobbing. Listening carefully, he stepped into the living room. Ahead was a dark alcove—maybe a sitting or dining area?—and that was where the mournful sounds were coming from.

He saw that there was a man huddled in one corner, next to the room's small fireplace. He was barefoot and wearing a white terry-cloth bathrobe. He didn't seem to realize Paul was even there!

"What's the matter?" Paul asked gently. "What is it?"

Clearly startled, the man looked up at Paul. "Are you Mr. Coste?" he asked, blinking in the dim light. "Will you please take your—"

"No," the assistant rector said. "I'm Paul Olson, Keith's brother."

The man stood up—stiffly, as if in considerable pain. "Very pleased to meet you, Mr. Olson," he said, shaking Paul's hand. "I'm David Carmichael." Then he looked out toward the front door. Paul could see he was clutching something in his left hand. "Could I ask you what time it is?"

Paul pressed the button on his digital watch. The red numerals glowed obligingly. "Eight twenty-one."

"Thank you," Carmichael sighed. "I wish he'd get here."

Paul didn't know what he was talking about. "Do you mean Keith?"

But Carmichael shook his head. He was clearly distracted, his mind elsewhere.

"That's Jennifer's car outside," Paul said. "Can you please tell me where she is?"

Carmichael glanced at him strangely, then looked away. "She won't speak to me," he whispered. "There's something wrong with her head."

Paul held his breath. As a minister, he had heard empty, toneless voices like this beside deathbeds and in hospital waiting rooms. The man in front of him wasn't merely distraught—he was in a state of shock!

Carmichael shuffled out of the alcove, toward the hallway, Paul following beside him. As the two men entered the light from the kitchen, Paul saw that Carmichael's left fist was cut and swollen. His lower lip was bloody, and his face was wet with tears. Dark bruises had risen on his cheek and jawbone. What had been going on over here?

"She's in there." David Carmichael raised his left hand, still clenched around whatever-it-was, and pointed to an open doorway under the stairs.

Paul instantly recognized Jennifer's wide, frightened eyes. She was on the floor just behind the sliding doors. She was lying on her left side, and her knees were drawn up against her chest, as if she were in great pain.

Paul automatically looked for a light switch, then realized there wasn't any. But there was enough light reflecting from the kitchen at the end of the hall.

"Jennifer?" he said, getting down on his knees beside her. But then he saw that her eyes were vacant, unseeing. Trickles of blood had run from her nose and right ear. Paul reached for her wrist, but her flesh was cold and inert. There was no pulse at all.

He raised his head. Farther back in the room, near

the windows, lay a man in work shirt and overalls, sprawled on his back. On the floor beside him was a bath towel, splattered with dark stains. The man didn't seem to be breathing. And there was something dark and smooth over his face.

Paul was searching for a pulse when he discovered the compound fracture. The shattered arm bone—ghostly white and faintly moist to the touch—protruded through the skin. Paul shuddered and moved his hand to the strange, leathery thing covering the man's face. It was wet, sticky, cold—and attached to the forehead!

"Oh, no!" Paul gasped. The man's scalp had been torn loose at the back of his neck, then pulled forward over the eyes and mouth. When Paul lifted back the flap of skin, he recognized the features underneath. It was Keith!

The assistant rector stood up slowly, fighting down his nausea and panic. In times of crisis, when a clergyman had to provide strength and sanity for others, Paul had taught himself to think logically—even coldly. That was what he had to do now. Later he'd have time to let his shock and grief sink in. But not yet, not now. Because standing behind him in the hall, dressed in that white terry-cloth bathrobe, was a maniac who had just killed two people!

Paul got a grip on himself and turned around. But David Carmichael was still standing in the hallway, gazing expectantly toward the front door.

Paul took a deep breath and started thinking. Carmichael hadn't mentioned Keith at all. But he had seemed concerned about Jennifer. Maybe that would be the way to handle him. . . .

Stepping out of the six-sided room, Paul managed a fairly cheerful smile. "I think Jennifer's all right," he said gently.

David Carmichael turned and looked at him. His

eyes seemed dazed—but also suspicious and mistrustful.

"She's going to want a doctor, though," Paul said. "Do you have a telephone?"

Carmichael nodded.

Be polite! Paul told himself. *Be very, very polite!* "If you'll show me where the phone is, then I'll call a doctor for Jennifer. Okay?"

Carmichael led the way up the stairs. As Paul mounted behind him, he noticed the bloody prints of bare feet that grew fainter with every step. Carmichael must have come up here immediately after the killings.

At the head of the stairs, Carmichael turned to the right and led Paul into a wide dressing room. In one corner sat a large exercise machine of some kind. Across the room stood an elegant Oriental table bearing a white telephone—and beside it, a Westchester-Putnam Telephone Directory.

"The doctor will want to look at those bruises of yours," Paul told Carmichael. "Don't you want to rest until he gets here?"

Carmichael nodded bleakly and walked into the bedroom beyond the dressing room.

Paul knelt and grabbed the telephone book. His hands were beginning to shake, but the number he was looking for was inside the front cover. Paul dialed it—and mercifully, it was answered on the first ring.

"Chappaqua Police," the voice said. "Sergeant MacIntyre."

"Good evening, *Doctor*." Paul kept his voice even and controlled. "This is the Reverend Paul Olson; I'm an Episcopal minister. We've had a slight accident here, involving two people. And I know my friend would appreciate it if you could stop by."

There was a second's pause, and Paul heard the beep that meant that the phone conversation was being recorded. "Are you with someone there?" the policeman asked. "Are you able to talk?"

Paul glanced into the bedroom. Carmichael was sitting on the edge of the bed, staring back at him.

"I don't think I should, Doctor," Paul replied. "But perhaps you could make a house call? We're here at—sorry, I don't know the house number. But it's on Sunset Brook Lane. The new house, right around the curve from the Olsons' at seven twelve?"

"Oh, right," the officer said. "That's six sixty-six! We'll send a squad car right over."

"Please tell your ambulance not to use the lights or siren," Paul said. "The patient doesn't need any more excitement."

"I read you," the sergeant replied. "Hold tight, Reverend!"

"Thank you, Doctor," Paul replied and put back the receiver. Then he jumped! Carmichael was standing right beside him. But the man looked wan and exhausted, even more so than before. Now there seemed to be an old man huddled inside that fluffy white bathrobe.

"The doctor's on his way." Paul smiled gently. "Why don't you go back in the bedroom and wait for him there?"

"But Coste will be here at eight thirty!" Carmichael said. "I have his coin for him. Will you give it to him when he comes?"

"Give him what?" Paul asked.

Slowly, painfully, Carmichael opened the fingers of his left hand. In his palm was an ugly old bronze coin. Around it, the flesh of Carmichael's hand was blistered and inflamed. When Paul lifted the heavy coin, a thin layer of Carmichael's skin came away with it.

"It hurts," Carmichael said.

Now the metal felt cool enough to Paul's touch. But

271

it must have been red-hot when Carmichael picked it up—so why hadn't he simply dropped it in the first place?

"The doctor will put something on that hand," Paul said. "Then you'll feel better. But *please* get some rest. Okay?"

Carmichael walked back into the bedroom, and Paul dropped the strange coin into his pocket. Halfway down the stairs, he stopped to listen. No footsteps! This time, apparently, Carmichael was staying in the bedroom.

Paul opened the front door and stepped onto the porch. He took a deep breath of the cool night air. So far, there were no headlights visible on Sunset Brook Lane. But the police would be here any minute. That first squad car would radio for reinforcements—homicide detectives, police photographers, forensic specialists. The entire house would be cordoned off; there would be roadblocks on Sunset Brook Lane. Paul and David Carmichael—and this Coste, if he showed up—would all be driven to the police station for questioning.

He pushed the button on his digital watch. It read 8:30 exactly. He would be lucky if the police let him go much earlier than 3 A.M. So if he wanted to pray, alone by himself for a few minutes, then he'd better make it fast.

He went back into the house and walked to the little room under the stairs. Then, deliberately, he turned his back on the sliding doors. He wanted to remember Keith and Jennifer the way they'd been last Christmas —smiling, healthy, full of love for each other. Paul closed his eyes and began to recite the Twenty-third Psalm.

He maketh me to lie down in green pastures only reminded him of the two bodies sprawled on the marble floor behind him. But Paul kept on. *Yea, though I walk through the valley of the shadow of death, I . . .*

Suddenly he felt that he was not alone—that something was watching him.

Paul opened his eyes. A crimson light was shining from the room behind him, casting his shadow on the wall. Was it a police car, out on Sunset Brook Lane? But the light wasn't flashing the way a police car's did. It was a steady, even radiance—and Paul saw that it was getting brighter and brighter.

He turned and saw that the intense red light was coming from *inside* the six-sided room! Squinting at the sudden radiance, Paul saw the bodies of Keith and Jennifer on the marble floor—as well as the enormous shape condensing in the air above them.

He watched in awe as the colossal figure continued to take shape before his eyes. The torso looked human, but the rest! It seemed to be part goat, part reptile. It was so enormous that it had to crouch over on its misshapen legs. Even so, its broad shoulders nearly brushed the ceiling.

Slowly it rotated its massive head and looked right at him. Its eyes—amused, intelligent—were more than a foot apart. The twisted horns above its brow had grown together to form a crown.

It stretched out one arm toward Paul. Then what must have been its lips rippled back, and it spoke his name.

Paul, it said. *Bring the coin here.*

Epilogue

Friday, September 14, 1979

SINCE MAY 4, DETECTIVE LIEUTENANT Francis DiMiglio had been following the Olson murder case in the newspapers.

From the very start, the antiques dealer had been the only suspect in the double killing. The night of his arrest, David M. Carmichael had made a rambling, disjointed confession, admitting to the investigating officers that he might have killed two people. As it developed, David M. Carmichael was entirely correct. According to the Westchester County Medical Examiner, he had fractured her sternum, plus a couple of adjoining ribs. Mrs. Olson had suffered a punctured lung, and must have been in great pain. But she could have survived those injuries with no trouble at all—until Carmichael crushed her skull between two heavy sliding doors. By then, of course, the woman's husband was already dead. Carmichael had broken his neck, then torn the man's scalp loose from his skull!

Lieutenant DiMiglio certainly hadn't foreseen anything like this. But he wasn't surprised, either. He'd seen with his own eyes the wreck Carmichael had made of his apartment. Somebody should have stopped to think what would happen if all that fury were ever directed outward, onto another human being. But that, in Francis DiMiglio's opinion, was the problem with the Police Academy. Cops were trained to figure out what *had* happened—not what was about to.

Paul Olson, the dead man's brother, was a priest or a minister or something. He was the one who had called the police in the first place. The shock of finding his brother and sister-in-law murdered was clearly more than he could cope with. When the first squad car arrived, barely six minutes after his call, the officers found Olson huddled near the bodies, completely hysterical. When a cop tried to comfort him, Olson came up swinging. They had to put him under restraint and shoot him full of sedatives. He was barely able to attend the funeral on Monday, May 7—which would have been the deceased couple's second wedding anniversary.

From what Lieutenant DiMiglio had been able to learn, there were some holes in Paul Olson's story. There was clearly something he was holding back; something he didn't want to talk about. But it was established that he and David Carmichael had never met each other before the night of the killings. And so Paul Olson was not charged as an accessory.

Booked on two counts of homicide, Carmichael had spent the night of May 3 in jail in White Plains. The next afternoon, he had been released on two hundred thousand dollars bail and allowed to return to his Riverside Drive apartment.

Then came the wave of publicity. Whenever somebody rich and well-to-do was arrested for murder, the newspapers always had a field day. And Carmichael's ritzy midtown antiques business—about to close for the summer anyway—had gone straight down the drain. The place was thronged with thrill-seekers trying to get a glimpse of Carmichael himself. The regular customers stayed home—who wants to buy old furniture from a man who might wring your neck?

Then came the arraignment. Carmichael's attorney entered a plea of not guilty by reason of insanity. Insane *at the time,* Lieutenant DiMiglio thought. David M. Carmichael might have been nutty enough in his own way. But immediately after his arrest, he had been in touch with reality—enough to start weeping over the woman he'd killed.

Someday, when the plainclothes detective had more time, he was going to sit down and ask his daughter Angela what made people so crazy in the first place. And by then, maybe Angela would have some answers! Because next week, Angela DiMiglio was starting graduate school in New Haven, going for her master's degree in psychology.

Sending Angela through four years of college on a detective's salary hadn't been easy. But Francis DiMiglio had never begrudged his daughter a single penny. She had graduated at the top of her class, and never given her parents any reason to worry about her.

The university dormitories were for undergraduates only, though. So Angela had to rent a place off campus. After several trips to New Haven over the summer, she met two other grad students who were looking for a third roommate to help share expenses.

This morning of Friday, September 14, Lieutenant DiMiglio helped his daughter load the family station wagon with her clothes and textbooks and drove her to New Haven. He parked the battered old station wagon right in front of Angela's apartment building, on the corner of Stiles Street and Hamden Avenue, and carried her suitcases upstairs to the two-bedroom apartment she was sharing with Cindy Trumbull, a drama student. But when Lieutenant DiMiglio walked in, Cindy was taking a bath—and apparently there was a boy in the bathtub with her. That was another thing Francis DiMiglio didn't like. This girl, Cindy Trumbull, had a live-in boyfriend.

Since Cindy Trumbull was still damp and unclothed, Angela had to carry in the rest of her boxes by herself. Her father unloaded all her stuff, carried it up the stairs for her, and then went back to the station wagon.

He climbed in behind the wheel and reached for the newspaper he'd brought with him from the city. What with helping Angela load the station wagon, he hadn't had time to read it. His eyes stopped on a story on page 10:

ACCUSED KILLER
FOUND DEAD,
TERMED A SUICIDE

September 13—David M. Carmichael, charged with slaying a north Westchester couple, was found dead yesterday in his Riverside Drive apartment. Police officers who investigated found the body hanging from a brass chandelier in the living room. A spokesman from the coroner's office said that death had evidently taken place several days before.

Carmichael, a prominent antiques dealer who lived

alone, had been about to stand trial for second-
degree murder. . . .

Again it made sense, Lieutenant DiMiglio thought.
Show a South Bronx junkie a roof that doesn't leak and
plumbing that works, and he'll think he's in the Wal-
dorf. But take a classier kind of guy like David M.
Carmichael, accustomed to expensive furniture and a
three-bedroom apartment. Put him in a cell with a
lidless toilet in one corner and a metal bunk that wasn't
an antique yet, but getting there. Something inside him
curls up and dies.

And nobody had picked up on Carmichael's self-
destructive tendencies. In the phony break-in DiMiglio
investigated, Carmichael must have stabbed himself in
the wrist and then wiped the blood all over his refrigerator. When the Chappaqua police arrested him, they
found a third-degree burn—apparently self-inflicted
by some unknown object—in the palm of his left
hand.

Lieutenant DiMiglio folded up the newspaper and
tossed it into the back of the station wagon. What the
hell was keeping Angela? He was eager to get back to
the city. Then, out of the corner of his eye, he saw the
building's front door swing inward. And Angela
stepped out onto the porch.

He got out of the station wagon. Whoever owned
Angela's building had tried to plant grass in the tiny
strip of earth between the curb and the sidewalk. But
the grass was definitely losing the battle.

"You have everything stowed away in there now?"
he asked.

Angela nodded. "It's lovely, Daddy," she said,
smiling. "I wish you could have seen Cindy's room. It
has this beautiful Chinese-style wallpaper with pheas-

278

ants and white peonies. My room is all freshly painted, and it's right next to the bathroom."

"That bathroom at the head of the stairs?" her father asked.

"Yes," Angela said. "The only problem with this place is, there's only one bathroom. And no shower—just this really ancient bathtub with claw legs. But did you see all that wonderful paneling under the staircase?"

Lieutenant DiMiglio shrugged. He let his wife worry about decorating and things like that.

"At the back of the house," Angela continued, "there's this big kitchen that everybody can use."

"*Everybody?*" the plainclothes detective asked. "How many people do they have in this building?"

"Well, there's Cindy and—and her other roommate, and me. And the two boys down on the ground floor. That's five of us. Oh, and just before you get to the kitchen, there's this little old-fashioned stained-glass-window-type room. When the sun goes down, Cindy says, it reflects the sunset and the glass glows all red. When I get my room fixed up, will you and Mom come up and have a look at it?"

"Sure, if you can get Cindy out of the bathtub! But they'll be working you pretty hard. Maybe you'd rather study."

Lieutenant DiMiglio gave his daughter a long, hard hug.

"Tell Mom I'll call her tonight, okay?"

"Will do, sweetheart. Good luck to you, now."

A few dead leaves were blowing down the street as Lieutenant DiMiglio climbed back into the station wagon. He started up the engine, but the traffic light at the Stiles Street intersection was still red. Impatient, he reached into his jacket for the change he needed for the tollbooths.

What the hell was this, in among the quarters? Lieutenant DiMiglio pulled it out and stared in surprise. It was a large coin, about the size of a St. Christopher medal, but dark and corroded. Had Angela slipped it into his pocket as some kind of joke?

The plainclothes detective felt a strange tingling in his fingers. But then the traffic light turned green. Francis DiMiglio stuffed the heavy round coin into his pants pocket. He'd look at it more closely when he got back to the city.

As he pulled the station wagon into traffic, he glanced back in the rearview mirror.

Angela DiMiglio was still standing there, waving from the porch of 666 Hamden Avenue.